Stardust, Always

D0711069

Writers Colony Press

Published by Writers Colony Press
Kindle Direct Press edition
Cover Designed by James Baldwin

Print Edition License Notes

This book is licensed for your personal enjoyment only. This book may not be duplicated either in part or in whole for commercial or non-commercial purposes without the explicit consent of the author(s) involved.

The stories within this edition remain the copyrighted property of the authors who contributed them, all rights reserved.

All proceeds from this book's sale are being donated to St. Jude Children's Research Hospital. If you are reading it and did not purchase it, please consider purchasing it either in paperback or eBook from Amazon, ordering it in to your favorite retailer, or donating the cover price directly to St. Jude Children's Research Hospital at:

www.stjude.org/

Also Published by Writers Colony Press

The Longest Night Watch
An Anthology for the Alzheimer's Association

Coming Soon
The Longest Night Watch, Volume 2
An Anthology for the Alzheimer's Association
... whether they want it or not ...

This book is dedicated to the memory of two men who made us believe in the power to be ourselves, and who faced their own mortality with dignity and humor—David Bowie and Alan Rickman.

And to all those who war against the traitors within their cells,

Stardust, Always.

All proceeds from this book go to support St. Jude Children's Research Hospital.

"Because of you, St. Jude is leading the way the world understands, treats and defeats childhood cancer and other life-threatening diseases. We won't stop until no child dies from cancer."

www.stjude.org/

Table of Contents

Foreword

Andrew Barber, Project Manager (Book)

"I got involved because 2016 sucked."—Clara Ryanne Heart, *Stardust, Always* contributor.

I got involved for similar reasons. I had barely begun to process the death of David Bowie before Alan Rickman had died as well. My family has also been affected by cancer. I was grieving, and wanted to do something to help. I'm not an oncologist or a research scientist—I'm a writer. My options were limited. But I wanted to do *something*.

It turned out I was not the only one. Both men had been a big influence on generations of writers. Several dozen members of the NaNoWriMo Participants Facebook group wanted to use their writing to help fight cancer as well. The group is notionally part of the National Novel Writing Month, but there's a community of writers all year round.

I had been involved with 2015's *Longest Night Watch* anthology, as had others on the *Stardust, Always* team. When Terry Pratchett died, we brought out a book to raise funds for Alzheimer's research. A lot of people wanted to do something similar based around David Bowie and Alan Rickman, in aid of cancer research, and somehow I ended up helping to organise it, alongside co-project manager Laura Hart. I'm never quite sure how these things happen, but I have no regrets.

We ended up with forty contributors from all over the world—from Britain to Australia, America to China, Mexico to Norway. Many more were working behind the scenes, on beta reading, editing, formatting, art design, marketing, and all the things that must happen to a book before it's ready to be born. This anthology exists because a great many people were generous with their time and talents.

We hope you will enjoy *Stardust, Always*.

Contributors

Amanda Parker Adams

Ms. Adams is a science fiction and fantasy writer in the Pacific Northwest of the US. She is owned by two cats, neither of which is a Siamese. Archivist, theater nut, and general weirdo.

She loves chocolate, sushi, and Guinness, but not in that order. She collects penguins (not the living ones).

Andrew Barber

After doing almost nothing with his writing for over 20 years, and being nagged by his daughter to enter, Andrew Barber beat 7,000 other poets to become the inaugural Poetry Rivals Slam Champion in 2010, and has since completed three volumes of poetry and four novels in *The Cybermancer Chronicles*. He was runner-up in the 2015 Individual Writer's Games, and captain of the Longest Night Watch team, runners-up in the Team events. He also writes satire, music, poetry reviews and computer programs.

Andrew was one of the organisers and editors of the *Stardust, Always* anthology, after contributing to the Terry Pratchett-themed *Longest Night Watch* anthology in 2015, in aid of Alzheimer's research. He wanted to get involved because he has already lost too many people to cancer.

Andrew's books and associated shenanigans are available here:

    www.lulu.com/spotlight/Cybermancer
    www.facebook.com/AndrewBarberAuthorPage

A. R. Harlow

My name is Anne Combs, and, my 'day job' is raising my daughter Riley, and attending college carrying a full course load, during the evenings. I have been a writer my entire life—scribbles on toilet paper rolls and the bottom of junk mail had been a common occurrence before I carried a notepad with me everywhere. Writing is breathing to me, as natural as the action of breathing in and out. It is derived entirely from my faith, which inspires me daily to do and be the best.

I have been a participant in the National Novel Writing Month for several years now, it has pushed me hard, and given me the drive and will-power to work through my first draft.

Ashlee Hetherington

Ashlee Hetherington is a dinosaur whisperer by day, and a fierce, magical volcano by night.

She's really just a clumsy flamingo who wishes her faery were still here.

```
Twitter: @artsyscientist
Blog: ashleebones.wordpress.com/
```

Becca Bachlott

Becca Bachlott lives in Maryland with her husband and two children. She is a super accountant by day and a super author by night. She has loved books from a very young age and started her writing career with stories about her friends in High School.

She is a member of the writing group The Red Herrings who won first place in The Writer's Games, hosted by The Writer's Workout.

Although she looks to be only 21, she is actually a child of the 80's and grew up watching Alan Rickman and listening to David Bowie. When asked about her favorite holiday movie, she would reply Die Hard without hesitation. St. Jude is her favorite charity.

Carol Gyzander

Carol Gyzander was a prolific reader of classic science fiction and Agatha Christie mysteries in her early days; since her family moved every two years, she had lots of time on her hands as the perpetual new kid. But she became adept at people-watching in order to fit in at each new school, and followed this up by studying anthropology—the study of people and their culture—and lots and lots of English literature at Bryn Mawr College.

Now that her kids have flown the coop, she has gone back to her early loves with an amateur detective novel and more science fiction in the works.

www.CarolGyzanderAuthor.com

Caroline Centa

Caroline Centa is a Paranormal Fiction Author who lives in Perth, Western Australia. She has always had an interest in writing but didn't get serious about it until 2012, when she began writing *Daughter of Hell*. Caroline has always been spiritual in nature, working for some time as a spiritual guidance reader, and spirituality and mythology features strongly in her work. She is a mother of two children and married to a very supportive man who has been her partner since she was nineteen. She has a very active lifestyle, enjoying gymnastics, rock climbing, archery and pilates on a regular basis, and loves playing board games with her friends.

Caroline can be found online at the following links:

Website: readingsbycaroline.net
Facebook: facebook.com/CarolineCenta
Twitter: @CarolineCenta

Clara Ryanne Heart

Clara Ryanne Heart has a background in human services and history. She also holds a Master of Arts degree in Adlerian Counseling and Psychotherapy with an emphasis in adolescents and military families. After working as a therapist for years, she returned to work as a professional ghostwriter.

The launch into 2016 struck Clara as particularly rough. After a series of crises throughout 2015, she started the year with her husband and toddler from a homeless shelter. When she heard of the *Stardust, Always* charity anthology, she leapt at the chance to submit a personal story, eager to help raise money to help in the battle against cancer.

Cornelius Q. Kelvyn

Cornelius Q. Kelvyn had long kept his writing in the shadows. He is delighted to have his story, 'Matronus', included in this anthology of wonderful authors. This story has been inspired by Rickman, Bowie, and others whom he has known who have battled cancer. For several months after the passing of a family member, he was repeatedly visited by a heron resembling the spirit of the one who had passed beyond. Some of the characters in this story are also featured in poems and short stories by Kelvyn.

```
Twitter: @cqkelvyn
WordPress: cqkelvyn.wordpress.com
```

D. R. Perry

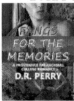

D. R. Perry prefers to choose love. However, one of the few things she actively hates is cancer. She lives and writes in Rhode Island with her husband, their daughter, and her little dog, too.—www.drperryauthor.com

www.amazon.com/author/drperry

Debbie Manber Kupfer

Debbie Manber Kupfer has been writing stories ever since she was small, but only started taking her writing seriously in 2012 when she finished undergoing treatment for breast cancer. She realized that we only have a limited time on this earth and if we really are passionate about leaving our mark we have to go after what we want.

To that end she started writing her fantasy series P.A.W.S., and the first book was published in 2013.

Connect with Debbie on her blog or via Facebook:

    www.debbiemanberkupfer.wordpress.com
    www.facebook.com/DebbieManberKupferAuthor

Diana Hudson

I live in a small town in Pennsylvania and love all things nature. In addition to writing, I enjoy hiking, photography, and various forms of art. I found my passion for writing at an early age with authors like Edgar Allan Poe and Stephen King.

I have personal reasons for wanting to be a part of of this project, as well as being a fan of both artists who were taken too soon. I lost my grandfather and one of my uncles to cancer. My father was diagnosed with prostate cancer in 2014 and shortly after surgery to remove it, he was killed in a car accident. My cousin Beth is currently battling cancer that has been deemed terminal.

So, I want to make a stand for all those who have passed, to those battling, and to those who are survivors. This is to those who refuse to give up!

Fiona Teh

Fiona Teh is an early childhood educator in an international school in China. She has degrees in both journalism and education and has published numerous newspaper and educational magazine articles. She is Malaysian by birth and grew up a third culture kid.

She is trained in Chinese martial arts and also enjoys rocking out on her ukulele with her music teacher/writer mom Margaret, and fellow writer and sister, Shu Lin. She thanks Shu Lin for her sharing her gift for plotting. You rock! She also thanks Margaret for passing down her gift for story weaving. Writing is healing and empowering for Fiona Teh. She hopes to reach the hearts of her readers in need of a bit of magic in their journey.

Georgette Frey

Georgette Frey currently lives on a small parcel along the Allegheny National Forest in rural Pennsylvania. When she isn't writing, reading or working with young people she is enjoying the wonders around her, either through a camera lens or via her family, which includes her partner, children, and both furry and feathered housemates.

Her personal narrative 'He Wasn't Sick in April' is about the month and a half from diagnosis to death of her father in 2014 of a rare cancer. The short bluntness of the tale is reflective upon the few weeks that changed the lives of her family.

Hayley Munro

Hayley Munro, in her own opinion, is a writer-extraordinaire who has dedicated her life to fighting worldsuck with words. She's a devout Harry Potter fan and 87% of her iTunes playlist consists of David Bowie songs.

She wouldn't be the person she is today had she not been introduced to either of those two things. She spends most of her time reading, writing about dragons, talking to cats, and speaking in the third person.

If you ever need find her, seek out the nearest hollow tree.

Janet Gershen-Siegel

Janet Gershen-Siegel is a published science fiction author and social media professional. Her most recent work is The Enigman Cave. Her experience with cancer and its devastating effects is all too personal.

She lives in Boston with her husband and more computers than they need.

`janetgershen-siegel.com`

Joshua L Cejka

Joshua Cejka has been writing for roughly 35 of his 41 years and loves every little last bit of it. Primarily focusing on mystery these days, he likes to stretch his legs occasionally, and is working on a series of books that combines the detective novel with fantasy.

Joshua Cejka is the author of the Meg Brown Mystery Series of books and the upcoming Stonemaiden's Cup. He live in Wisconsin—for the moment—with his two cats, Dharma and Emma, and a desk full of effluvium which he occasionally must combat before it destroys him.

Kate Post

Kate Post is a writer, poet, and Kentucky native woven with Wyoming threads. Her pieces have appeared in *The News-Enterprise and Notations*, and she has worked in editing at *New Madrid Journal of Contemporary Literature*. At 21, she has a head-start on grandmotherly skills like cooking, knitting, crocheting, baking, and yelling at kids to get off of her lawn.

When she's not channeling her inner Betty White, Kate can usually be found re-reading *The Princess Bride*, re-watching *Firefly*, or attending a comic convention (sometimes in costume!).

Further reading:

```
katepost1.wordpress.com/
Twitter: @notanowl211
```

Katelyn Sweigart

Katelyn Sweigart is a Californian who grew up on a ranch full of rescued animals. She's been a multimedia journalist, a dungeon master, a foster parent for dogs, and a magician's assistant. Like many, cancer touched her life multiple times.

She was thrilled to have a chance to use her love of writing, David Bowie, and Alan Rickman to benefit St. Jude's.

Find her on Twitter @katelynsweigart

Kell Wilsen

Writer, although this is my first piece to be properly published, and not just posted on a writing website. Working towards being a freelance writer and web developer, with the help and support of story-minded strangers on the web.

So, when some of those helpful and supportive strangers suggested using our combined talents to make something that would commemorate the lives of two great men and raise money for charity at the same time, I joined right in.

Kelly Kuebler

Hailing from a small town in Michigan, Kelly Kuebler is a 2011 graduate of Siena Heights University where she received a BFA in Creative Writing. An avid writer and photographer, Kuebler has previously worked for Michigan Concerts as a freelance reporter. She has interviewed and photographed numerous notable musical artists. She is currently studying professional photography with the New York Institute of Photography.

Stardust, Always marks her first appearance in a major trade publication. Her piece ('Dying is Harder on the Living') is a tribute to her late grandfather Walter, who passed away from bone cancer in December 2014.

When she isn't writing or glued to her camera, she enjoys antiquing, producing videos and collecting entertainment memorabilia.

```
www.kellykuebler.com
Twitter: @officialkellyk
```

Lacey D. Sutton

Lacey D. Sutton is a prolific writer and even more prolific editor. Meaning that this is the second piece of hers to be published, and not just subjected to endless rounds of revision. As a day job she wrestles with tSQL code, making data dance to her clients' whims, and her night job involves being at the beck and call of a small child and two giant cats.

She is an annual attendee of the Sirens Women in Fantasy Conference, and a seven-time winner of the NaNoWriMo writing challenge. Cancer hurt her mother and claimed the life of a dear friend last August, and Lacey is still very, very angry. This may have influenced her short story 'Oubliette'. OK, it totally did.

```
Twitter: @LaceyDSutton
Facebook: Lacey D Sutton (writer)
www.shadowandclay.com/
```

Laura Hart

Laura Hart is a mother of two who spends more time with her kids than writing. She got involved with this anthology because cancer has touched her family and changed it forever.

So many people were inspired by the lives of David Bowie and Alan Rickman, she wasn't surprised when their passing was also an inspiration. By helping with this project, she felt that she could make some difference, in some way, to some person.

Laura Roberts

Laura Roberts can leg-press an average-sized sumo wrestler, has nearly been drowned off the coast of Hawaii, and tells lies for a living. She is the founding editor of Black Heart Magazine, the San Diego Chapter Leader for the Nonfiction Authors Association, offers affordable editing services for indie authors, and publishes an annual anthology about the intersection between love and pop songs at Buttontapper Press.

She currently lives in an Apocalypse-proof bunker in sunny SoCal with her artist husband and their literary kitties, and can be found online at:

        www.Buttontapper.com

Lora Hughes

 My name is Lora Hughes and I live in Hertfordshire, England with my two children. I got involved with *Stardust, Always* as I was a fan of Bowie's music in my youth and enjoyed Alan Rickman in the Harry Potter movies. I was devastated that they both died so close together from 'the big C'. After their deaths, this quote from Alan Rickman resonated with me:

"And it's a human need to be told stories. The more we're governed by idiots and have no control over our destinies, the more we need to tell stories to each other about who we are, why we are, where we come from, and what might be possible."

I posted it to the NaNoWriMo group, adding 'wouldn't it be great if this quote could inspire us all to write more?'

I knew David Bowie had a love of books and members in the group suggested writing an anthology in memory of Bowie and Rickman. The idea caught many people's attention and basically it went from there!

Mayra Pérez González

Mayra Pérez González is a wordsmith, professional daydreamer, papercut survivor, and an admirer of Bowie and Rickman since childhood. She grew up in both suburban Los Angeles and rural Mexico. With a degree in Spanish Literature from UCLA, Mayra strongly believes that the pen is mightier than the sword. She is fascinated by languages and knows Spanish, Italian, and Ancient Greek.

She is the Editor-in-Chief and Founder of Books & Quills Magazine and writes for La Gente Newsmagazine. Mayra is very good at getting lost, forgetting, procrastinating, saying completely irrelevant and random things, laughing, and being awkward. She's very bad at hiding her emotions, surviving in any sort of apocalypse or dystopia, and writing any sort of bio.

www.mayraperezglez.com

Michelle Valens

Michelle Valens is a writer from the Midwest who also enjoys other things, She got involved with the *Stardust, Always* project because of her love for the Harry Potter series. She also lost her father to cancer several years ago and wanted to do something for other people going through the same thing, When she's not writing, she is known to be taking photographs or creating digital art.

Paul Lansdell

My name is Paul Lansdell and I live near the Dartmoor National Park, South West England. At the end of 2015 I was diagnosed, for the second time, with cancer. I share the company of people I've known, loved and admired.

It was whilst awaiting the start of my treatment that I wrote *And Then, Sit With Me*. The poem questions the suggestion that, should I survive, I would somehow be better than them; I won, they lost.

Today, I continue to walk my road, knowing that some of the finest people are waiting for me at my journey's end.

Paula Hayward

Paula Hayward is currently finishing a Bachelor's in history with a focus on medieval history, part of the reinvention of her own middle age. She is mother to one young adult son and keeper of one big dog. She was attracted to this project as a long-time fan of Bowie and Rickman and as a 20+ year survivor of Hodgkin's Lymphoma.

Her future plans include finishing her degree, conquering a pile of rough drafts, and surviving.

R R Virdi

R.R. Virdi is the author of The Grave Report. He is an avid fan of science fiction, fantasy, and especially mythology and urban fantasy. He has worked as a mechanic, in retail, the fitness industry and the gaming PC world. Ronnie has a deep love of all things mechanical with a heavy emphasis on automobiles, especially American classics. He enjoys building things and tinkering with computers from his home in Falls Church, Virginia.

There are rumors that he wanders the streets of his neighborhood in the dead of night dressed in a Jedi robe and teal fuzzy slippers; no one knows why. Other such rumors suggest that he is a professional hair whisperer in his spare time. We don't know what that is either.

```
www.rrvirdi.com
www.amazon.com/R.R-Virdi/e/B00J9PZ1YW
www.facebook.com/rrvirdi
```

Rachel A. Brune

Rachel A. Brune served five years as a military journalist with the U.S. Army, including two tours in Iraq and a brief stint as a columnist for her hometown newspaper. After commissioning as a military police officer, she continued to write and publish articles for a number of military and civilian news publications.

She continues to serve in the Army Reserve, as well as write and publish short stories and novels in a variety of genres. She blogs her adventures, writing and otherwise, at:

www.infamous-scribbler.com

S. R. Betler

S. R. Betler is a writer from Kentucky who enjoys writing low fantasy, poetry, and dabbling with fan fiction. When she's not writing, she's listening to music, reading, watching movies, and exploring nature. She first fell in love with David Bowie after watching Labyrinth and Alan Rickman after Die Hard, both of which have inspired her as an author.

She's had friends and family battle with cancer, not all of whom have won in the end, and is honored to contribute to this anthology in remembrance of those affected by the disease.

Facebook author's page:

www.facebook.com/S-R-Betler-735755803188872/

Sophia Diaz

Sophia Diaz has been writing for most of her life, both prose and poetry. She is an avid reader in a variety of genres, not to mention a movie and music enthusiast. She recently graduated from Florida International University with a Bachelor's in English Literature.

When the idea for this project came up, she was ecstatic. Here was a way to honor two remarkable men and raise money for a noble cause. She is proud to be part of such a project.

Stacy Whitmire

Beast. That word, when applied to a cancer, rings in your head. "A Beast" is what my oncologist called my melanoma when I was diagnosed in Feb. 2015 at 26 years old. I had one hell of a year and saw things I'd never seen before. After the year I've had—a whirlwind of sickness, biochemotherapy, and surgeries, but also friends, family, and love—I knew that I had to be a part of this anthology. I have incorporated in this story (although completely fictional) something of who I am, what I have gone through, and my beliefs. David Bowie and Alan Rickman both thought that life should be humorous and mysterious.

As my dear friend Holly said to me after she read my story, "Humor is what keeps us going." I think I believe that.

Suzanne Wdowik

 A person's death is a tragic event. An artist's death is something more nuanced. With the passing of Alan Rickman and David Bowie, we grieve the loss of two amazing lives, but we also celebrate the gifts they've left us with. I joined this project because while cancer has affected many of my loved ones for the worse, my loved ones have affected me for the better, and if I can share just a bit of what they've left behind, I can make the world a little more magical and a little more meaningful.

As Ray Bradbury said in Fahrenheit 451, "Everyone must leave something behind when he dies ... It doesn't matter what you do ... so long as you change something from the way it was before you touched it into something that's like you after you take your hands away".

Tony Hillier

 It's fun and cathartic to write, which I have done in bursts all my life. In Kolkata I published in the city's newspaper magazine. I published a book of photos, poems and drawings in a Kenyan school with each contributing pupil having their own copy.

Self-appointed (but thankfully accepted) Swindon Community Poet for the last 15 years. I enjoy juggling with words and sharing them 'hot' with the people who inspired them. I read my Bowie tribute poem at a music venue for a Bowie tribute night in aid of a cancer charity. In my opinion, every community should host a 'Community Poet' to use the art to record and reflect upon community issues and events and to have fun.

Photo credit—Chris Bourton

Trine Jensegg

Trine Jensegg is a 30 year old Norwegian nerd. She started telling stories at the age of 5, slowly building a steady fanbase of stuffed animals. It was suggested that she should write the stories down, and she hasn't stopped since. Now she's expanding to a slightly more alive audience. Like you. Her stories usually falls within the fantasy genre, but has been known to stray. Like her.

When she's not writing, but should be, she spends her time questing and / or getting her heart broken in video games, or pretending she's in a musical. She is currently living in Oslo with her cowardly cat Hiro.

Virginia Carraway Stark

Virginia Carraway Stark has a diverse portfolio and has many publications. Getting an early start on writing, Virginia has had a gift for communication, oration and storytelling from an early age. Over the years she has developed this into a wide range of products from screenplays to novels to articles to blogging to travel journalism.

She has been published by many presses from grassroots to Simon and Schuster for her contribution to 'Chicken Soup for the Soul: Think Possible' as seen on ABC. She has been an honorable mention at Cannes Film Festival for her screenplay, "Blind Eye" and was nominated for an Aurora Award.

virginiastark.wordpress.com/about/
www.facebook.com/Virginiacarrawaystark
virginiastark.wordpress.com/contact-me/

Tucker McCallahan

Tucker McCallahan is an author, editor, and researcher. An outspoken proponent of LGBTQ rights and polyamory, Tucker has lived all over the country. Currently Tucker lives in the poly community House That Love Built unearthing obscure facts, blasting music at inappropriate levels, amassing the world's largest collection of sex toys, and feeding an aquarium full of gay fish.

Zoé Perrenoud

Zoé Perrenoud was born in Lausanne, Switzerland. She has an M.A. in Creative Writing from Bangor University and is currently working as a freelance writer and translator. Her work has appeared in the *Aesthetica Creative Works Annual*, Newcastle University's *Crossing the Lines* collection of short stories and on the website of Delano magazine.

She wanted to get involved in *Stardust, Always* to immortalize the passing of two major artists and to help raise funds for cancer research, in honour of her father-in-law, Bernd Seligmann, who passed away in 2011. Zoe lives in Luxembourg with her husband and two cats.

Editors' Note

As you can see from the contributor biographies, this anthology brought together an international group of authors, and is intended for an international audience. Thus, while we corrected grammar, we did not concern ourselves too much with spelling where the difference was simply British vs. American English standards. We recognize that this might colour your reading, but please bear with us.

The editors who donated their time to this book are Andrew Barber, Ashlee Hetherington, and Lacey Sutton.

Stardust, Always

From Stardust

S.R. Betler

When I met him for the first time—and the last—I was already dying; I just didn't know it yet. But then, aren't we all? We knew nothing of each other except that we wound up at the same bus stop on a dreary Monday and that he had the good sense to bring an umbrella, whereas I did not.

I had never seen him before—I would've remembered the bowler hat and the vintage suit—but he strode up like he owned the place and sat down beside me unapologetically.

"Did you know there are approximately seven and a half billion people alive at this very moment?" he said, staring out into the rain, as if it were a perfectly normal conversation starter.

"That's a lot of people," I replied. There was nothing else to do, and who knew how long of a wait we had ahead of us, so I decided to humor him. After all, what was the harm?

"If you look at it from the perspective that we're just two out of seven and a half billion, then sure, that's a lot. But those seven and a half billion who are alive now represent only a small portion of the more than a hundred trillion people who have ever lived. With numbers like that, what are the odds that you and I would even exist? Yet here I am, and there you are."

"Are you saying we're just happy accidents?"

"I don't believe in accidents."

"So then it's fate?"

He laughed, and as he did, his smile dug little furrows in his face—evidence of his age. He wore them well, like badges of honor that lent him the air of a person who knew what he was talking about.

"Are those my only options?" he asked.

"Well, if you don't believe in chance, and it's not fate, then why else are we here?"

He gripped his umbrella and lifted the tip of it skywards, towards the surging mass of rain clouds that had lingered over the city for the past three days.

"We exist because somewhere up there, a star died," he explained.

"Oh? How is it that a star dying leads to you and I?"

If there was a correlation there, I couldn't see it, but he seemed so sure. His tone was as matter-of-fact as if he were explaining that the Earth was round, and the look he gave me belied his amusement—as if I had argued that it was, in fact, flat.

"Well, what is it we're made of?"

What were humans made of? Earth, according to some religions; energy, according to others. Atoms, if one were to ask a scientist, or, perhaps, a handful of common and easily attainable elements—oxygen, carbon, hydrogen, nitrogen, calcium, and phosphorus. Nothing truly special. But which of those was the answer he was looking for?

Before I could come to a decision, he laughed again, tapped his umbrella on the ground twice, and announced with gusto, "Stardust, of course!"

"Stardust?" I asked.

"Everything started as stardust at one time or another. It's just a matter of how far it's come since then. It's easy to forget because we don't *look* like stardust, and we certainly don't feel like it, but everything begins somewhere, doesn't it?"

"So if we're made from stardust, what are stars made of?"

"Us," he said as if it explained everything perfectly. If he had any sense of the paradox that was kicking around the cogs in my mind, he didn't show it. He just stared off into the distance, smiling at something only he seemed to fathom.

"How can that be? Stars existed long before humans, so what were the first stars made of?"

"Bit of a chicken-and-egg problem, don't you think?

Does it matter what order things happened in so long as it holds true now? We all come from stardust, and when we die, somewhere down the line, it's stardust that we ultimately become."

"I wonder—" I began, fumbling for the right words—words that seemed to come so easily for the stranger. In that, we were not so similar. I had always loved the stars as a child, but it seemed that with time, as so many grown-ups do, I had let my childhood fascinations fall by the wayside. Out of sight, out of mind, as they say. With all the worries of today, tomorrow, and yesterday, what use would one have for a ball of gas so many light-years away? "I wonder, if you could ask and they could answer, if a star would mind dying, knowing how many hundreds of lives would be born from its death."

"Well now, *that's* a question. Now you're thinking." He slapped his thigh as he laughed, the deep-bellied sort that caused his umbrella to tap the ground as his whole body shook. "But I think the real question is would *you* die knowing that your death could give life to a star that would, in turn, bring life to hundreds or possibly thousands or maybe even *millions* of other creatures?"

"Well, I don't know. I don't suppose I've ever thought about it."

I could die for my family, sure, in a heartbeat. For a stranger? Possibly. At least, I'd like to think it was in me. But for a star?

"What about you?" I asked. It seemed like the sort of thing he thought about often, so I ventured that he'd have an answer. I wasn't disappointed, as he cocked his head and looked up towards the sound of rain splattering against the bus stop roof.

"On a dreary Monday? Sure, why not? It's not like it's Friday and I've got the whole weekend to look forward to." He laughed again, and this time, I couldn't help but join him.

There was a sudden roar a block over, and a minute later, the bus appeared at the end of the street, plowing through the fog like a beast with glowing eyes. It bellowed as it slowed, plunging headlong into the puddle in front of us. The man beside me threw open his umbrella as water splashed over the bench. A dreary Monday indeed.

I squelched as I stood and gathered my briefcase, which had the benefit of being waterproof. The driver opened the doors, took one look at me, and issued the most insincere apology I had ever heard.

"You know, you should really invest in one of these," the old man said with a grin, shaking his umbrella and sending droplets of water splattering in all directions. "Comes in handy."

"Aren't you coming?" I asked as I motioned to the bus. He hadn't moved from his spot. In fact, he had settled in and made himself right at home on that bench, like a king lording over his kingdom.

He waved at me dismissively and chuckled.

"No, no, you go on. I'm waiting for someone. Thought they'd be here by now, but I guess you can't rush these things."

"Well, it was nice meeting you."

"You, too."

Maybe I should have said more. Asked for one last nugget of advice, one more thought to wrestle with throughout the day. Left him with a parting joke, perhaps. Or maybe, even, simply asked for his name. But I didn't.

Instead, I climbed onto the bus and slid into a seat in the back, tucking my briefcase onto my lap. He waved a polite farewell as the bus carried us into the fog, towards the bowels of the city, and I returned the gesture, wondering who he was and if we'd ever meet again.

I couldn't imagine who he was waiting for, but as far as I could tell, they never made it. The next day, the obituaries reported the death of a John Doe who had dozed off on a bus stop bench and passed away in his sleep. No one ever showed up to claim the body, though I heard through the grapevine that a good Samaritan donated the money for a tombstone with the instructions that four words—and only four—go on it:

FROM STARDUST, TO STARDUST

My bank account felt rather empty afterwards, but it was the least I could do.

Two weeks to the day, I was diagnosed with cancer and began treatment shortly after. It became all too clear to me why someone might pick a bench, any bench, on a dreary Monday and stare off into the sky—rain be damned—and strike up a conversation with a stranger.

Just how my story plays out, well, who's to say? But when it rains, I still think of that old man, and on clear days, when the stars twinkle and dance, I swear I can hear him laughing. One day I'll join him, though I 'm not sure when or how. Together, we'll take our place among the stars.

Stardust, Always

Change and the Great Beyond

Laura Roberts

Ch-ch-ch-changes
keep on coming,
daily, weekly, monthly;
change is inevitable
(except from a vending machine).

The only thing we have to fear
is change itself.

Change gets in your eyes,
change is the new change,
old change is the best change,
change in my cup or else -
we are coming up.

Changes are coming,
changes that speak louder than words.

Change is good.
Little yellow change,
Change for a change...

There is nothing as loyal as change.
It's so easy to be change,
and so hard to be a (wo)man.

Write change, edit change,
there is nothing to change;
you just sit at a typewriter and bleed.

Either that change goes, or I do.

Stardust, Always

Give change a chance.
Let's change,
all of us
together
now
in the revolution,
where change is required
and change is inevitable,
and change is nothing to fear
because change keeps on changing
every

      single

           day.

Melody and Magic

Caroline Centa

"But gods cannot be human!" Elohim shook his head and leaned into the plush back of his chair. His eyes connected with those of Djehuty. Djehuty's obsession with the humans spanned over many cycles and he now took human form for his appearance. Over time, he'd taken on more forms than any of the others; an ibis, a baboon, and now the dark-haired, brown-eyed male that sat before Elohim.

"I don't see why not?" Djehuty said.

"You're too powerful. Only part of you could inhabit the soul vessel to live as human. And, well, the parts must stay together."

Djehuty looked to the ground and sighed. He felt a piece of him was missing. For most his existence, he spent his time researching the humans. They were fascinating beings. He wanted to show them he was more than the written word they knew him as. As he watched them evolve, connecting to each other through electronics and radio waves, he watched the media world form and wished the humans would recognise the part he played in it all. But the higher gods would not have it.

"I know no one has done it before, but I've heard of a theory that will allow a god to live among the humans. If I separated into more parts and lived as multiple humans …"

"That could work. The planet is small enough that your parts will be close enough to survive."

"I could be born as twins!" Djehuty smiled.

Elohim shook his head. "That won't work. It is not possible to separate your soul into multiple parts and send them to the viable lives at the precise same time. There will be moments between sending one part and the next. Negligible

31

difference from our end, but almost a year on the planet."

"But I can go?" Djehuty was behaving like a human child, causing Elohim's heart to melt. He could not help but make decisions that made others happy, and it broke his heart when he had no choice.

"There will be conditions. I need to know first what you intend to do. I know you're a god, but after Khara …" Elohim shook his head. "The chaos he is still causing … . And we've not been able to call him back yet."

"I understand." Djehuty nodded, perhaps a little too enthusiastically.

"And you'll be on call. If we need you back here, you will need to come home."

"Yes, yes. Of course."

"Go to the hall of records and fill in the details. You'll be given two bodies to inhabit. Both male. Record how you intend to live their lives and I'll review them as soon as possible."

"Thank you, Elohim." The chair scraped across the marble floor as Djehuty pushed it back. Elohim raised a quill from his table and dipped it into a pot of ink before recording this conversation on the pages which lay on his desk.

* * *

On his way back to the hall of records, Djehuty visited the kilns to see the Clay Gods. The Clay Gods created each human from a ball of clay, ready for each life, while Djehuty wrote out the life it would live. He wanted to waste no time preparing the lives he would live. Once everything was ready, one of the gods (most likely Elohim, in this case) would then inject a soul into the clay mould and send it to the assigned parent. It was a convoluted equation to create life.

The Hall of Records held details of every human life and, as the God of Writing, Djehuty knew it well. It was his duty to record the lives of the humans. Djehuty enjoyed writing the stories. Sometimes experienced souls gave input into the lives they wanted to live, but other times new souls would be born. It was his job to create a life for them. It was through creating these lives that Djehuty's obsession with being human had developed. He wanted to write a life for himself.

Djehuty's brother, Yinepu, was already in the hall, slouched over a large oak desk. A massive, leather-bound book lay open in front of him, the stained pages speaking of its age. It was the jackal- headed god's job to follow-up on the lives of the humans when they ended. To ensure that the souls followed their lives accordingly and passing on the details to those at the scales of judgement.

"New death?" Djehuty asked as he sat at the desk, opposite Yinepu.

"The humans are at war with one another, thanks to Khara. We've had millions coming through. I've been run off my feet. You should see the Hall of Purgatory. I don't know if I remember a time it was so crowded. How about you? Got any new lives?"

"Only my own."

Yinepu raised his eyebrow at his brother. "Your own? Well, your timing is impeccable. How are we going to rebirth all these souls if you're off gallivanting on the planet? Who's taking over your job?"

Djehuty shrugged his shoulders. "That's not my problem. Elohim has already approved my births. But I'll write up a heap of lives and you can tell whoever takes over to distribute them as they see fit. Just let me know the total expected from this war and I'll get onto it."

The shake of Yinepu's head was barely noticeable as he returned to his ledger. Djehuty opened the leather-bound book sitting on his own desk. It was a mirror image of the one in front of his brother. The two books were magical and never left the table. As the gods wrote in them, their words materialised as books in the vaults below. These formed the Akashic records and were only accessible by a few beings. However, most of the books could be called up to the shelves in the Hall by the gods. That was unless they were in the restricted vaults. That required special access.

33

Djehuty looked over at Yinepu's book and watched as the words he wrote disappeared off the page.

"Do you know if they're any closer to recalling Khara's soul?"

"We think so. That would put an end to this mess," Yinepu replied with a sigh.

Djehuty picked up his quill and wrote his name at the top of the page in hieroglyphics. He loved the old language and thought it was suitable for writing out his lives. He then rested the tip of the feather on his face, enjoying its softness. What did he want from his time on the planet?

He decided that he wanted both his lives to be born to working-class families. That would allow him to experience what being human was truly about. Djehuty pulled out the map next to his book and had a look at the countries. Where would be a good place to live?

"Hey, 'pu?" Djehuty asked. Yinepu looked up at his brother. "Where would you recommend a life for a simple working-class boy to be born?"

Yinepu shrugged his shoulders. "Who knows? They're all much of a muchness."

"Well are any of them nicer than the others after they get to purgatory?"

"People vary no matter where they come from. You get good from everywhere as well as the vile. Although I am quite fond of the British accent."

"Right. I'll go there then." Djehuty returned to writing out his life, deciding he would dedicate one to music and the other to theatre. Both allowed him to explore the world of language without writing. He hoped his influence in those areas would then be recognised and he could earn himself a new title.

* * *

"So you're ready to be separated and born?" The bearded god asked Djehuty. He was adding final touches to two male figures made from red clay, and Djehuty watched with curiosity.

"Yes, Prometheus." Djehuty smiled. "The lives are written and approved. I am giddy with anticipation to meet my human parents. Elohim has told me both my mothers will be named Margaret. I think that is lovely."

"So what do you plan to do while you're down there?"

"I wish to add another epithet to my name. I am already known as The Scribe and the Lord of Words, but I am so much more than that. I hope that with these lives, I can expand into the world of music and theatre. I want to touch the lives of many through the spoken word and I want humans to recognise that they need only to be true to themselves. By being individuals, they can achieve so much. I want to inspire people. I want to be responsible for the growth of their wonderment. I want to make a difference."

"Doesn't everybody?"

"Yes, but it's not every day a god gets a chance to have a go." Djehuty said.

"So who's doing your job up here, while you're gone?"

"Apparently some guy named Major Tom was given the role. It's only for one cycle, so he won't have lots to do. I've already written lives for all those who were killed by the war and are waiting for rebirth."

"Major Tom? I've not heard of him." Prometheus' eyebrows narrowed as he looked up at Djehuty.

"Neither have I. I will meet him before I leave. In fact, I should head off and do that now. I wanted to know how much longer until the vessels will be ready. I am eager to get the process started."

"They'll be ready by the time Ra clocks off and Hekate takes over." Prometheus replied.

"That's not very long then. I'd best get a move on."

Djehuty turned away from the Clay God, his white robes billowing behind him as he walked away.

* * *

The cheers from the Hall of Judgement resounded through the walls to the altar in Elohim's ceremonial room. Djehuty raised his eyebrow with surprise.

"Sounds like something good just happened." Djehuty said to Elohim. Elohim was measuring out various coloured liquids into different vials. He barely showed any emotion as he nodded in reply to Djehuty. "What do you suppose it was?"

"Khara's finally been recalled. The war will begin to close now."

"That'll be good for me then?" Djehuty asked as he fidgeted in the leather seat, sat opposite the alter Elohim stood at.

"Depends on what you want to achieve," Elohim said.

"I want to bring change to the people. I want to expand expression and inspire people to live true to themselves."

"For what purpose?" Elohim put the vials in his hands on the table and leaned forward to look Djehuty in the eye.

"I want to be the God of Expression. Not just the God of Language."

"Very well. It is time." Elohim said. "Have you sat with Metatron and explained what he is to do in your absence?"

Djehuty chuckled to himself at the mention of Metatron. He had misheard Gabrielle, Elohim's messenger, when he told Djehuty of the replacement. To think there was someone called Major Tom in the heavens who could do his job. "Yes, yes. He wasn't jubilant about having to do my job. Something about being stuck in a tin can instead of being able to explore the universe."

"He's spent long enough gallivanting around the place. It'll do him well to stay in one spot, considering sending him to Wisconsin did no good. I really shouldn't have invented loopholes."

"Why did you?" Djehuty asked.

"Why did I what?" Elohim asked, returning to the vials on his desk.

"Invent loopholes."

"It's not exactly free will if there are no loopholes now,

is it?"

"I guess not. So how long until I'll be born?" Djehuty shifted in his chair.

Elohim picked up one of the vials. It was full of a dark, blue liquid. Djehuty thought it rather reminiscent of ink. "This one will separate your soul into two." He then picked up two smaller vials, one filled with fluorescent green and the other blood red fluid. "These will anchor your souls to their designated bodies. The figures from the office of Prometheus should be delivered in a moment and then we can complete the process. Are you sure you want to go through with this? Life as a human isn't all it's cracked up to be."

"I am sure. I know what to expect. I write the lives, remember. I am the creator of the stories."

"Creating and living. They are two different things. You would do well to remember that."

A timid knock on the door caused both gods to turn. A small brown creature with large ears and a pointed nose held out two small, clay figures.

"Delivery from Prometheus, sirs." The creature's voice was high-pitched.

"Thank you, Nym." Elohim rose from his chair and collected the clay figures before patting Nym on the head and ushering him back out of the room. "Well, it's time." Elohim returned to the table and picked up the vial of blue liquid. "Drink this."

Djehuty nodded as he took the vial and poured it into his mouth. Other than a slight tingling sensation, the liquid didn't make him feel any differently. "Is it working?"

Elohim nodded and raised the other two vials. He poured a drop of the red liquid onto one of the clay figures and then repeated the process with the green liquid onto the other figure. "You will have to drink these two as well," he said, handing what remained to Djehuty.

The room swirled around him the instant the liquid touched his lips. A cascade of colours swirled around him before fading into dull stars and ending in darkness. Within moments a soft beat floated to Djehuty's ears. No, there were two. They thumped rhythmically, then he felt them separate. His consciousness faded, and he was no longer Djehuty.

* * *

HAMMERSMITH, LONDON. 1945

A young woman stopped dusting her house to touch her bulging abdomen when the announcement for the end of the war came through the radio. She was grateful that her baby would not be born into the disaster of the world. She glanced over to the small boy playing with wooden blocks on the floor.

"Did you hear that, David?" She asked. The boy looked up at his mother. "The war is over."

"What does that mean, Mummy? Why are you crying?" He stood and ran to his mother, wrapping his arms around her legs.

"I am happy. It means we won't have to live in fear anymore."

* * *

BRIXTON, LONDON. 1946

"I'm pregnant, John," the woman announced.

John put his head in his hands and shook his head. "But I can't marry you, Peggy. Not yet. I'm still technically married."

"That's okay. We will work it out. Together." Peggy put her hand on the man's shoulder. "This baby is a blessing. I can feel it already. However long it takes, we will marry and become a family."

The man turned to wrap his arms around the woman. "You're right. I love you, Peggy. And this baby will be a testament of our love."

A Villain with Heart

Clara Ryanne Heart

"I can't do this!" I growled and dragged my pen across the notebook. The ragged gash left in the paper curled. The shadows along its jagged edges twisted into mocking smirks.

"What are you trying to do?" Steven asked.

"I'm just trying to write and the words aren't working for me."

"Maybe I can help."

"That would require too much talking." I loved my husband. And his ability to calm me down when everything else seemed to work against me was uncanny. But this was no ordinary problem. The thought of trying to explain it to him pained me. If only he could read my mind instead of requiring the backstory.

"Oh no ... The *horror.* Talking to your husband? Shut up and tell me which words are hurting you."

And then it happened. That tingle just below my temple. Near the top edge of my jaw. I pinched the bridge of my nose and clenched my eyes. I would only have a few minutes before the tingle grew. The paper would feel too bright. My computer screen would burn through my retinas and sear my optic nerves.

If I was ever going to finish this, it would have to be now. Before the migraine could take over.

I slumped out of the room and down the hall into the kitchen. Steven's socks slipped across the hardwood floor behind me. I smirked at the memory of our first night in this house. "Still think you're a ninja?"

I rummaged through the cupboard. Moving dishes and mugs from one side to the other. Why I needed to collect so many different coffee mugs when I only ever used one made no sense to me. One favorite mug that liked to hide and laugh.

Wait a minute, that wasn't the mug laughing. That was Steven. I turned around to see him leaning back against the dishwasher. My favorite mug dangled from his fingertips.

I took in a deep breath and leaned into his chest. "Migraine ...," I whimpered.

He wrapped his arms around me, just as I knew he would, and pressed his lips against the top of my head. "Okay. That's your brain's way of telling you that you need a break. Come on."

He led me back out into the front room and dimmed the lights. "I still have so much to do." I couldn't stop myself. Every word twanged into a relentless whine. I flinched at my own voice.

The tingle grew.

"It's fine," Steven whispered with a grin. "Lay down here. I'll grab your mask and maybe I can help you with some of it."

I forced my lips into a smile and obeyed. A few minutes later, a cooling mask hid the room from my view. The steam of a fresh mug of coffee carried its aroma straight to my sinuses. I leaned back into my seat and groaned in contentment. Papers rustled from the other side of the room. Seconds later, the sofa cushion billowed under me and my weight shifted slightly as Steven lifted my feet and placed them into his lap.

"Okay. So who are we working on today?" Steven whispered.

"Xiuhcoatl."

More rustling papers before Steven continued. "Aztec god of destruction—."

"No. He's a weapon of destruction."

"Weapon of destruction. Sorry. Okay, so who is he to Celyna?"

"Main antagonist. But a minor villain."

"A minor villain?"

"Yea, like he's a threat but not really the main threat. So

at some point in time a larger threat will surface."

"Ah, hence the name. This larger threat is using him?"

"Exactly."

"Okay. So what's the problem with Xiuhcoatl then?"

I stared into the back of the cooling mask and listened to more pages being flipped. Steven's fingers rubbed along the bottoms of my feet as he read through my notes. "Seems okay to me. Looks like a real bastard."

"Yea, but I didn't just want him to be a bastard. I want him to be ... I don't know. I wanted him to be the type of villain Alan Rickman would play. You know?"

"Ah. Okay."

I'm not sure how much longer after that I dozed off. But I did. Steven studied my notes. He read scene after scene of my novel, making notes of his own while I napped. When I awoke, my migraine was on the decline. The stinging tension behind my eyes finally loosened enough for me to remove the mask.

"Feel better?" Steven asked.

"I think so. Even better, I think I figured out the first part of what I should use as my pseudonym."

"Really? And what's that?"

"Clara."

"Clara? Like The Doctor's companion, Clara?"

I giggled and sat up straight. "Yes. Exactly like The Doctor's companion Clara. And also exactly like Clara Clayton."

"Clara Clayton. Clara Clayton, Clara Clayt—wow. That is really hard to say over and over again." Steven chuckled.

"Remember? The school teacher from Back to the Future?"

"Oh Doc Brown's little hubba hubba."

"Yes. Actually if I could choose to use the name 'hubba hubba' I would. But for now I'll stick with Clara. What do you think?"

Steven pinched his lips in to a thin line and glared at me. His eyes darted from one side of my face to the other. Finally, he tucked a lock of my auburn hair back away from my cheek and nodded. "Yea. I like Clara. I think that'll work just fine."

Days passed before I was able to return to working on my novel. Yet when I did, Steven's notes were, as always, front and center and not at all helpful.

"I love you. You got this. Don't ever give up."

Okay. So his notes were helpful. Just not always in the way I expected them to be.

I decided to skip a few scenes and work on other revisions. I needed to make Celyna stronger. To justify why she would be granted her freedom. Something that would catch the eyes of other characters without making her shine with a spotlight. Lucien still needed more motivation to help Xiuhcoatl. And I had to double check through Zedekiah's interactions with Celyna. My beta reader didn't like the hint at a love triangle there. And I couldn't blame her. I hadn't meant for it to seem like a love triangle, but really just close friends.

Now I needed to go back in and make sure that relationship was defined the way I meant for it to be.

"How's it going?" Steven asked as he entered the room with a pile of laundry. "Did you figure out what you wanted to do with Xiuhcoatl yet?"

Socks and sweatpants tumbled out of his arms and onto the sofa with a less than graceful slump.

"No, not yet. I decided to leave him alone for now and handle some of the other bits of feedback instead."

"Ah."

"Hey, so I was thinking about my pseudonym, and I think I should have more than just a first and last name."

"What do you mean. Like you want a middle name, too?"

"Yea. I was thinking Ryanne."

"Ryan? Like your nephew, Ryan? The one with autism?"

"Yea. What do you think?"

"Clara Ryanne. I like it. But it doesn't really matter, does it?"

"What do you mean?"

"I mean ... no one's going to know whether it's 'Clara Ryanne' or 'Christopher Randolph'."

"Christopher Randolph?"

"I mean, don't authors all just use initials now? To hide their gender because men sell better? So won't you just be C.R. Author?"

I stared down at my fingertips hovering over my keyboard. My nails clacking against the letters as I pounded out new words. "I know a lot of authors do that. I'm not one of them. I want people to know I wrote this as a woman. And I'll sell just as many copies as any man would."

Steven stopped moving. Two mismatched socks adorned his hands as he gazed at me. "Good for you," he said. He crossed the room and leaned over to give me a kiss.

The static electricity beat him to it.

As I rubbed my lip and laughed, he peeled a third sock from his chest. "Anyway. So what do you think goes with Clara Ryanne?"

"No idea," I said with a sigh. The computer screen glared at me as the blinking cursor laughed.

Later that night, I decided to abandon my novel. At least for a short while. I sank into the sofa and curled up into Steven's arm. "Can we watch *Project Runway*?" I asked.

"You know, I have learned more about fashion than I ever thought I would care to know. And yet I bet I still couldn't thread your sewing machine."

I laughed at his sarcasm and snuggled in deeper. "Okay, fine. How about *Die Hard*?"

"Now you're talking," Steven said and snapped up the clicker. "You're going to let me watch it, right? We aren't going to get ten minutes into it and then you need me to get up to make popcorn? Or coffee? Or grab you a water?"

I pondered over his question and rocked from one side to the other. "Yea ..."

"Yea, you need something? Or yea we can watch it?"

"Yea, we can watch—actually now that you mention it, popcorn really does sound good."

Steven laughed and knocked his shoulder into my arm, bumping me back against the side of the sofa. "All right," he said. "You get drinks, I'll make popcorn. And we meet back here in four and a half minutes."

"Deal!"

And three minutes later we were back on the sofa and the opening credits were playing. Soon, the sounds of gunshots and screaming drowned out the chomping noises of our popcorn. My heart fluttered as Hans introduced himself to McClane.

"You see. *This* is the type of villain I need. You see how well he flipped over from terrorist to victim? That's what I need."

"Oh shit," Steven muttered as he clicked the pause button on the clicker.

"No, really. This is why I'm having such a hard time with Xiuhcoatl. I need him to be something deeper than just a villain. He needs something. He needs heart."

"Hey, that's it."

"What's it? Are you about to make fun of me for ruining a movie again?"

"Not even close," said Steven. "But I think you just finished building your pseudonym."

"I did?"

"Yea. Clara. Ryanne. Heart."

"Clara Ryanne Heart," I whispered. A smile crept across my lips. "Yea. Clara Ryanne Heart. I like it."

"Okay. So problem solved. Now we can finish the mov—."

I leaned over and gazed at Steven. Just raising my eyebrows was enough to make him realize my time in front of the television was over.

"We aren't finishing the movie are we?"

I shook my head and kissed his cheek. "Nope. I have things to do. Websites to build. I need a blog. A Facebook page. A Twitter account. I need to get a real presence set up."

"Really? Even though Xiuhcoatl's such a mess?"

I laughed and cracked my knuckles over my keyboard. "Oh, believe me ... Xiuhcoatl will have plenty of heart."

Steven shook his head and hit play on the clicker. The cat curled beneath his fingertips and soon enough his attention was gone. I turned back to a fresh internet browser and logged into my Facebook account. "Create new page," I whispered as I aimed the mouse at the button.

Stardust, Always

Always

A. R. Harlow

One word sums up Alan Rickman:
'Always'.

Always striving to make an impact,
Always speaking articulately,
Always riveting.

Always engraved in my heart
As Severus Snape,
Seeming to embody pure hatred,
But making the greatest true sacrifice
For a love he could never show.

Always inspiring, always changing,
Always growing in our hearts,
Inspiring our souls to take flight,
And changing the way
We view the world around us.

We can make changes too,
Even if it is just ripples in the water.

Today, I am starting ripples.
Tomorrow, we will all turn those ripples to waves.
Next week, we will set the waves free
In all the seas of the world,
And we will make a difference that lasts

Always

* * *

For my mom Paula, daughter Riley, husband Matthew, and friends John and Tiffani for encouragement, inspiration, support and love.

Stardust, Always

The Call of the Sea

Fiona Teh

The grey sky grumbled like a bad-tempered old man as thick black clouds knitted together over Emerald Isle. Deep in the middle of the East Bay marketplace, Roan Stirling swayed slightly as she hunched over trays of raw dough. She was dressed for the middle of summer in a thin cotton dress and a plain faded blouse. Huddled under a much- patched tent, Roan made uneven dough balls, eyes glazed in the midday heat. She was listlessly working up a short fantasy about the cool seawater and her legs, dancing to a beat in her mind. As if to spite her, a single stinging smear of sweat dripped into her unfocused eye, rudely destroying her daydreaming. Roan yelped and dabbed at her eye with one hand while shaking her fist at the air. Nearby, Aunt Orla and her daughters twitched at the sound.

Oh blast it all, she thought irritably. I'd gladly give my last copper to be soaked in ice water! Her feet were swelling and she winced as she gingerly slipped her thin summer shoes off and stopped for a rest. The Healer had warned her this might happen but did it have to show up during the hottest time of the day?

If Uncle Breff had his way, he'd have made her stop hours ago. "Eh, you're a young lady now, oughta be spending time flirtin' with young lads," he would admonish, his kind green eyes clearly tired of his wife's sharp ones. Roan would have gladly run off then.

But not to flirt!

Roan had just turned seventeen and was, in the eyes of the good people of Emerald Isle, now eligible for marriage. She was not keen on flirting with the lads, however, never mind securing a husband. Her childhood friend Eileen Matteo did enough flirting for the two of them. That suited them both very well; fair Eileen did at least enjoy the attention the hopeful suitors gave her. She loved to play the soft lily role and watch the lads run around making grand romantic gestures. It was rather funny, really. Roan knew full well that Eileen was no soft lily. She had seen her lug heavy baskets of fruit for her father when he needed help. When she said that as much to Eileen, her friend had just smiled, eyes twinkling with mischief.

Whatever game Eileen was playing, Roan was happy to let Eileen take all the attention from the hopeful potentials while she hid in the shadows. Roan could not evade everyone completely, however. There were a few lads who inexplicably preferred Roan's quiet nature and might have mentioned as much to their mothers, much to her disgust.

"It's a shame Roan's not as honey-tongued as that sweet girl Eileen," Mother Rivers, the washerwoman declared regretfully to her friend.

"Lucky she's a hard worker," clucked back Mistress Han, the spice merchant's wife. "I doubt she's got much of a dowry, what with a gypsy for a mother and no knowledge of a father to speak of. It is a sure bet Breff will leave his fried dough business to her!"

Both women had sons they wanted to marry off and had recently rested their interested eyes upon Roan. The women weren't necessarily mean-spirited, just somewhat careless with their words. Roan did not like to admit it, but it stung when they talked about her so crudely.

They were not the only women with matchmaking desires. Recently Roan caught some middle-aged bachelors staring at her with odd expressions that made her feel uneasy. If any men or meddlesome mothers had made their intentions clear to uncle Breff, he did not share this with Roan. Uncle Breff was a reserved, cautious type of man and did not say much to anyone. In that way, Roan was similar and preferred to be left alone.

For the most part, Roan ignored the women who made it a daily sport to harangue her ears. "Jes' pay no mind to them, love," Uncle Breff would say, apologetically and awkwardly. "They're just gossipy old hens clucking their tongues." Roan knew he meant well, but uncle Breff was often baffled by such things, and seemed awkward and apologetic when he talked about them. Roan refused to ask aunt Orla for help either. She was rather of the prickly sort. Who knew what she might say or do?

If only they knew I wouldn't live long enough to give them grand-babies, Roan thought without animosity. *They wouldn't be so quick to nag me, and they might just leave me be!*

It was true that Roan was neither sweet of tongue nor as fair as many of the girls from the Emerald Isle. Her gold complexion and dark hair came from her mother's Gypsy heritage, and she had inherited Niomi's magic too; a poor exchange for the few memories she had of her mother. The Traveling Bard had returned home one day, thin and sick, with a body-eating disease beyond the reach of healers, and a tiny baby in her arms. Her brother Breff had taken one look at the mother and child, and made room for them in his tiny home. As Niomi grew weaker, baby Roan grew older.

While Niomi's magic had been her song, Roan, they soon discovered, danced. While people accepted her gift with pleasure, no one really gave her too much attention. After all, she was just a commoner, like the rest of them. Quite a few people had the gift in some form or degree, but nobody else had dance magic.

Whenever Roan danced at public festivals and wedding parties as a paid entertainer, people expected and desired for things to happen. She manipulated little spell nets that could find the right person with the right spell. Sometimes her spells reached certain people needing extra courage. Other times her spells suggested creativity. Very often, young brides and their grooms would ask her to dance a spell for fertility.

Her spells were as playful and airy as her dance steps, and she never lacked dance partners, male or female. Roan was a shy girl, but she shone like a star when she danced. Before Niomi died, she had made Breff promise that when Roan came of age, she would have free choice of what she wanted to do. She had looked into Roan's eyes and told her to 'be free'. Roan had been too young to fully comprehend her meaning, but growing up, she always felt like she was constantly waiting for something to happen. In the meantime, she drifted.

Uncle Breff had recently wrenched his back while hauling sacks of flour, and was forced to stay home to rest, leaving his wife and niece to tend to the fried dough stall at the market. His wife Orla Hawkins was not exactly unkind, but she was not exactly thoughtful either. She had left Roan to work without a word, while her own two daughters flitted about uselessly.

Marla, plump but sweet of face, sidled up to her mother and smiled prettily, "Mum, Lucie and I are just going to get ice lollies and check on Breff. Is that alright?"

Lucie's eyes glittered with cheek and she got up from where she had been sitting and hurried to her twin's side. Fluffing her soft brown curls, slightly damp from sweat, Lucie hooked her skinny arm around her mother's waist in an amiable way. "I'll see if he needs anything," she said softly.

For a moment, the trio exchanged quick looks. Breff Stirling was a kind and hardworking baker and a good husband to his wife. He was equally a good stepfather to the mostly flighty twins when they moved into his tiny little dwelling he shared with Roan. They seem to adore him and in turn, Breff showered them with proper affection.

Roan had no reason to be jealous of the attention they received; Breff clearly loved her too. Having a family unit other than Roan in Breff's life actually gave Roan a chance to leave Emerald Isle, at least when she found the courage. She was most afraid of breaking his heart for she knew he loved her; she was also the only direct link left to his sister.

Then there was also the problem of that blasted illness,which Roan could not shake.

The Healer had said little, except for grave hints that Roan should prepare for the worst. Roan remembered the look in Uncle Breff's eyes the first time she had fainted. She had never seen him so distraught. It was ample proof that she had the same body eating illness that had eventually taken her mother's life. Knowing that had only made her grit her teeth in defiance, despite her fear. She was not going to let sickness hinder her plans!

"Look at that sky. A storm is surely brewing! Lucie, here, coins for your ice lollies but hurry home—we won't be long behind you." Orla sighed. Her voice was soft and genteel from her time as a lady's maid, but it rippled with a slight unease as she looked at the darkening sky.

The twins leapt to their feet, swirling their thin homespun summer skirts of blue and yellow. They waved to Roan as they skipped away, arm in arm. "See you later, Roanie!"

they called breezily.

Someone cleared their throat loudly and Roan blinked quickly. "Wool-gathering again Roan?" Aunt Orla eyed her from the other side of the fried dough stand, her sharp eyes narrowing. Not for the first time since summer began, Roan thought about leaving.

"Just making sure the dough is perfectly shaped, auntie," she replied smartly. She felt sweaty and cross, and for the first time that day, waves of sickness started to hit her hard.

Roan closed her eyes for a moment to regain her balance and swallowed away the sourness building up in her mouth. She stepped outside the tent, and for a long moment, Roan kept her eyes shut tight and tried to regulate her breathing, the fabric of her dress bunched in two fists as she fought yet another wave of nausea. The Healer had warned her that this would occur more often, just like the swelling of her hands and feet. Roan forced herself to breathe, but she was anxious. Orla bit down on another sharp comment as she watched her step-niece struggle.

When the first few fat drops of rain hit her eyebrow and slid onto her eyelid, Roan lifted her floury hands into the air and let out an oath of thankfulness.

"Bless you Great Lady Aiyu, Goddess of Rain, for your kindness and reprieve from this dry spell!" Roan kissed her fingers and raised her thin arms towards the sky. Like most Emerald Isle dwellers, Roan prayed to a variety of Gods and

Goddesses. Great Lady Aiyu had been a bit cross of late with her patrons and hadn't deigned to produce much rain.

"Oh, go on then and have your walk by the beach," Orla muttered brusquely. "I can't stand to see that sour face anymore! I'll pack up by myself. Make sure you get home before it starts to storm."

For a moment, Aunt Orla's critical gaze wavered, and she looked as if she wanted to say something else, something nice. Then she shook her head and turned away, her lips pursed. Aunt Orla was never really good with words. Roan drew in a deep breath and moved slowly. Her dizzy spells were getting more frequent, but she was not going to miss out on the chance to frolic at the beach. She pulled the yellow headscarf off her hair and stuffed it into her skirt pocket.

Aunt Orla beckoned to Scab the street urchin and ordered him to start stacking things into the rusty wagon nearby. Scab—dirty, impish and no older than eleven—had been hanging about the marketplace waiting for such an errand. He grinned crookedly at Roan and picked at the dried blisters on his face. Roan rolled her eyes and hid a smile as she slipped him a piece of the honey drop he loved so much. With a grin of absolute pleasure, he popped it into his mouth, away from Orla's sharp eyes.

Silly with joy at her sudden freedom, Roan sprang up and turned towards the sea. She gave a happy yip, grabbed her poncho and dashed out into the heavy air, weaving expertly through the cacophonous throng of vendors and harried-looking customers in the marketplace. Everyone there knew and liked Roan, vendors and customers alike. They waved to her absentmindedly, calling her name as she ran past their stalls.

She streaked perilously through the people, animals and carts kicking up the dust of East Market Street, and paid no mind when Eileen and her brother Thomas waved to her from their packed wagon. Roan was anxious; the rain was picking up, and already the wind had started to whistle. She was eager to get to the beach quickly.

She hurried past the path that led to the gate and the

beach area towards the face of a little hill. There she followed a narrow, curved hill path to a broken set of steps that dropped steeply. As she reached the last step and the raging sea came into view, Roan stopped and stared.

Lo! What a magnificent sight! In the brewing storm, the azure sea crashed against and into the slippery black rocks. Nobody came to this part of the Emerald Isle. The sea was a dead drop from the piles of sharp rocks that made the edge of a cliff, beside the short hill that also carved into a cave. It was also a known playground for the Merfolk of Emerald Isle because of its forlorn state.

Amongst this mess of seaweed, driftwood and rocks, there was a small clearing of grainy sand. This was Roan's spot. She clambered down to the clearing eagerly, pulling off the shoes that no longer fit her swelling feet. With an urgent cry of sheer pleasure, she flung her arms into the air and dug her toes into the soggy, rough sand. Purple magic streamed steadily from her as she danced a few steps forward in preparation. Roan lifted a slim leg in front of her and raised her arms to a pose, pulling her leg sideways with practiced ease until it rested against her standing leg. Flushing with anticipation, she lifted her leg until she stood on her toes.

In the deep glimmering ocean, curious Merfolk sensed the magic to come, and popped their heads above the dark frothy waves to watch. Roan, not realizing she had company, lifted her chin and leapt into a magic dance. As a dance mage, she knew all the square dances it was possible to know, as well as the faster jigs the older people enjoyed. This dance was something altogether different. Roan had seen a version of this once when her mother had taken her to see a visiting dance troupe. The dancing girls did amazing things with their bodies, lifting their legs, splitting and leaping with such grace. Roan let her body do the creating while she focused on the feeling she desired.

Amused and very much mesmerized, the watching group of merfolk cheered, their musical voices blending with the sounds of the waves. Naia, a very young mermaid eager and quite new at her own magic capabilities, was entranced, and giggled with delight as Roan's strange purple magic tickled her senses. She playfully hurled her own power forward to join Roan's.

Her gift came in cool briny aquamarine and twirled around Roan's, like a baby tidal wave, shocking Roan's body for a few seconds. It felt amazing. With a soft laugh that was filled with relief, Roan glanced down briefly at her energized feet. She turned towards the singing Merfolk and launched a series of quick turns en pointe, testing out the mingling of powers.

Rejuvenate! Roan commanded her magic boldly, as she took two quick steps to the left and lunged forward into a grand leap, splitting in mid-air and then landing back down again with a soft thud. Naia realized what she was up to and bade her own power to boost Roan's.

Her body hurt. Determined to fight this, Roan envisioned the healing warmth of purple bolstered by the surprising appearance of aquamarine, reaching into her veins and through to her blood path and into her heart. Her magic surged forward, purple intertwined with aquamarine, working as a team. The whirling colorful magic spun into a tight watery net, creating tension before bursting into thousands of droplets up in the wind and rain and showering down again.

Naia shook out her seaweed-hued hair with utter delight and called her power back. Buzzed, she giggled and dived deep into the ocean. Her sudden departure jolted the others to follow, leaving Roan suddenly quite alone.

Her dark hair flew back as lash after lash of rain battered steadily against her face. She hurriedly pulled the poncho over her head and dashed into shallow cave, cut by the sea into the rocky hill. Crouching, she folded her legs into her chest and wrapped her arms around them. She shivered, but not with the cold. In a short time, she had worked up her emotions into a mighty storm inside her. "Bother," she said, half crossly and half in relief, before surprising herself and bursting into tears. She had never tried to heal herself before.

"It won't last." A deep voice spoke, startling Roan.

Still crying, Roan snapped her head up. A tall, thin man

stood rather stiffly at the edge of the cliff. He was just steps from where Roan crouched. He had dark shoulder length hair the color of chestnuts. From her position, Roan could see that he wore a cloak made of sealskin. It was an odd picture.

Gasping with slight fear and awe, Roan jumped to her feet. "You're a Selkie!" she exclaimed, backing away and covering her mouth, eyes agape. In all her young life, Merfolk were the only sea creatures that had shown themselves to her freely. She had certainly never seen a Selkie before.

"Silly girl, I'm not here to do you harm," he said somewhat haughtily. The man wore the loose brown tunic and trousers that most young working men favored. He did not wear shoes.

"What doesn't last?" she asked, curiously. At this, the Selkie chortled rudely. Bristling,

Roan narrowed her eyes but did not look away from the strange creature. She was going to be brave! The Selkie clasped his hands in front of him, unblinkingly. He had solemn blue-grey eyes that made Roan think of storms.

"Your spell. It will not last," he said shortly.

Roan frowned and nodded reluctantly. "I think I know ... sir?"

"I'm Tam," he said, bowing stiffly in the rain. Roan fought to hide a smile. He really was a strange creature.

"Tam ..." Roan let the strange name roll out. "How do you know what my magic can do?" she asked crossly.

Tam merely sent her a dry look and shrugged languidly.

"I'm a Selkie. I know magic. If you so desire, we could make a bargain. A healing spell." His eyes glittered as he leaned forward, smiling slyly.

"To heal me completely?" Roan asked incredulously and also hopefully. She should not bargain with an immortal. But ... to be healed! She would be mad not to consider other possibilities.

"Aye. You're a mortal with a mortal illness. Give up your mortality. Choose to live under the water." Tam gestured towards the ocean. "If you choose to accept my bargain, you will have to give up your family. You can never have a mortal lover. Also you will no longer be a dance mage. No legs." He nodded to her legs pointedly.

Roan gasped at this. "And what do you want in return?" she asked, with gritted teeth, for he must want something.

"You can get me information. You'll be new to the underwater realms. As a new element you'll have no known allegiances. You'll report to me discreetly."

"And if I don't get you the information?" asked Roan defiantly. The Selkie merely stared unblinkingly at her before answering.

"You will have a year and a day as a Seeker. Should you fail to deliver, you will regain your mortality as well as well as your illness. You are to meet me here, before the sun fully reaches the horizon with an answer, for anytime after, I shall be gone."

With that, the Selkie turned his back towards her and dove into the ocean without a second look. Roan watched as he changed into a great grey bull seal and disappeared into the water.

Trembling, Roan fled. With only the safety of home in her mind, Roan stumbled blindly up the slippery steps and ran headlong into tree roots and brambles.

Uncharacteristically clumsy, the minute she got home, Roan fell into the mudroom in her haste, bumping in her aunt.

"Good gracious, lass. Look at you, soaked to your skin! I said hurry home, not dawdle! "

Roan hurriedly peeled off her wet things, leaving them strewn in a wet clump. She could smell the heady scent of meat pies baking in the hearth and the warm bread cooling. "I lost track of time." She mumbled, licking her lips with anticipation of a good supper.

"Lost track of time, she says. No doubt lost in her dancing spell. This child will have the death of me."

Shaking her head with exasperation and relief, Aunt Orla picked up Roan's wet things and pushed her towards the tub of steaming hot water. "Have a yourself a good soak before you freeze," she ordered sternly before leaving her.

"Yes madam," Roan said, surprised and touched that a bath had already been drawn for her. Uncomfortable feelings of guilt and … love gnawed at her. Could she give up her family for the sake of her health?

Roan slid into the tub and shuddered with pleasure as she soaked away her chills and dark thoughts.

Dusk crept in and Roan found herself very busy with supper and then the cleaning up after. Marla and Lucie entertained her with girly chatter. Uncle Breff was feeling better and hummed cheerfully while he rocked in his old wicker chair. Even caustic-tongued Aunt Orla was cozy in her corner, mending a basket of things. It had stopped raining and Eileen dropped by as she often did in the evenings. Roan's mind did wander, from time to time. The Selkie's promise of immortality was too incredible to forget. It was the solution she had been looking for yet- how could she give up her gift? No more magic meant no more dance healing.

How could she give up the gift her mother had passed on to her?

It was not the right time to think about this. Eileen had coaxed Roan to dance, not that she needed much convincing and Lucie got out her little fiddle. Bits of magic drifted out in pockets of warmth as Roan twirled first with Eileen then with Marla. And look! Was that a smidgen of smile on Aunt Orla's face?

Roan lost herself in this moment. It wasn't until bedtime when Roan suddenly realized with sinking feeling that she only had a few hours left before she had to make a decision.

"I don't know!" She said out loud in horror.

"What don't you know?" Lucie asked curiously as she braided her hair with deft fingers.

Roan had forgotten that she shared a room with the girls.

"I don't know what I am to do!" She wailed softly and felt as if her heart was breaking.

"Blessed saints, are you quite alright?" Marla cried, alarmed at Roan's sudden plight.

"What if I never healed?" Roan groaned, hiding her face

under her pillow.

The girls were quiet as they glanced at one another. Roan finally lifted her face and stared gloomily. "I'll take care of you," said Lucie.

Roan sat up and stared at Lucie and Marla. "Why?" She asked the younger girl.

"We're family. That's what we do. Help each other. Except, I really don't like to work at the fried dough stall anymore. I really would prefer to be a lady's maid, like mother was." said Lucie, wrinkling her delicate nose. Roan could not help but laugh with relief as tears threatened to spill. "I'm just being daft, don't mind me. I think you'll make a very nice lady's maid."

When a sharp rap on their door sounded, the trio giggled and soon all chatter died out.

Roan felt for the first time, a real connection with the twins, like she belonged. She stared tiredly out of the window. It had started to rain again and their bedroom window flew open. Roan leapt up quietly to shut the latch. As she reached forward she heard the roar of the ocean.

Frowning, she cocked her ear. Visions of playful mermaids reflected prettily in the rain drops that fell along the window pane. The Selkie shimmered amongst the merfolk and gestured with his arms in mockery. He beckoned. The rain smelled salty. A fat drop of rain fell onto Roan's arm, leaving behind a fish scale. Alarmed, Roan dabbed the spot that glittered on her skin. "No!" She said. With fierce determination, she glared straight into the Selkie raindrop image. With a definite tug, she shut the window and locked it.

When Roan woke up, the sun was high in the sky, birds were chirping rudely and somewhere in the house, she heard the sounds of breakfast being prepared.

Roan sprang up, stretched, and danced.

The Man Who Fell Back To Earth

Andrew Barber

They were the best of dark, stormy nights; they were the worst of dark, stormy nights. There had been a pattern to them, although nobody could work out what it was. Nobody on Earth anyway, although one came close.

Even Enoch, falling through the clouds with lightning zapping around him, half-deaf from the thunder, had less idea of what was going on than he would have liked. All he really knew was that he would meet a messenger who would help him work out his mission on Earth. God really did move in mysterious ways. Enoch wondered if he did it deliberately. He put his hands over his eyes again, and wondered why it was so important that he be naked. He was freezing.

Parachutists have a rule of thumb for calculating altitude based on the animal kingdom. When the legs of a horse become visible, the observer is about 1,500 feet up. When they can see those of cows, it's around 1,000. Sheep legs can be discerned at 500. Good advice is to pull the rip cord when the cars are the size of ants. When the ants are the size of cars, it's usually a bit late.

Enoch had neither rip cord nor parachute, so the last advice would have been particularly useless; if he'd known how close he really was to the rapidly-approaching ground, there was little more that he could have done to panic anyway. He was already screaming at the top of his lungs with his eyes closed and his fingers in his ears.

He felt himself slowing down, as a freak gust of wind from below seemed to hold him aloft before dropping him neatly on his feet in a field. He opened his eyes slowly, trying to compose himself. His breathing was still laboured.

"Dave!" said a whispered, urgent voice in the dark.

61

"Wake up! A bloke just fell out of the sky ..." There was the sound of a thud, and a rustling, followed by waking sounds of indignant surprise.

"Did you just elbow me in the ribs? I was fast asleep!"

The reply came in the same tense whisper. "Keep your voice down! Dave, there's someone out there. I'm serious. He just dropped out of the sky."

"What? What are you talking about?"

"Look!" She pointed, and there he was. He was looking at their tent like he'd never seen one before. He started approaching them. "O.M.F.G. He's naked!"

Dave roused himself and started getting out of his sleeping bag. "I don't know what you think you're doing, mate," he shouted, "but you can stop right there, or I'm going to start getting annoyed ..."

Sandra, his girlfriend, tried to get back in the tent, but Dave was already getting out, and it took them a couple of attempts before they managed it. Eventually he was standing up outside.

Enoch had stayed where he was. "I come in peace," he said.

"You're very naked for an ambassador," said Dave.

"Everyone starts out naked," said Enoch. "This is my rebirth."

Dave crossed his arms. "Are you some kind of religious nut?"

"I ... I don't understand," said Enoch. He was shivering.

"He's going to catch his death of cold, no matter what he believes," said Sandra. She looked at the night sky. It was still dark and stormy, and rain was coming down in sheets.

"He's not our responsibility," said Dave.

"He will be if he dies," said Sandra. "Give him your sleeping bag."

"I don't want strange naked men in my sleeping bag."

"Fine." She picked up her own. "Here you are, mate. Warm yourself up with this." She called him over to the tent.

Dave snorted, and got some underwear out of his rucksack. "At least put these on first." He saw Sandra's look.

"And here's a T-shirt. And a towel."

"You are very kind," said the man "Call me Enoch."

The variously-happy campers introduced themselves.

"Where am I?" asked Enoch.

"Just outside Swindon, mate." Dave was still looking him over suspiciously.

"Er, Swindon?"

"You don't know Swindon?"

"No ..."

"No, you don't look like you're from round here ..."

"*Dave!*" Sandra looked embarrassed. Was she going out with a bigot? They had only been together for two months, and this was their first trip away. The weather had already been a challenge.

"Well, he doesn't. A naked man of—let's be honest— Middle Eastern appearance falls mysteriously from the sky ... Don't *you* have questions?"

"Well, okay, yes, I do." She turned to Enoch. "I *did* see you fall from the sky. Well, I heard you first. I'm surprised my boyfriend didn't ..."

"I was asleep!"

"Anyway ... I heard someone shouting, although I didn't understand the words, and then I saw you land, miraculously unscathed, with your fingers in your ears."

"He probably escaped from a CIA black renditions flight ..."

"Dave, I saw him slow down, so he could land unhurt." She looked closely at Enoch. "How were you able to do that?"

"I believe the Lord wanted to protect me," said Enoch.

"I knew it! He *is* a religious nut!" He paused. "I'm still not sure *which* religion ..."

"You seem like one able to divine the truth in people," said Enoch, looking at Sandra. "And you have already seen something miraculous. I fell through that storm from Heaven, and yet I am unharmed."

"You *fell through that storm?* With all the lightning and stuff?" Sandra was amazed.

"I did," said Enoch, "because the Lord has a plan for me."

"And now he reckons he's one of the Blues Brothers," said Dave. "He thinks he's on a mission from God."

"I *am* on a mission from God. I am Enoch, son of Jared, father of Methuselah."

"Methuselah from the Bible?" Sandra was looking doubtful now.

Enoch looked pleased. "I had been led to believe that the mortal realm had lost its faith."

Sandra's face couldn't decide between scorn and concern. "I wouldn't say I was faithful ..."

"You'd bloody well better be," muttered Dave darkly.

"But I've heard of Methuselah," continued Sandra, ignoring him. "Wasn't he really old?"

"Was he? That's nice." Enoch smiled. "I was called to Heaven when I was only 365, so I missed most of his childhood."

Dave started sniggering, and pulled out his phone. He would do some research on this 'Enoch'.

"Er, yeah," said Sandra. "You don't look like you're 365 years old."

"That was when I was on Earth, but the Lord called me to Heaven."

"Are you saying you've come back from the dead?" Sandra rolled her eyes. This was getting weirder and weirder.

"No," said Enoch. "I didn't actually die. I was called to Heaven to become an angel."

"I thought you had to be dead first?" This wasn't making a lot of sense to Sandra.

"Usually, but the Lord makes exceptions sometimes. Well, twice. Me and Elijah."

Dave snorted. "God even put his only begotten son through a mortal death. What makes you so special?"

"I wouldn't like to say," said Enoch, "in case it was my humility." He smiled.

"It says here," said Dave, looking at his phone, "that this 'Enoch' is revered in Islam. Are you a Muslim?"

"Of course he's not a bloody Muslim, Dave. He was in the Bible."

"Oh sorry, my mistake," said Dave, rolling his eyes. "It says here that 'after becoming the angel Metatron, Enoch gave the Ten Commandments to Moses'. Was that you as well?"

"There were so many messages back then," said Enoch wistfully. "Nobody seems to care much any more. I was ready to deliver the answers, but nobody was asking any questions. Not the right questions, anyway. That was why the Lord gave me back earthly form, so that I may walk among you, and heal his creation directly. I am here to meet a prophet. Are you the prophet?"

Concern joined the suspicion on Dave's face. He tilted his head to one side and looked at him. "Is there anyone we need to contact for you?" he asked very slowly. "Do you have a carer?"

Enoch looked at the sleeping bag, then around the around the tent, and at his new hosts, but he wasn't really sure what was going on. "Er, you two?"

"Hold on, mate," said Dave. "We're not your carers. Do you have someone who looks after you?"

"The Lord protects me, while I do his work."

Sandra and Dave exchanged a look. The rain was still heavy, and if they weren't going to send him out in it naked, it would have to be in their own clothes. It looked like they would be entertaining him for a while yet.

"So what is the work you have to do?" asked Sandra. Dave shook his head. "Don't engage him," he mouthed.

"The Lord has noticed that some of his creation are unhappy, and fight wars with each other."

"Has he noticed that most of them are religious wars?" asked Dave, ignoring his own advice. "You'd think he might have done something about them by now. We've had them for ages."

"He's surprised that they're still going on. He has a different concept of time."

"Says the 365 year old man ..."

Sandra ignored her boyfriend. "So how are you going to

stop war then, because to be honest, you're not the first to try, and we still keep having them ..."

"I now understand my mission," said Enoch looking at Dave. "I will be the Lord's emissary on Earth, and I shall remove the need for religious wars by unifying religions."

Dave laughed. "I don't think you realise what you're taking on here ..."

Enoch smiled. "I am aware that it will be challenging ..."

"Challenging? Mate, you don't know the half of it. There are dozens of Christian denominations, and they don't all get along. Protestants and Catholics have been fighting for as long as there have *been* Protestants and Catholics. Neither of them agree with the Eastern Orthodox, who are also Christian but disagree about when Easter should be, and have done since about the 11th century. All the different branches of Judaism do their own thing. One side of Islam is practically at war with the other, and neither likes the Jews much. Come to think of it, nobody seems to like Muslims much either, not even other Muslims, if they're the wrong type of Muslim. The Hindus don't get along with anyone from a different class of Hinduism. There are about a billion Buddhists who follow a religion without a god, and billions more who believe in no god or religion at all. Even Star Wars fans have their own religion. And the Flying Spaghetti Monster. And don't get me started on the Scientologists ..."

"I think you might be over-simplifying, Dave," said Sandra.

"I am. I *am* over-simplifying. The true picture is a lot more complicated."

"The true picture is the one with billions of individuals in it," said Enoch. "Free will, remember?"

"I'm still not sure whether what you're saying is true," said Sandra, "but Dave is right. It's going to be difficult. If I hadn't seen you fall to Earth, I'd think you were just a lunatic."

"But you *did* see me fall to Earth. Well, you saw me fall *back* to Earth, anyway. I've been away for a while."

* * *

Sandra decided to leave Dave at the campsite. It was his tent, but her car, so it seemed a fair arrangement, although not to Dave. Enoch was still wearing his clothes.

"You and Dave are ... unmarried?" asked Enoch, as they drove away.

"Don't start," said Sandra. "He was being a dick, but I *did* see you fall from the sky. He didn't. If *I* hadn't, you would not be in this car right now."

"This world is indeed ungodly."

"So where do you want me to take you?" asked Sandra. "Because to be honest, I'm out of my depth here. I've never met an angel before."

"I am no longer an angel," said Enoch. "I return to the world as a mortal man, just as I left it."

"But you've been back here since, haven't you?" asked Sandra. "I saw a movie that had Metatron in it. Dogma, it was called. Ha! The guy who played you said humans didn't know anything they hadn't seen in a movie, and here I am, not knowing anything about you except what I saw in a movie. Funny old world."

"It's true that Metatron came down to the world of men, but Metatron was no longer Enoch. You would know it as 'transubstantiation'." Her face said otherwise. "Possibly," he finished softly.

"Right ..." Sandra would skip over this bit. "Anyway, where are we going?"

"I need to speak to the leaders of men," said Enoch.

"Well, we're not going to be able to just walk in there," said Sandra. "I'll take you to the police, and you can work it out with them."

The police were primarily concerned with how he entered the country.

"Do you not have *any* ID, sir?" asked the desk sergeant. Enoch shook his head.

"I told you, he just fell out of the sky!" said Sandra. "I

was there. I saw it."

"Have you been drinking, miss?"

"No, of course not. I drove here."

"Why did you leave your boyfriend for a man you'd just met? Did you know each other previously?"

"How could I have known him?" asked Sandra. "He used to be an angel."

"I'm sure a lot of young women say that about their boyfriends ..."

"He's not my boyfriend! I just met the guy. He used to be an angel. A literal angel, with wings and stuff. It was him that told Moses the Ten Commandments. Tell him, Enoch."

"Sandra speaks the truth," said Enoch. "I was the voice of the Lord that the children of men could hear. I was the Recording Angel."

"Thought that was Charlotte Church ...," muttered the desk sergeant.

"I was the voice of Balaam's donkey, when it addressed its master with the Word of the Lord. The Lord was angry with Balaam, so I drew my sword and compelled the beast to speak."

"See?" said Sandra. "He can just whip out his sword and make donkeys talk as well!" She paused, and looked at Enoch with something approaching awe. "So there were talking donkeys in the Bible too? It wasn't just Shrek?"

At that point, the desk sergeant made his decision. They both seemed to believe what they were saying, and if they didn't, it served them right for wasting police time. He took them into custody and called for the mental health team.

Five hours later, two doctors and a nurse arrived. They spoke to Enoch first.

"Hello," said one. "Do you mind if I call you Enoch?"

"Why would I mind?" said Enoch. "It's my name."

"As you wish," said the doctor., making a note on her pad "I am Dr. Panwar. This is Dr. Sharma and Jackie, who's a psychiatric nurse."

"Are you leaders of men?" said Enoch. "I would like to speak to them."

"I am, er, head of the team, yes. What would you like to talk about?"

"The world has lost its way," said Enoch simply.

"How do you mean?" asked Dr. Sharma.

"There are too many wars. Dave said so. The Lord has charged me with preparing his creation to accept his love, but there are many divisions of a religious nature."

"I see." Another note on the pad. "And who is Dave?"

"Dave is also the Lord's emissary, to help me learn my destiny. Dave knows much of the world, and speaks as a prophet. I met him in a forest. Near Swindon. After falling naked through a thunderstorm. It's been quite a difficult day ..."

"You fell through a thunderstorm ... Where did you fall from?"

"Heaven. God released me from my duties as an angel and commanded me to live among men as a mortal man again. I've been quite looking forward to it."

Dr. Sharma looked at her colleagues. "I assume we're in agreement?"

There were two nods.

Dr. Sharma made another note on her pad. "These thoughts aren't helpful, Enoch, but we can give you the help you need ..."

* * *

Up a hillside in Wales, a mystical sect of worshippers had no knowledge of this. They had been so sure they'd read the prophecy correctly. They were actually remarkably close. They had the right date, the right time and they'd only been out by a fraction of a degree on the line of longitude. They had spent a lot of time reading the 'apocryphal' books of Enoch, books that true believers knew should really have been in the Bible. Enoch was man become angel, his 'flesh turned to flame, his veins to fire, his eye-lashes to flashes of lightning, his eye-balls to flaming torches, and whom God placed on a throne next to the throne of glory, and received after this heavenly transformation the name Metatron." It said so, in the Third Book of Enoch.

They knew the true message of the Bible, once those books were in it. Humanity is something to overcome. Why settle for mortal form, and three score years and ten, when it's possible to become an angel? And if an angel, why not a god? According to the Talmud, Metatron alone could sit in the Presence of God, apparently because he was the Heavenly Scribe. But what if the first century rabbi Elisha ben Abuyah had been right? What if there *were* two powers in Heaven? The rabbi had been made apostate for that. What if he was the one that really understood the nature of the divine?

That sect in Wales believed so. They always had. They checked their calculations for the thousandth time, swore at each other, and the weather, gave up, and went to the pub.

* * *

Back in the Swindon police station, the desk sergeant left his shift with a relieved sigh. It was mostly boring, apart from those two lunatics at the end. Even the doctors thought they were mad. They'd let the girl go, although not without a prescription. 'Enoch', though, seemed in need of some restraint. In their considered medical opinion, he was 'floridly psychotic' and had been committed for his own protection.

He fumbled for his phone when it rang.

"Hello?"

"Hi Jack. Ha ha! You get it?"

"Every bloody time ...," he muttered. A policeman's lot was really not a happy one. Not this policeman, anyway. His wife's niece was a trainee journalist, so he apparently had to be her informant, just while she was getting started. The alternatives were too horrible to contemplate. He put a smile in his voice. "Hello, Lorraine, how are you?"

"Not so bad. It's a quiet news day, so I thought I'd see if you had anything more interesting than 'local boy loses bike' to put on the front page. It wasn't even a nice bike."

"Mostly quiet, thankfully," he said. "Not much to report apart from a couple of nutters. A guy and a girl. The guy thought he was an angel."

"An angel?" Lorraine laughed. "That's a new one. Did he have wings?"

"No, he only used to be an angel. He's back to being a man again now."

"What about the girl?"

"I think she just thought angel-man was a better bet than her boyfriend, so she gave up on him. Maybe she's looking for a father figure. He's 365 years old apparently."

"Good effort." Lorraine could already feel the story forming. "So he was born around the time of Shakespeare? He'd have seen some changes."

"More than you think. He spent most of his life as the angel Metatron. He's actually Noah's great-granddad."

"This just gets better and better. Tell me more ..."

* * *

Sandra had not been impressed with the police, and launched an online campaign to help Enoch. Lorraine's piece went to press on the front page of the Swindon Advertiser; it really was a slow week. And a computer programmer called Bob had rather an extravagant reaction when his obsessive search for 'Enoch' and 'Metatron' showed some new hits online. He threw his laptop at the wall, screamed loudly about the unfairness of it all, and started phoning his friends.

"I see where I went wrong," he said. "I am so sorry. He's in Swindon."

"Why the bloody hell is he in Swindon?" said Trevor, the leader of the Order.

"Why is anyone?" Bob had often wondered about this. It's not usually somewhere that people go to deliberately.

"I mean, why isn't he where you predicted he would be?"

Bob prepared to launch into an explanation, then took a

deep breath and stopped himself. "Have you ever tried coming up with a predictive computer model based on 13th century Arabic interpretations of non-literal Gnostic texts that were once written in Aramaic? Nobody else could have done this."

"You *didn't* do this, Bob. You said he would land up a hill near Abergavenny. We had to go all the way to bloody Gwent and look at the rain for seven hours."

"I was very slightly out on one co-ordinate .... Anyway, we know where he is now. We're going to Swindon."

* * *

The case didn't attract a lot of attention, and mental institutions are mostly concerned with keeping people inside. Getting out can be a challenge. Getting *in* is much simpler. The Order of New Age Gnostics were able to visit Enoch simply by claiming to be his relatives.

Not all of them, of course. The hospital would let in anyone, but two-by-two, like animals on an ark. Just Bob and Trevor. The rest waited in their vans.

"Are either of you going to say anything?" asked Enoch, looking from Bob to Trevor and back again.

"Forgive me, my lord," said Bob. "I did not know how to speak to an angel."

"I'm not an angel," said Enoch.

"But you became an angel," said Trevor. "You ascended and spoke for God."

"Yes."

"And now you're back on Earth again," said Bob.

"I noticed that," said Enoch.

"So how do you do it?"

"How do I do what?" Enoch looked from one to the other. They both had the same questions and were taking it in turns to ask them.

"How do you become an angel?"

"I don't know," said Enoch. "How did you become a

human?"

"What?"

"I've been talking to the people here, to learn more of the Lord's creation." Enoch looked around the courtyard, the broken men shuffling in holey socks, and all of them smoking. There was nothing else to do. "Barry, the large man in the corner, believes that 'karma' makes all the big decisions, including whether we're born as humans or not. Karma seems to be just another word for the Lord's divine justice. Lucy, who broke that chair over there, is now in 'lockdown', but before she went, she said that science has all the answers. Apart from medicine. She didn't like medicine very much at all. Science might also be another word for the Lord providing answers about his Creation. I came here to unite the world's religions, but they are not as different as Dave the Prophet thought. They just call the same things by different names. Names have power. We are literally in Paradise here. Paradise means 'enclosed garden', and here we are." He looked from the high walls to the single tree.

"Who is Dave the Prophet?"

"He was the messenger when I first came back to the world. I was expecting to meet someone when I arrived. He gave me my mission."

"You were expecting to meet *us?*" said Bob. "I predicted your arrival, based on your writing!"

"You read my books?" asked Enoch, surprised. "I didn't think anyone would understand them. That was when I was trying out my poetry. I was very young, no more than 150."

"Your mission is not to teach men to unite their religions," said Trevor. "It is to teach men to become angels, and *overcome* their religions."

"I don't know how to teach men to become angels," said Enoch. "I was chosen."

"Then teach men how to be chosen!" said Bob. "What do we have to do?"

"You know what to do!" shouted a man on the other side of the courtyard. "You just don't want to do it!"

"That's Sister Rosetta," said Enoch. "He's a nun."

Bob and Trevor looked at the man, and his beard. "That's not a nun," said Trevor. He paused. "Er, you *do* know you're in a mental hospital, don't you?"

"This is exactly what I was expecting," said Enoch, looking around.

"I wish I could say the same," said Bob, looking at Enoch.

* * *

Sandra continued her online campaign to free him, but with little progress. Her petition got less support than those wanting Kanye West to be sent to Pluto and the Queen of England to be renamed Queeny McQueenface. Even the petition to carve Donald Trump's face into Mount Rushmore was more popular, although the artist had admitted the hair would be a challenge.

Sandra had also reached out to religious groups. She'd spoken to her local priest, the imam, the rabbi—she even found an arch-deacon online who was willing to talk—but she was wary. She had already spent several hours in a police cell waiting for a psychiatrist she didn't need.

She *knew* Enoch was real. She was a first-hand witness to a genuine supernatural event—she had seen it with her own eyes—and yet nobody believed her. She looked at the Bible that she'd bought. She'd even researched it a little. And the other faiths. Billions of people believed in stories of their gods (sometimes the same god), and they could not comprehend that something similar could actually happen nowadays, even the ones who had been waiting for such a thing, often for centuries.

And what happens when the long-prophesied message from God *does* arrive? They lock up the messenger for being mad, because believing these things happened to someone *else* a long time ago is normal. Believing they happened to *you* is apparently a sign of schizophrenia. Enoch's doctors were quite insistent on this point.

She wondered how Enoch was doing. She'd visited him once, at the start, but she found the hospital distressing. She didn't want to think of anyone living like that.

She wondered if they were living at all.

* * *

Bob, Trevor and the rest of the New Age Gnostics made their way disconsolately back to Glastonbury.

"I really thought we had something that time," said Bob.

"You always do," said Trevor.

"And one day, I'll be right," said Bob. "Incidentally, it's your round."

He watched Trevor walk to the bar, and looked around the pub. He was in a pub just like this when he'd first become inducted into the Mysteries of the Craft. It seemed a long time ago now.

Maybe he never would be an angel. Maybe he no longer wanted to be. Seeing Enoch in the hospital had been a shock. What would they say about *Bob*, when they discovered he'd spent 20 years working on a computer system that could turn mystic texts into dates and map co-ordinates? He'd finally come up with an answer, almost. They had found someone who had fallen from the sky, as the prophecies seemed to suggest, although he was in the wrong place, and had now been diagnosed with psychosis.

There but for the grace of God go I, thought Bob. It got him wondering.

Maybe, one day, he *wouldn't* be right.

* * *

Sandra started to visit Enoch, she wrote letters on his behalf, and she began to organise his appeal. She couldn't do anything until he'd been in there for 90 days, but she wanted to be ready.

Had she still been with Dave the cynical prophet, she might not have bothered. He would have complained about the government, ranted about austerity and cutbacks, and said that Enoch would be released as soon as someone worse off needed the bed, because there were only twelve of them for a town of 200,000 people. He would have been right. Perhaps he *was* a prophet.

Two weeks later, Enoch was free again. They stood by her car, and she smiled.

"I must be as mad as they say you are," she said. "You told me you were a 365 year old man who was once an angel, and I believed you. Since then, literally everybody else has said you were a madman, and I still trust you more than most men I've met. Why is that?"

"You've met the wrong men," said Enoch. "Thank you for letting me stay with you."

"Don't make me regret this," said Sandra. "I've only just got Dave off my back."

"Don't be too hard on Dave," said Enoch. "He was doing the Lord's work, and the way of the prophet is hard."

Sandra laughed. "If I ever see him again, I won't be telling him you said that."

They got in the car and drove past the pub, which was called The Rat Trap.

"Odd name for a tavern next to an asylum," said Enoch.

"Swindon is an odd place," said Sandra. "What are you going to do now?"

"I'm going to figure this out," said Enoch. "I'm going to work out people, and what they want. I'm going to talk to people, and read about people, and really *understand* them. Then I'm going to figure out how to make them happy."

"I'm glad Dave isn't here," said Sandra with a chuckle. "He would have had something to say about the task you've set yourself."

"Dave's role is complete. What do *you* think?"

Sandra glanced in his direction, then made the turning, easing the car into the traffic. "How long have you got?"

"I'm still only 365," said Enoch. "Most of my family

lived to be over 800, so at least 400 years, if it pleases the Lord."

"You're going to need more time," said Sandra.

She gunned the engine and they headed back to town.

* * *

Dedicated to Shirley, Gen and survivors everywhere

Stardust, Always

The Unpardonable Adventure

Virginia Carraway Stark

Emma was happy to escape the house and go outside, if only for a few hours. The house felt stale and dim to her. She played with her pen debating if she could escape studying before tossing concern for the future to the wind. *Screw finals! I'm going to die if I stay in this house!*

The sky was stormy and a wind blew but it wasn't raining, not yet. She tied up her runners and then, after another look out of the curtains, guiltily ran back through the house to her bedroom with her runners on to grab a sweater. Her shoes were barely dirty and she didn't want to take them off and on again with so few moments of her childhood left.

She ignored the smudges she left on the floor, there would be time enough to be an adult all too soon. She didn't want to do this thing called "adulting". All her friends were excited to be leaving home and heading off to college, university, trade school or to work full time at whatever crap job they were working at now. She had been accepted into most of the universities she had applied to, not that she had shot for the stars on that, State University was good enough for her, she didn't even want to go! She knew that she didn't want to go and yet her parents persisted in calling her ennui with University applications a "phase" that she would "regret in a year or two, little Miss!"

"Where's a sweater when you need one?" she exclaimed in frustration. She threw the mini piles of laundry around, sorting through the dropped clothes for something warm. Outside she heard the wind start to blow against the eaves and she cursed under her breath. If she didn't get out of here she would go mad. There was so much expectation and tension to succeed at something she didn't even want to succeed at. If a storm settled in she would go out anyway. *A bolt of lightning would settle all of this nicely,* She thought with some satisfaction. She imagined her parents coming to her funeral—no, it wouldn't kill her. They would come to the hospital after she recovered from her coma, they would cry when she explained why she was out in the storm and finally hear her unhappiness...

And the moon will rain canapes too—while we're in the realm of fantasy. She snorted. If she got hit by a bolt of lightning her Dad would "arrange" for her to have chance to take the finals again.

She threw open her closet door, deciding to grab a light coat and stopped dead in her tracks. A man was standing there in the darkness of her closet. His unkempt hair obscured his face, his hands were folded in front of him, his head bowed. Emma gave a yipe of fear and slammed the door shut.

There was no sound from the closet, no movement as you would expect if you slammed someone in your closet and gave a girly shriek. "I'm being silly. I didn't see what I thought I just saw. I'm just imagining things. I imagine things too much," she said the words out loud into the empty room.

She often spoke to herself but it was rare that she ever got a response back. Muffled by the wood of the closet door she heard a resonant voice say, "You're not imagining me. I'm very real, Miss Green and it was rude to slam the door on my face."

Emma's large eyes grew larger and her pale skin paler. She would love to think she was imaging things, but that voice ... it sounded so real. She still needed a something warms to wear as well. That was the final deciding factor, she picked up a ceramic knick-knack and opened the closet door. The man looked up this time and his doleful eyes and disinterested expression made her feel more than a little silly to be threatening to hit him over the head with the unicorn she had gotten for her thirteenth birthday.

She lowered the unicorn to her side. "Who are you and why are you in my closet?"

"At last, some reasonable questions," he said with a sigh. "I am a spirit, and I've come to warn you that you're about to have an Unpardonable Adventure," he answered. "I think you'll need a jacket, a sweater won't be warm enough." The man held one of her coats out to her, balancing the hanger on his index finger.

"What sort of an adventure?" she asked, taking the jacket and wondering how he knew she had been looking for a sweater.

"I already told you, an Unpardonable one," he replied, his voice as still and implacable as a lake of mercury.

Emma couldn't help but think that the spirit looked like a famous and recently deceased actor. The actor had played in some of her favorite movies. He looked different in person, but she supposed that could also be because he was dead now.

"Please, tell me more," she asked. She reached out a hand to touch him, to see if he was real and he batted her hand away. The contact felt real, more real than most real life contact felt, like he had struck her inside her skin in direct contact with her flesh and nerves.

"Of course I'm real you silly child, I handed you your coat, didn't I?"

"Umm," she started, feeling as silly as he said she was.

"Well, why are you standing around?" he asked. He was wearing a long, black shirt with a mandarin collar, it was untucked and hung over a pair of vertically striped black and white pants.

"I've never seen a spirit before, I want to know more!" she exclaimed. She wasn't afraid anymore, she was exhilarated as though she had met a living celebrity.

"I've already come and warned you, don't tell me you're a greedy girl as well as a silly one," he said scathingly. He muttered under his breath after, "This one should be a simply Dreadful Adventure at this rate."

"I don't know how not to be a little greedy," she willingly confessed. "You're a ghost of one of my favorite actors ..." She paused, interrupted with his snort of breath.

81

He blew his hair out of his eyes. "Favorite actors, I hardly think that's accurate, I just played a few roles in some movies you happened to see. I'm quite sure you have no idea of my career."

Emma flushed, trying to think of a movie she had ever watched just for him, after a minute she said, "I watched, um, that one with the singer in it who turned out to be girl-god because it had you in it."

He looked at her, gauging her. Finally he responded, "Very well. You're going to have an adventure that will help you decide what path to take. That's all I'm going to tell you, I didn't have a very long part in that movie and you don't remember the title. Good luck to you then, you'll need it."

With that he grabbed the doorknob inside the closet and slammed the door. Emma tried to pull it open but it was jammed. After a bit of wiggling the old brass knob opened revealing an empty closet. She went through it, despite the fact that it wasn't very big and it would be hard for even a dead actor to hide in there, spirit or no.

Outside the weather was still changeable, one minute sun and the next a brief drenching of rain. Her conversation with the man in the closet had taken longer than she had thought and it was getting late. Her parents would be home soon and she knew they'd want her to do her chores and have dinner with them if she was here when they came in. *There's still a chance I could get struck with lighting,* she thought with a smirk.

Her encounter with the shade of the dead actor had cost her valuable time and she heard the crunching of wheels turning into the driveway. One of her parents was home early! She ran downstairs and out the back door, diving through the hedge that blocked their backyard from the alley. She put her head down and ran down the alley and out into the street liking the feel of her hair whipping across her face and the wind's hands pushing back against her.

She ran down the street to the park, ignoring the now steady raindrops that hit her nose and her freckled cheeks. They were tiny droplets and nothing to worry about anyway. She let her long dark hair stream behind her, enjoying the sense of her feet hitting the sidewalk and the wind whipping her hair.

She got to the park before the rain set in and ran to the swings. She got one going, pumping her legs and said to the park, "An Unpardonable Adventure. I wonder what that even means? Can an adventure ever be pardoned? Can you help it if you have an adventure? Who would have the right to declare something 'Unpardonable' anyhow?"

The familiar voice whispered on the wind, *The whole world will judge it Unpardonable. Silly girl.* His voice sighed again with the rising wind.

The storm had found her now. The wind whipped her hair and the rain pelted her face. She loved the feel of it. This was a million times better than figuring out how her final English essay should go or studying math.

"I could live in the winds and the storm forever!" she declared defiantly to the empty park. No one but her would ever be in the park in weather like this.

A noise louder than anything she had heard before and a light brighter than anything she imagined hit her. She was knocked off the swing and hit the turfed ground with a thud. She was dazed, smoking slightly, but she opened her eyes, her vision was blurred and she saw the spirit's face close to her own, still wearing the same doleful look as before he shook his head ever so slightly. "I did try to warn you, you know."

Emma faded out again. She couldn't keep her eyes open. The rain soaked her through and when she woke, things were not as they had been.

She sat up, dazed by the lightning that had struck her. The storm had passed and more than that, it was also dark out, very dark. There were no streetlights, only the light of the full moon and the stars to give her an idea of where she was.

A light slowly lit up in the darkness, it was, or seemed, to be far away. A distorted light in a large crystal ball, it grew brighter and lit up the tall, slim man holding it. Emma couldn't tell if he was moving oddly or as if his form was being distorted by the large orb he held. Rays of light were beaming out of it now in flashes, illuminating her surroundings in gasps and bursts.

He had to have been closer to her than she had thought at first because he was at her side so quickly he startled her. He had a strong smell to him, like incense and loam and the rich smell of pine smoke. His eyes caught her in the light over the orb. It was large, almost the size of a punch bowl. She could see images swirling inside.

She reached out her hand and touched the sphere. She could see the edges of images and she glimpsed her own face peering out at her, distorted with the streams of movement from pictures she couldn't pick out.

The man pulled the large glass ball from her hand and tossed it away from them, the orb spun in the place where he had been holding it. Emma looked after it longingly and started after it but he put a hand on her shoulder.

"Mustn't touch, little girl, it isn't yours."

"But it had my face in it," she replied.

"That doesn't make it yours," he said, a snide tinge of humor to his voice.

"Who are you?" she demanded. She felt like she was being made fun of. The man before her reminded her of a spider with his long legs and arms and his venomous eyes. *If a spider could smile, it would smile like that,* she thought and put out her chin in defiance.

"I'm the King of Unpardonable Adventures. I believe you were told I would be coming to see you. What you weren't told was that I am also the Servant of Saturn and the Lord of his Magic. Now tell me, Emma, what do you want to do?" he asked and leaned over her shoulder, his long legs moved him so quickly he darted about her faster than she could follow.

"I want to go look at what's in that crystal," Emma said determinedly.

"And?" he inquired.

"And look in it," she finished, puzzled by what he expected her to do with it.

"That's not very exciting," he said. His frown was as staged as a tragedy mask and she once more felt that he was making fun of her.

"What else can I do with it?"

"Those things would be Unpardonable," came his inscrutable and annoying response.

Emma walked towards the ball and the King of the Unpardonable flicked it away from her with an easy motion of his fingers and no matter how quickly she tried to walk it was always a step or two away from her.

She stomped her foot and turned to face the man. "I demand that you tell me what Unpardonable means. Not the word, but the way you and the other one warned me about it. What is an Unpardonable Adventure?"

"It's something that will change you forever and leave you separate from all that is normal and grown up for all time," he explained, for once his face serious, almost kind.

"What does it do?" she asked.

"What doesn't it do?" he replied. "It will show you other worlds and forbidden horrors and delights. It will show you what it chooses to show you and in a night you will live ten lives."

"That doesn't sound unpardonable to me," Emma said. It was what she had always wanted. To stay in the realm of the child, to know secrets and see mysteries. She never understood why all characters were like Wendy and came back from adventures and grew up and became normal.

He smiled as though she had spoken her every desire out loud. "They return to their normal lives because anything else would be Unpardonable. They would be set aside, sundered from their families, their loved ones, all that is 'normal' for all time." His voice was gentle, he stroked her hair and she didn't flinch from his touch.

"I don't want to be normal," she said, steadfast in her faith.

"So many say that and so many are lying to themselves. My dear, your path here can continue to the rest of your life, your life as you were meant to live it, or you can choose the magical path and nothing will ever be the same for you. You will have advantages beyond your belief and will be spurned by those you think love you and turned away from every source of aid. The Universe will lay your every need at your doorstep but humans will close their doors in your face. They will talk about you. They will say all manner of things about you. They will be right to say them, even the lies, because you have become Unpardonable."

"That doesn't sound all bad," Emma said, more hesitant than before, the tall, thin man was built like a spider. His words and the closeness of him was intimidating.

Like a flash he was by the orb, spinning it lazily on his hand. "It's far from all bad. It's far from all good. The only definite thing is that once you take this path you will be amongst the Unpardonable and it is a decision once made cannot ever be unmade."

Emma set her chin. "Show me," she demanded.

"It's your funeral," he said and sent the orb to slowly spin towards her. He was behind her now and whispering the words in her ear.

He paused as though listening to his own inner voice. "It's your birth as well—you will never be the same my inviolate little child. Remember, once you look, you must not look away. You must see it all or your sanity will be destroyed."

"Remember?" she said, her eyes pulled away from the ball. "You never said anything about losing my mind!"

"Oh, yes, you will. I may have forgotten to mention it, I myself am highly Unpardonable and sometimes forget the niceties of those who are still pardonable. People like yourself," he said with the hint of a mocking bow.

"How long do I have to look?" she asked, her blue eyes looked up at his eyes, one was blue and one green, she saw. His left pupil was greatly larger than the right.

He spun the crystal. "Let's see, shall we? This isn't a negotiation for sane minds."

Emma watched the colors swirl together. What she saw is difficult to explain to the Pardonable.

She saw her own face coalesce out of symbols and sigils that looked so arcane that she wondered if they were made up or real symbols. They formed together, she recognized the symbol for Mercury and for Saturn and triangles facing up and down, wavy lines and then there was this girl. The girl was her.

All around her the world was a wondrous place. She was the Emma in the glass now and what was there seemed more real than anything she had ever seen in the 'real' world.

She was walking down a dirt path, grass and trees grew up on either side, a respectful distance away from the path. She watched all these things form, not from anything explainable but from all that made them what they were. The grass was the chemistry that made up grass, it was the chlorophyll, it was the sun's light itself, it was the sun, it was a cool day and bare feet, it was the steak that had been the cow that had grazed on the grass, it was the seed it had sprouted from, it was the dead sticks of grass it would one day become. It was emerald green and perfect, it was blighted and wrong, a symbol moved one way or another changed it to right or wrong.

It's all how I think about it. She realized as she watched the same thing be true of the trees, the sky, the path, even a bird that sang in a tree. All things were made up of all that they were and all they could be. Their possibilities and their failures not counted against them, they were independent of potential and the passing of time.

It was down this road that Emma walked, whole empires of history unfolded in front of her. The pyramids were built in front of her and she watched Rome fall to barbarian hoards. She caressed the soft skin of Cleopatra and saw that here she was one way and there she was another. Here she made one choice and avoided the bite of the asp and here her body was already cold. Here she was forced to march in Augustus' Triumph and she impaled herself on a sword while the Romans cried out for her blood, for her beauty and her death.

All things were possible. All things had happened and had never happened. The storm was gone and the moon was full and close and as Emma watched, admiring her cratered face and she saw something falling. Holding out her hand she caught a cracker with something on it, a sniff told her what it was: caviar! Little bits of food were raining down all around her and Emma laughed and bit into it. The moon was raining canapes!

That was how Emma Walters became Unpardonable.

After an unknown time she woke up in the park. The orb was still in her hands but the King of the Unpardonable was gone, or at least, she couldn't see him. The orb was shrinking and melting like it was made of gelatin that had gotten wet and was melting away. She set it on the ground and it merged with the soil.

A peace and beauty had descended on the girl who had left her house a normal child and was returning as something other. She walked home, it was early morning, dawn's first light was peering over the horizon like a child who peered into an orb and saw more than she intended.

The secrets of the universe danced in her mind. Her eyes had changed from large and innocent to having an unfathomable look to them. To look only in her eyes one may have mistaken her for someone very old but her beautiful face was, if anything younger looking and more refreshed than when she had searched for her sweater the night before.

She had lost her shoes and her sweater at some point in her adventure. She had lived multiple lives while on her adventure, how could she possibly be back here? How could she be in this place? The place of her childhood.

Her feet knew the way home and the dew on the ground was refreshing. Her gaze was a thousand miles away and her mind too high up for the Pardonable to reach or see.

She let herself into her house. She hadn't done her homework, she hadn't done her chores. She started to laugh. How could such silly things matter after all she had learned? The moon was setting and dawn had come. Coming home at dawn when she had been expected to be home studying for final, she was just beginning to see how having such adventures could make one "Unpardonable".

She tried to sober herself up. It was like she was up too high, looking down on the world from the clouds. Like a girl reeling in a kite she lowered her perspective enough to understand that she was just a girl here and she had things that needed to be done. Upstairs a door opened and slippered feet padded over hardwood floors. Her mother appeared at the top of the stairs. She looked ready to start into one of her patented rants on misbehavior. It was bound to be something she had rehearsed as she had tried to fall asleep, listening for Emma to come home all night.

Looking at her, Emma could see that her mother had had little sleep. Some of this was a sort of vindictive pleasure at having a chance to vent at her pretty daughter. Her mother was losing all her illusions of being a young woman as her daughter blossomed before her. Aside from that, and in fact but most of her recriminations stemmed from genuine love and concern. Emma had never disappeared for an entire night before.

Her mother opened her mouth and Emma looked at her, expectantly, patiently. Her mother closed her mouth again. There was something different about her daughter, something compelling and repellant at the same time. She wondered briefly if Emma had lost her virginity during her lost night out but her motherly intuition told her it was something else.

Instead of her planned lecture she said, "Your father and I were worried when you didn't come home last night."

"Yes, I suppose you were," Emma replied after a pause.

"I don't ever want you to do that again," she said, feeling she shouldn't leave all of her speech unsaid and at the same time feeling as though she was now talking to a stranger.

"Do that again?" Emma asked, a tad bewildered. "I don't think that happens more than once ... or maybe it does, I suppose I hadn't thought that far. For everything I may have only seen the borders of a vaster land."

"I don't know—" Emma's mother started.

"What I'm talking about," Emma finished, tendrils of fatigue seeping into her voice. "I know you don't, Mom. It's alright though, I'm home and safe and I won't stay out late unless I have no choice."

She was coming down from her height where she could

touch the moon and collect the canapes that rained from her luminescent brow.

Her mother was speechless, her forehead furrowed. "And tonight you had no choice? Emma, I don't know what you mean—have you been drinking?" she asked hesitantly. Emma had never come home drunk before. She had always been so good and now her daughter was so close to graduation and she didn't know how to handle this sudden disparity in idea of her daughter and the new reality standing before her.

Emma laughed, "I'm not drunk but I feel a little like I am. I had a choice in this, but if what I have done is Unpardonable, then we will have to work something else out. I can't change the unchangeable and who knows what the future will bring."

Emma looked at her mother with a deep affection before she spoke again. "Once I was an egg sitting in your ovary and now I'm standing here with wet feet, with that hanging over my head, how could I ever make a promise to you?"

Emma's mother could think of nothing to say to the stranger at the foot of the stairs. Her daughter's answers were impossible to understand and her gaze—it made it difficult to be angry with her. She felt like Emma was older than her and she was the one coming to her as a child. Her mother felt shameful herself for her selfish thoughts, her angry thoughts. She felt more than a little frightened too. The fear overshadowed all her other feelings, competing only with the shame for dominance.

Emma understood. It wasn't exactly as though she was hearing all of this, it was more like she was feeling the vibrations of her mother's very atoms. She felt compassion for her mother. Emma had just become a very complicated young woman. She opened up the downstairs closet to put away her shoes. She was somehow unsurprised to see the man in the mandarin collar with the dour face and sallow complexion handed her a towel. She closed the closet before her mother could glimpse him, if her mother could even see him at all. Emma briefly considered opening the door again and leaving it to swing wide. What would her mother think of that?

It was a cruel thought and she quashed it. She couldn't think it was okay to hurt people with knowledge and force the metaphysical onto their frail minds. She'd have to watch for him, it seemed he was lurking in nearly every closet in the house! The thought made her laugh a laugh and not even her mother's unimpressed expression could stop her. The idea of cautiously peeping into doors forever to make sure a spectre of any famous actors crept into the closets. It was like living in the desert and checking your shoes for scorpions. Who knew what actor might strike next? Michael Jackson could come moon walking out of a door at any moment to bring something unexpected.

Emma's giggles turned into peals of laughter.

"Have you lost your mind?" her mother asked.

Tears from laughter had been squeezed on her cheeks and Emma wiped them away as she got control of her laughing. "I think I have, and, it's marvelous," she replied.

Emma dried off, her face deliberately sober as she refused to think of Prince or someone else coming out would it rain purple tomorrow? Knowing that possibility was endless filled her heart with a joy she had never known under the restrictions of what some might call being "normal" or "good" and others simply called, "Unpardonable".

Her mother watched from the bannister, wanting to flee, but afraid to leave. That was her little girl down there and she sensed that she was slipping away from her. Emma watched her mother as well, she could hear her wondering and now it was like reading her mother's mind. It wouldn't be right to leave, but I don't want to be near her, she seems different. Wild. Like a tiger had come home instead of her little girl.

You're being paranoid. You should go to bed, Emma thought at her mother.

Her little girl with eyes that glowed with a preternatural light and smile that played at the edges of her mouth as though she were about to laugh at any moment at a joke only she understood, walked up the stairs. She kissed her mother on the cheek ignoring the hurtful fact that her mother pulled away from her when she did.

"I should go to sleep, I'm tired," her mother said, shying away from her daughter. Her mother walked away as quickly as could be pardoned and closed her bedroom door behind her without another word to the feral creature that had come home to her. Emma watched with bemusement and went to her own room, closing the door quietly behind her. Her mother's withdrawal from her was hurtful but she had been aware that there would be a steep price to pay for the gift she had been given. She knew she had only touched on the edges of her gift.. and the edges of the price.

She looked around. Her room was familiar and strange. It was like visiting a place that had been abandoned and then remembering in jerks and spurts all that had happened here. The teddy bear she had loved, the homework, still laying open on her desk, a montage of her and her friends on a pink background. They were still her friends, but she had the Unpardonable taint to her now and they would know. Maybe one or two would forgive her but most would find her a novelty at best or something to be frightened of or detested at worst.

She changed into her pjs and looked up at the ceiling. She could still see the symbols that made up everything dashing together, falling apart. Making and unmaking all around her. She could see into her parents room by removing the wall then a symbol replaced here or there and her solitude was restored, her parents none the wiser for her meddling. None of the Pardonables would ever see what she did, but they would feel it, and every time she breathed and saw the air, watched her hand move, saw the cancer eating at an old man, or the laughter of a child come out in rainbows of color: she became more Unpardonable.

Her Unpardonable Adventure had only just begun and she could hear the laughter at her, with her. Two men laughing, one with a warning and one with an orb, neither of whom would ever be forgotten. They had set her feet on this path and as the years past she would have moments where she blamed them and even hated them for making her beyond the norm. Mostly, however, she would get to know them and love them with a heat unknown to anyone who hadn't had at least one Unpardonable Adventure. This was only the beginning and Emma would have many more adventures even after she was old and gray.

As the next day came and the one after that, her life turned from respectable young lady to having adventure after adventure. It wouldn't be for many years that she could look back and tell you the sum of how much that night had changed the course of her life. The Man with the Warning appeared to her many more times in the future as did The Man with the Orb. I would tell you more about what happened, but if I did, you might slip a bit yourself. It's easy to find you've become unpardonable, it can start to happen from things as small as listening to a song, or reading a story. You discover that you yourself are magic and not meant for things of the normal world where all the people are alike and pardon each other. You will find yourself unpardonable. It's more than likely I've already said too much.

Be careful when you open closets, as we all know, a doorway to nowhere can lead anywhere. Be careful in places like parks that are close to nature, the trees and the earth itself is bursting with its own unpardonable magic. Don't imagine what could be lurking at the bottom of ravines or that faerie live in old rotted tree stumps and drink nectar like butterflies. Never think any of those types of thoughts. If you want to stay safe, stick to parking lots and paved pathways, never be alone where your own thoughts could lead you down those Unpardonable pathways or you may discover yourself at the start of your very own, Unpardonable Adventure.

Stardust, Always

And Then, Sit With Me

Paul Lansdell

I'll talk not of defeating
winning
overcoming
or of battles with C

I've walked this path with many
Some, not this far
A great number, on further than me

Of none, do I consider to be
"Beaten"
"Losers"
"Failures"
or of deserting the fight

So, I'll talk of walking this road
As far and straight as I am able

Then I'll sit with Billy, Paddy, Patricia and our mothers
with untold others
And, on the roadside
we'll talk of where our paths led
and well the lane was trod
and how we made our way

To those that walk on
I'll cry:
"Step on! Walk well! And step on!"

Stardust, Always

For, when you tire of the path
So sit with me

Yet, still, there'll be no talk of success, failure, beaten or
beat, won, lost, defeated or retreated

Perhaps never met, we are still companions of a road
For what's met, is met as met
and we have walked well, my friend. Together
we walk well

The Last Patient

Janet Gershen-Siegel

"You're my last patient."

"What?" The four-word sentence made no sense.

"I'm dying of lung cancer."

I remember fighting the urge to repeat myself and ask, 'What?' again. Instead, I asked, "How long?"

Weeks. "When the time comes, you'll be transferred to another doctor. Actually, she is my ex-wife."

It was September of 1981. I was nineteen years old. I was too young when I started college. It's hard to put together a truer sentence. I was foolish, quirky, vulnerable, and all too trusting. Whatever skills and experience I had picked up in a small suburban high school were utterly useless in a big city university.

I did things, and took risks, that were itchingly, twitchingly, mind-bogglingly stupid. It was Dr. Richard Brodie's task to keep me from doing too many of those things. He was a psychiatrist.

But I was nineteen. And I remember thinking to myself, *I'm not tall enough for this ride.* Yet I was on it, anyway.

When I had returned to the suburbs the previous May, Dr. Brodie had been fine, as normal as I suppose any teenaged girl would have ever noticed. He was in his fifties, and smoked a cigar during our sessions, and resembled Ed Asner. When I returned in September, he had seemingly shrunk to half his original size. I must have stared, for so he told me. He also asked for me to call him Dick. No longer would he hold himself at arm's length.

We continued meeting until mid-October. I would tell him my latest dumb doings. He would listen and often laugh a bit. I got to call him by his first name. He would hug and kiss

97

me on the cheek in greeting and farewell, and I would do the same in return. And so Dick and I would get together every Thursday afternoon at an old hospital building near the fens and campus.

Just before Halloween, I got the call. It was his ex-wife, and I had become her newest patient.

I asked her if I really had been his last patient, and if I had been, then why was that so?

She confirmed: I had been. I was his only teenaged patient. The others were middle-aged, dealing with divorce, coming out, suicidal thoughts, or the like. For Dick, I had problems, yes, but they were a lot closer to the question of who would be my date on a Saturday night. They were serious to me, but much more readily solvable.

She said that for Dick, in the last month of his life, talking with me was a little like seeing the future.

I am, more or less, Dick's age now. With Rickman, yes, but especially with Bowie, we have been able to see the future.

Thirty-five years ago, a sacred trust was unexpectedly given to me, to be a friend and confidant to the man who was supposed to be mine. I did what I could, but I was not ready for it. And so today, I give it to you, if I may, all you artists, you musicians, you actors,. But I also give it to you accountants and engineers and librarians and chefs and soldiers and everyone else, too. Even if you feel you aren't tall enough for this ride, I urge you to get on it anyway. And I give to you, if I may, the task of showing the world the future, in whatever way you know how.

And for Dick, wherever he may be—I am proud to have been your last patient.

Dying is Harder on the Living

Kelly Kuebler

It's a proven fact that even years and odd ages have never been kind to me.

In 2002 my father almost died in a car accident.

In 2004 I have what is probably the worst birthday I've ever had. Don't ask me about it.

In 2010 I began falling down the slippery slope of depression.

You get the picture.

Skip ahead to 2014, probably the worst and most trying year of my life. My serious boyfriend moved away (and told me around my birthday). My grandmother was diagnosed with early onset Alzheimer's, and my paternal grandfather was diagnosed with prostate and bone cancer.

My grandfather was a simple man who only needed the basic things in life, and always had a charm about him. He lived on the original Kuebler farm that my ancestors established when they moved to Michigan from Swabia, and never had any desire to leave it. He saved everything; if it was broken he said he could use it for parts. I mean—the man drove a junky old van until it literally committed suicide by blowing up outside of a bar one day. He never wanted flashy cars, a big house or a fancy job. He was perfectly content living on the farm and going to the Bridgewater Bank every once in awhile for a cup of coffee. He was like Mayberry in human form.

The things I really admired the most about him were his patience, dedication, and positive attitude. The man had patience of steel. We're talking about a man who married a woman who spent all of his money, tore him down, and henpecked him up until the day he died. This woman shot at him at one point and HE STAYED WITH HER. Quitting was simply not in his vocabulary. He always believed that hard work paid off. He never said anything bad about anyone, and if you complained his reply would always be, "So what are you going to do about it?" Never would he give you the sympathy you were looking for, but no matter what it was, he could always find a way to help you out with it. He had an outlook on life so unique that I have yet to meet anyone else with the same perspective.

He died ten days before Christmas: December 15, 2014.

I helped my father write the obituary, prepare his eulogy and pick out photographs for the funeral. Every inch of the way I was a rock, devoid of emotion and going through the motions. It was my first real brush with death and funerals. It simply hadn't sunk in; I was still expecting to see him at Christmas.

Then I found a photograph that I didn't know even existed of my grandfather and me, circa 1993.

I cried my eyes out and felt the stitches holding me together rip apart.

It would take two hands to count the number of people I've known who have either survived cancer or have lost their battle. But none of them have impacted me the way that my grandfather's battle did. I never allowed it to get to me or see the truth of the situation until I was holding this photograph in my hands. I felt such a rush of emotions that it was overwhelming. Guilt, for not getting to know him better and for not spending more time with him. Anger, that he had to live a life with someone who didn't appreciate him. I felt an incredible sadness that I can't even begin to describe but can only compare it to being hollow.

This photograph, this 4" x 6" photograph, made me realize everything that had happened in the past 6 months. The time he spent being incapable of working on his beloved farm, the excessive weight loss and being a prisoner in his own body; he didn't deserve it ... any of it. My classmate didn't deserve it. The kid I used to babysit didn't deserve it. Nobody deserves to whittle away from an incurable disease, and nobody deserves to watch someone go through that.

A friend and co-worker once said to me "dying is harder on the living than those that are doing the actual dying." I always agreed with what she said but never actually felt those words until I was watching the reality of it. Though I wasn't around to see the ugliness of the battle or to be with him in his final moments, I still watched my father endure having to make the difficult decisions while trying to remain strong for everyone else. I knew all he wanted to do was to breakdown from having to watch his father become a victim of terminal cancer. He had to take care of my ailing grandfather, deal with the estate and worst of all take my grandfather away from his beloved farm to place him into hospice care. I know he is still haunted by the look my grandfather gave him as they wheeled him away, never to return home again. The living are the ones who have to watch helplessly as their loved one falls victim to a disease and still somehow be strong enough to smile through the pain.

Though all of this was painful to watch unfold, I eventually found his death to be a blessing in disguise. He was free of pain and onto a better, peaceful place. It was the biggest awakening and realization I've ever had.

After his death, I felt a tremendous amount of emotional pain because of the weight of the guilt I felt from not getting to know him better. As a child it was always out of my hands since the two sides of my family are pretty close to being the Capulets and the Montagues, but after getting a driver's license there weren't any more excuses. I just never bothered to visit. You just think that they are always going to be there; that just because they are your loved one, that they are somehow immune to death.

Since his passing, I've grown to be more appreciative and grateful for those around me. I've learned more about my heritage and my roots so that I can understand myself as a person. I try to be more like my grandfather in everyday life now more than ever. I don't complain to just vent but rather try to talk things out and find solutions to the said complaint. I take more chances in life, appreciate the little things and have stopped lusting over things I don't need. He taught me how to enjoy life again and that was the greatest gift he could have given me. Happiness is found in the simple things.

Now that it is 2016, unfortunately my bad luck curse is still present. My boyfriend lost his job, my sister's fiancée broke off their engagement, and we lost two icons: David Bowie and Alan Rickman.

Music and film will never be the same without these extraordinary souls. They each gave their lives to creating art to make the people of the world happy. I hate to admit I'm not a big fan of Bowie but I did enjoy his music (plus I wasn't around during the Bowie era). His music is what made him so iconic and is one of those artists whose work will stand the test of time. I do greatly admire Rickman's talents. I first saw him as Professor Snape in Harry Potter and grew to love many more of his roles over the years. He was one of those actors that captivated you in such a way that you believe their characters to be real and alive rather than an actor pretending. They give such a spirit to their characters that it feels magical watching their work on screen. He was part of an elite group of artists who could do just about anything that was thrown at them, and do it with meaning, conviction and full dedication. In my opinion, he never had a bad performance; an extremely rare thing with such an extensive career. He was truly one of the best.

Though I never met Bowie or Rickman, I feel the world got to know them through their work and we all felt like we lost a family member of our own when we heard the news of their passing. As fans, we can't help but feel a little lost knowing that we won't be seeing or hearing new material after those final projects have been released.

Is it harder to live in a world where we aren't graced with the beautiful talents of Rickman and Bowie? Of course it is. There is always a void when you lose icons; the fabric never looks the same. Is it hard pressing on without my grandfather around? Yes, absolutely. It is hard to live in a world where your loved ones are not. It is hard to not see them or talk to them or get to know them better. So yes, I believe that dying is harder on the living because we have to endure the pain of not being with them.

To push through that pain, I find comfort in knowing that Bowie, Rickman, my grandfather and everyone else I've lost are all up there looking over us and enjoying their retirement from life. They are all in a peaceful place where they can be eternally happy and watch over those they love most. I know my grandfather's spirit is with me, I can feel it at times, especially when I'm upset or feel like giving up on everything. I believe our lives don't end with death. We merely just go to another state of being. One day you and I will join them —hopefully when we're 98 and die peacefully in our sleep. Then we all can be stardust … always and forever … happily ever after.

Stardust, Always

Bare Bones

Stacy Whitmire

It sucked being an only survivor. Sure, she had Bones for company but he had a bit of a snarky, sarcastic personality that wasn't always endearing. At least she had him though. There had been a time before she knew Bones, when she traveled alone, and it was one of the most miserable experiences of her life: alone in a desolate wasteland. Despite his snarkiness, she was glad to have him.

"I swear you're taking us in circles," Bones said.

Miri rolled her eyes and sighed. "Oh, do stop complaining already. If you think you know any better, then lead the way, smarty pants."

Vast desert stretched out before her, that's all there was anymore. Buildings were in crumbling ruins and trees laid flat, partially disintegrated from the shockwave. A thick cloud covered the sky, but the heat of the sun was just as strong as ever, beating all around her, the clouds trapping the heat in the atmosphere. Today the heat was particularly suffocating. Her body felt like it was roasting, her blood boiling just underneath the surface, ready to bubble over at a moment's notice.

Miri closed her eyes for a long moment and, in the darkness of her eyelids, she began to spin. She fell to her knees and sat back on her heels, her body curving slightly forward as her head continued to spin.

"Whoa, Miri! Watch it!"

"Sorry, Bones," she whispered, "I just need a minute."

"Here, you need to drink some water."

"No … we need to save it."

"*Drink* some *god-damn* water."

Miri sighed heavily and reached for the water canteen.

105

How did life get like this? She knew. It was just too unbelievable. An entire race wiped out, or at least she could only assume, since she hadn't seen another survivor in years. She used to be a part of a group, but for one reason or another they died or went on their own way until she was the only one left.

She remembered the day like it was yesterday.

They had heard about it for weeks, but no one believed it. Some idiot decided the human race was corrupt, and deliverance could only be brought about by death. To save us all, he concocted "The Meteor," also known as the doomsday device. It was a bomb, but no ordinary bomb. It had the magnitude of a large meteor strike on earth which, when properly placed, could destroy the world.

On the news, the broadcaster had said, "Officials assure the public that nothing of this magnitude could exist, and that mankind just doesn't have the type of technology available to create a single bomb that could destroy the entire planet. We have a leading nuclear physicist here with us today weighing in on the subject. Phil, is a bomb of this magnitude even possible?"

Phil chuckled and leaned forward. "Linda, it's laughable! While we might have the capability to create something to affect a large geographical region, in no way could it wipe out the entire human race. The world is a large place, and for all of those watching and worrying over this possible threat, this is a simple case of fear mongering; a war tactic by radicals to cause worldwide hysteria. Come on now, folks! Let's be realistic and maintain some sanity!"

Feeling reassured, no one took the threat seriously and returned to their normal lives. Well, except for those paranoid freaks, and luckily she had known a few of those. Miri had refused to believe them. When they insisted she come to their bunker she told them she had class and couldn't miss it. It was so long ago now that she no longer remembered what class she had been taking, she just remembered her eyelids drooping as she leaned on her hand, elbow propped up on the desk, trying to take notes with her other hand and fighting the haziness of sleep.

There had been no notice, no time to think or react. The only sound was of the wind screaming through the air, and then the building was leaning, cracking, and breaking, the ceiling thrashing down in chunks. Chairs and people flew to one side of the room, and Miri was no exception. Everything started in slow motion as Miri stared at the wall, and then at the ceiling. Things snapped into overtime as a force field of air pushed her from her seat and she went flying, crashing into other people around her.

Miri woke to the sounds of the wounded crying out for help, as if from a far distance, and the sounds coming from her own lips. A ringing sound filled one of her ears and a thick dust coated her throat as she tried to breathe. She brought her forearm up to cover her mouth as she gathered her bearings, but the dust still found its way into her nose and mouth. Coughing, she reached for the hem of her shirt to pull it over her nose but it was caught on something. When she looked down at her torso she saw the big piece of concrete pinning her down and was momentarily surprised, and then concerned when she realized she didn't feel the pressure of it on her.

She groaned and tried to call out for help, a rough rasping sound choked out of her mouth. Was that even the word she had been trying to say? She tried again but, looking around, she saw everyone else crying out, just like her ... .

Now is not the time for this.

Miri opened her eyes.

"Miri, did you hear me? Now is not the time for this. Get up. We have to keep moving; we need to find shelter for the night. Come on."

"Ok, Bones." Miri absentmindedly checked her satchel, making sure it still hung just behind her right hip. Wouldn't want to lose it. Before standing back up, she returned her canteen to her belt. Her first few steps were staggering as she regained her feet. She focused mainly on her feet. Her shoes were ragged but still holding up well from the last store she had raided. With effort, she lifted one foot and pushed it forward, just one step in front of the other, afraid of what she might think if she looked ahead.

Was there anyone left? If there was, she was determined to find them or die trying. She wasn't sure how long she had been searching, or where she had searched. There were old signs strewn about, the big freeway ones that said where you were headed or where you are, but those were largely unreliable. However, she knew that there was no way she had passed Atlanta just two weeks after leaving Ogden, her hometown right outside of Salt Lake City. In fact, she was pretty sure she had been heading west towards California, but who could say for sure anymore?

"Bones, tell me something funny."

"You want to hear a joke, do you?"

"Yes, Bones, please. Anything to keep me going right now."

Quick as a whip, Bones asked, "What happens after an apocalypse and there's no food?"

"Uh … everything dies? Bones, what kind of joke is this?"

"You become a bag of bones."

"Oh *do* shut up." Miri smiled a little to herself as she continued to trek through the muck. "That wasn't even funny anyway."

After Miri found a respectable shelter for the night and rested up, she felt a bit more energized the next day. When she came across a chasm, it seemed like a smart idea to find a crossable area and jump rather than to try to make her way around it. There were crumbling buildings on either side. If she found a place where the chasm wasn't so large, she could easily go from one side to the other. She didn't know how large the chasm was, but it went as far as she could see through the destruction and it would save her a ton of time rather than trying to find a way around it.

Heading along the edge of the chasm, it didn't take long to find an area where a metal beam stuck out over the chasm, held in place by the crumbling building it came from. It looked like the perfect spot to attempt a jump, and the best spot she had come across yet. She inched along the beam, not really lifting her feet up, but shuffling one foot forward. It was hard to resist the urge to bend down to stabilize herself, to cling to the concrete, but she knew she couldn't make her leap from that position.

When she reached the edge she set her stance, "Ok Bones, on three. One. Two. THREE!"

Miri squealed as she pushed off, the metal beam slipping from its position as the concrete slab holding it started to crumble and break at its base connection to the building. Air was forced out of her body as she slammed into the other side, her hand scrambling for a hold. She hadn't cleared the jump. Her body dangled over the pit, dirt biting into her face as she clung with all her strength.

"Aghh! Help! Bones? Oh my god, Bones?! Are you alright?" Miri looked around frantically, searching for a way to pull herself up. "There's got to be a way."

Her body slid another inch, her arm muscles straining and burning as she dug her fingers into the tough soil. Miri gritted her teeth and stubbornly set her jaw. "No."

Rock slid beneath her feet as she tried to gain a hold on the cliff side. She threw her foot out to the side and found a solid rock sticking out. She jammed her foot onto the rock as hard as she could.

"Don't fall. Don't fall. *Don't fall.*"

Her foot found something solid she could put her weight on. With one foot safe, it was easier for her other foot to finally find a place to rest as well. Slowly she crawled her way up the edge of the cliff. Her fingers clawed into the topsoil, refusing to give way. Grasping for air, she finally reached the top and flopped onto the ground, rolling onto her side. Every inch of her body ached from the strain, her muscles shaking and screaming at her. It hurt to breathe as her chest heaved trying to catch up to the moment.

Electricity jolted through Miri as she bolted upright and swung her hands to her side, searching her lower right hip, "Bones! Oh my god, no! Oh my god."

Miri scrambled to her knees and scanned the ground. Her satchel didn't make it with her. Ignoring her screaming muscles, she threw herself at the edge "BONES!"

She looked down, her breathing still coming in ragged pants, her heart aching with a deep stabbing pain, and her muscles barely supporting her weight as she peered over the edge. Tears started to form in her eyes making it difficult to see.

"Please, oh please."

There it was. Barely hanging on by the strap.

"Bones! Just—just hang in there! Please don't fall! I'll get you, hang in there!

Miri looked around her. A few feet away was a hooked pole, and she threw her body in that direction, crawling along the ground as fast as she could, her body not strong enough to propel her to stand. Pole in hand, she returned to the pit and peered over again. There was the satchel—still there.

"I'm going to get you Bones, don't worry."

Forcing herself to move, Miri twisted so that half her body was on solid ground. As her right arm held out the pole, she reached out to the satchel to hook it and pull it up. She gritted her teeth with the effort, barely allowing herself to breathe. Her entire body was shaking, her arm screaming in rebellion. A spasm shook through her arm and she almost dropped the pole as her arm flopped down the side of the cliff. She stared at her arm, imagining it moving in her head, and slowly she began to tense her muscles back up.

As the pole hooked around her satchel, Miri precariously pulled it up the side of the pit. Rather than risking her arm muscles, she rolled her body away from the cliff, allowing the pole to be brought towards safety without much effort. Sobbing in relief, Merri snatched at the satchel and clutched it to her chest. Tears began flowing freely down her cheeks.

"I'm so sorry, Bones. I'm so sorry."

Miri sat up and scooted away from the pit. Once she was at a safer distance she rocked over Bones' body, cradling him to her chest. Her heart shattered into a million pieces as her body swayed back and forth.

After some time, Miri stopped rocking and she knew she had to count. She released the satchel from her chest and peered into the bag of bones. She remembered back to when she was alone, before she had met Bones.

It was a different time. One where she hadn't been sure if she could even use her voice anymore, or that it at least wouldn't sound like a toad. There were no birds to talk to, no plants to coax into life. It was all complete ruin. Every once and a while something would flash just out of her field of vision; something else had survived, and Miri wasn't too sure she wanted to know what it was.

It had been months, more than she could tell—the sky was an endless cycle of faded grey turning into pitch black— since she had lost the last member of her group. She was starving and in serious need of finding a food stash. Anything. A grocery store, or even a convenience store would do. Just something, anything, that had possibly survived the onslaught. The last time she had eaten had probably been a week before. Her water was also almost gone. She recalled how her mouth was so dry it felt like she had popped a cotton ball in it. Her lips were no better. They were cracked and had felt like used sandpaper.

She remembered how hard it was to focus, to continue putting one foot in front of the other. It almost felt like that now, but at least now she had Bones to keep her company, and a bit of food left. With each step she took, her legs felt like they weighed twenty pounds more than usual. Her stomach had been so empty, she walked half-curved over, not even able to straighten her stomach muscles into a standing position.

Step. After Step. That's all that was left.

She thought back to a half-remembered quote and how it so aptly described her: staring senselessly, lost, and without meaning, doomed to roam this way for the rest of eternity. Who would have known the world would come to this? Perhaps she had died, and this was truly hell. Maybe no one had survived the blast.

Softly, she recalled singing in her harsh voice. Her lips

had tugged as she tried to form the words to parts of a song. The lyrics had been a bit hazy, after not having heard any music for several years. The last part of the song she could remember had caught in her throat as she sang of dying alone.

The world had flipped as her foot caught on a piece of debris. Miri's body flew forward, her chin scraping along the ground, and when she finally stopped, she didn't have the will to get back up right away. Instead, she stayed unmoving and barely breathing, her energy and will to live completely sapped from her soul.

It took her a long time—she couldn't tell how long, not with the sun hidden behind the grey haze—it felt like eternity before she opened her eyes. A loud cry had escaped her throat and she scrambled backward, as quickly and as far as her body might allow. She remembered the terror that clutched at her heart. Crouching about a foot away from her original spot, she eyed the skull with its empty sockets staring back at her.

Someone had died right here. In this very spot. Probably just like her—too exhausted to go on, parched, and without food. The jaw was slightly agape, as if surprised. The bone was completely devoid of any flesh; the surviving animals had probably picked it clean.

She stared down at the skull morosely. We are the dead. She was just as dead as the guy who died here without a breath left. The only difference between the skull and herself was that she still had flesh on her bones and breath in her body.

She continued to eye the skull for a moment. Inching closer, not sure what possessed her to do so, she hesitantly reached forward and moved the mandible as she said, "Hi, I'm Bones."

A small giggle escaped Miri and her hand snapped over her mouth. It wasn't funny. Then the giggle turned into a laugh, which turned into a stomach-holding roll as she couldn't contain her hysteria. Had she *really* just used a skull as a *puppet*? When the laughter finally died down she began to cry. Was she truly the only one left? There had to be someone out there. Not just this skull lying here, staring up at her, her only piece of company.

She had laid on her side for a long time, the tears rolling as she stared at the skull.

Everyone was gone.

"Tell me a joke, Bones."

Her finger reached out and tentatively moved the skull's mandible.

"Alright." Bones paused as he pondered for a moment. "Alright. Knock, knock."

Miri groaned through her tears. "Really, Bones—"

"Knock! Knock!" he repeated, with emphasis on each knock.

"Ok, fine. Who's there?" She choked over the words as she stared at her fleshless puppet, barely able to see through her tears.

"The Meteor."

"Bones ..."

"*The Meteor!*"

Miri hesitated, not sure she wanted to answer. "The Meteor who—?"

"—BLEW UP YOUR WORLD!"

Despite herself, Miri laughed with tears leaking out of her eyes, and knew she had just found a friend.

Miri shook her head, bringing herself back to the present, tears still flowing, "If it's not all here I can find you new ones, Bones. It'll be ok. Don't leave me. I know sometimes we don't get along. I don't mean it, Bones. Please be ok. I'm so sorry."

Carefully, Miri reached in and, with a shaking hand, she pulled out the first piece, the skull that always sat on top. "I've gotta count. I need to count. You've got to all be there. I'm so sorry, Bones. What if I lost a piece of you? I'm so sorry! I'll count. I'll make sure you're there. Ok, here's one."

Next she pulled out what she thought to be part of the collar bone, "Two." And with hands that were shaking so hard she was afraid she might drop a piece, "Three."

"It's ok, Bones. I'll make sure you're whole. We'll still be together. Come back to me."

Painstakingly, Miri counted each one, not exactly knowing their names or how many of each were actually in the human body. All she knew for certain was that she had over fifty different bones. Not enough to make up all the bones in the human body, but enough for Bones to exist.

"I promise you, Bones, after this I'll find you two more. I'll make it up to you."

Miri crouched over her pile of bones for a long time. She counted fifty. There was definitely fifty. Maybe she should recount; she couldn't be sure until Bones spoke to her again. She rocked for a moment, staring intently, with her hands clasped in front of her just under her chin.

"Come on, Bones! Come on!" Miri screamed, frustration and fear consuming her body, "Bones! Please!" Her rocking increased in fervency. Her stomach twisted and churned as nausea consumed her.

"Oh, my god. Come on. Come *on*." The words repeated over and over again as she rocked over his bones. She pounded the ground beside her, over and over again. With a final wail, Miri collapsed next to Bones. Completely exhausted, she stared at him as she had the first time she had met him.

Slowly, she reached out and moved his mouth, "That was quite the tantrum Miri, done yet?"

Miri giggled.

Holding back a sob, she asked, "But you're with me, right Bones? It's the two of us again?"

He only had one word for her, and one word was all she needed.

"Always."

A Truer Portrayal Never Witnessed

Sophia Diaz

He was there from the start,
A man in the dark.
Hidden from the world
For the crimes he created.

When first introduced,
His gaze was beyond cruel.
It was easy to blame him
For the wrong that came then.
But what we were led to believe,
Was all just a scheme.
Yet once the truth surfaced,
His behavior never lessened,
And the hatred only greatened.

As the years went by,
We learned truths and lies.
He was a victim, he was a villain,
He was fury at its limit.
His hatred was a combination,
And the repercussions recoiled
On an innocent little boy.

But there was more to see,
Than the darkness, the hatred, the ever-present sneer.
There was guilt beyond anything
Another has ever felt.
A moment's weakness, a haunting action,
Has brought him from villain to man.
A plan was struck to change the war,
Another painful sacrifice the world would never know.

Stardust, Always

This man was brought forth
From mind to eye.
A character come to life,
A truer portrayal never witnessed.
For many years, he has been more.
An angel, a villain, a movie star,
A lover, a caterpillar, and so on it goes.
A man of many faces,
Giving the world quite a show.
And, as the curtain closed,
We bid adieu, and promised you'll be in our memories

"Always."

Goblins & Glitter

Katelyn Sweigart

"What made you want to be a pediatric oncologist?" Ally's mother wiped her nose with a tissue and hugged herself around the middle. Her tired eyes never left her daughter's sleeping face, hidden under an oxygen mask.

Dr. Jones glanced up at her from the equipment she was checking.

"When I was five, my older brother was diagnosed with bone cancer," she said. "He was fifteen."

A stricken expression tightened the already pained look on Ally's mother's face.

Dr. Jones took a seat across from her and Ally, in one of the very comfortable armchairs they provided at the hospital. She decided a story would maybe … not distract, but occupy the parts of the mother's mind that ran in vicious, downward circles.

"My parents didn't know what to tell me," Dr. Jones began. "They were very … protective. I was the only daughter of four children, youngest by five years. They coddled me and thought I was fragile."

They both looked at Ally. Her knitted beanie was like a knight's helm. A battalion of stuffed animals kept watch over her while she rested. Her forearms were thinner from chemo, her knees a little knobbier, but no one would call Ally fragile.

"So they made up this story. Your brother was bad, so the goblins are making him one of them. They showed me the x-ray and pointed at the mass and said, 'See? That's because of the goblins. They want to turn him into a goblin too.'"

Ally's mother wrinkled her nose, and Dr. Jones chuckled softly.

"I think saying 'cancer' would have been less scary to me than 'goblins' at that age," she admitted, resting her elbows on the arms of the chair and lacing her fingers together. "I was born in late June. 'Cancer' was the thing my mother read out loud to me from the horoscopes. Goblins were nasty little creatures that hurt people and stole children. I don't know what they were thinking. They don't even remember telling me."

"They were probably sleep-deprived," Ally's mother suggested with a huff. Her eyes were red and puffy. There was a full-body fatigue of a person who consumed too much caffeine in lieu of sleep.

"Sleep deprived and having to answer to a confused five-year-old asking why her brother was sick. Young children think cancer is caused by something very specific, like a thought or action. Or it's contagious."

"We had the talk with Dana," Ally's mother said. "Her younger sister. She's eight, but we had all those help books and the psychiatrist to tell us what to say. I keep thinking we're being bad parents, not being able to pay attention to her like Ally, away at the hospital all the time. My husband's with her right now, so I can be with Ally and not feel so bad. She thought cancer was just from cigarettes."

Dr. Jones leaned over to return a stuffed horse to its post by Ally's elbow.

"My brother was going through teenage rebellion when it happened," she continued. "Little five-year-old me heard the fights they had. Staying out late. Getting caught with drugs. Talking back, yelling. By saying my brother was bad and cancer was the result, it was scaring me to be good. Then I got it into my head that I needed to rescue my brother."

* * *

Gwendolyn Leah Jones found out goblins were real when she was four years, eleven months old.

"Max was really bad, so the goblins are trying to take him away," her dad said. He held up a see-through black piece of paper with lacy white bones. It looked like a Halloween decoration.

He pointed to a frilly bit of bone. "See? The goblins did that. We're trying to make sure the goblins don't get him, so we have to take him to a special hospital."

Gwen squinted at the x-ray then up at her dad. "Goblins?"

"Yes. And it's very, very important you be a good girl so that the goblins don't come after you, too."

Gwen was a good girl. A very good girl, in fact. Her mother always said so. Usually after one of her big brothers did something bad like track mud in the house or let their laundry hampers get full of stinky clothes or stay out way past Gwen's bedtime.

Gwen was such a good girl, that she realized she needed to rescue Max.

She went to her bedroom, then to her bookshelf. She pulled out the big fairy tale book her Nana gave to her when Gwen said she could read now.

It was blue and felt like the couch in the living room. Smelled like it, too. Like new boots. Gwen traced the gold letters with a tiny finger and opened it up to the Table of Contents, but it was far too long and she got lost.

Gwen jumped up and went to her nightstand, where *Harry Potter and the Sorcerer's Stone* sat. According to that book, goblins worked in banks. She opened it up and grabbed her reading bookmark.

Max made it for her out of purple and green construction paper. They would sit on her bed, and he would read Harry Potter line by line, making her follow along with her finger and the bookmark. It helped keep her eyes from skipping ahead and getting all confused...

Except now Max was in the hospital and couldn't help her read anymore.

She took her bookmark, laid it flat across the page, and dragged it slowly down.

Fairies, Goblins, and Trolls, chapter 3 ... Goblins, page 94.

On page 94, there was a drawing of a squash-faced

creature with spindly arms, beetle-black eyes, big ears with lots of hair sticking out, a whippy tail, and red pants.

Did all goblins wear red pants? She turned the page. The goblin on this page looked like a chihuahua standing on its hind legs with a hooked nose, bulbous eyes, freaky little claws, and no pants at all. But it had a little hat, like a garden gnome. It was brown.

Gwen sighed. She was going to have to do a lot of research.

* * *

Her mother and father told her to be a good girl, so instead of actually fighting the goblins, Gwen the Glitterwitch outwitted them. No one got in trouble for being smart, after all. Smart-mouthed, maybe, but Gwen didn't know the difference.

Instead of a sword, Gwen had a spellbook full of magic words. It was actually a My Little Pony diary—with a heart-shaped lock she broke open with a butter knife because she lost the key. And then she copied big words out of the G section of the dictionary, because G was for "Gwen" and "good girl." Then she realized G was also for "goblin" and "germs" and started copying from the A section, because "alakazam" and "abracadabra" were magic words.

In the pockets of her witch's robe (her mother's green satin kimono), she had her Dust (different colors of glitter in finger-sized vials from her arts & crafts kit). When Gwen threw a handful of her Dust and said a magic word from her spellbook, magic would happen (and the nearest surface would instantaneously be utterly fabulous).

Her book, Nana's fairy tale book, said goblins lived in the mountains, in caves, and the dark places under things. After careful research, she concluded the goblins who were trying to take her brother were the Dark-Places-Under-Things sort.

Very, very quietly, Gwen crept into Max's bedroom.

It smelled like old pizza and the stuff in a blue bottle her mom liked to spray on everything. There weren't any clothes on the floor, except for his gym shoes. She shut the door very slowly, happy when it didn't creak. She didn't turn on the light, allowing the cold moon to illuminate her way.

Bookcase, desk, chair, fake treasure chest, night stand ... bed.

Scooting closer, Gwen examined the bed. It had red sheets and pillows and a black blanket. The red bed skirt was hitched up near the foot, like a theater curtain partially drawn, revealing inky darkness beneath.

As she stared, the darkness skittered away, deeper under the bed. She choked off a scream, covering her mouth tightly with both hands.

No. Gwen the Glitterwitch was brave. She dropped her hands and fisted them in the pockets of her robes, around her vials.

Then she got onto her belly and wriggled under the bed. Her questing fingers met something hard and greasy.

She had found the pizza. The book hadn't warned her about old pizza in the Dark Places Under Things.

Wrinkling her nose and wiping her hand, Gwen pulled out a tiny black flashlight she had found in the everything drawer in the kitchen, clicking it on. Crumpled socks, dust bunnies, and the icky pizza caught the thin beam. She wriggled in some more, crawling on her elbows, inching deeper under the bed.

That's when she found the little door.

It was jammed into the wall, broken plaster dusting its stone frame white. The door itself was made of wood the same dark color as their dinner table. A thick metal ring hung above a crooked keyhole. Gwen pulled the ring, but it was locked.

Putting the flashlight between her teeth, Gwen dug in her pocket and pulled out a handful of silver Dust and her spellbook. She opened it one-handedly and said the first word she saw. She tried again without the flashlight in her mouth, tossing some of the silver Dust at the door.

"Aspirate."

The metal sparkled like new nickels and the lock popped open. Slightly ajar now, a rich earthy smell leaked out. She grasped the metal ring and pulled. Her flashlight caught dirt and hairy roots.

Gwen entered the Goblin Kingdom, squirming on her belly with the flashlight in her mouth again.

The tunnel was tall enough to stand in once she was through the door. She scraped mud off her knees, straightened her robes, and looked around. It was a pretty boring tunnel, so she started walking.

The first goblin Gwen met had bulgy, mottled cheeks like bruised apples and white hair like a dandelion tuft. He—or she?—dug at the dirt, pulling out worms as big as garter snakes and slurping them like spaghetti.

Gwen didn't scream this time. She grasped a handful of magenta Dust and threw it at the pudgy cheeked goblin, yelling "Amaranth!"

The glittering cloud swirled and the goblin was caught in a web of cotton candy. It screeched like a tea kettle and tried to eat its way out only to recoil as soon as the sugar melted on its purple tongue.

"ERGBLEK!" The goblin spat. "That not cobwebs, that CANDY! Disgusting!"

"You nasty little goblins are trying to take my brother away!" Gwen accused.

The goblin blinked little red eyes at her, head tilting. "Say what now?"

"I'm Gwen the Glitterwitch, and I'm here to save my brother!" She put her hands on her hips and gave the goblin her best Angry Mom look.

"Ooooooh," the goblin pursed its lips, making its cheeks even bulgier. "That not my department. I'm Mud Inspector. Gots to make sure mud is the perfect ratio of water to dirt to icky-squicky things. You be wanting Childnabbers or Toddlertakers. How old is he?"

"Fifteen."

"Oh. You want Ol'Factory then," it tapped its pinched

nose. "Prolly the Department of Body Odor. They always gots teenage boy socks and gym britches for Super Smelly Stuff vats."

It pointed a blunt finger down the tunnel on their left. "Just follow tunnel 'til you get to sewers, then follow rotten egg smell. Ol'Factory right by the spa and hot springs."

"Um. Thank you," Gwen said, because good girls were polite.

"Don' mention it."

* * *

The Ol'Factory looked like someone tried to make a building out of yellow-green silly putty and egg cartons. And mostly succeeded.

The second goblin Gwen came across had an appropriately huge nose for his line of work—which according to his name tag was "Tramplefungus, Foul Stench Engineer."

"Anemochorous!" Gwen flicked a handful of neon green Dust at him. He let out a ferocious sneeze that knocked him off of his feet and right into the Ol'Factory's slimy walls.

"Not again," he wailed, trying to unstick himself and snort a dangling booger back up his nose. "And why does it smell like key lime pie?"

"I am Gwen the Glitterwitch, and I'm here to rescue my brother," she declared, fists on her hips and chin jutted up. "Take me to your leader."

Tramplefungus blinked at her. " ... Uh ... my supervisor's at lunch."

"I want to see your manager," she said, remembering what her father always said.

"Oh dear," he fretted. "Um. Okay. Could you help me down?"

Gwen reluctantly took Tramplefungus's outstretched claw and heaved. He dislodged with a squelch. He adjusted his tie, cleared his throat, and mumbled, "Follow me please."

She followed him through the Ol'Factory's front entrance, where he swiped his keycard and gave her a visitor badge—a piece of sticky yellow flypaper.

"You can keep it when you leave," Tramplefungus whispered. "For a snack."

"I have a couple candy bars."

Tramplefungus sniffed disparagingly.

Inside, the Ol'Factory did look like a factory, full of bubbling vats of every color you wouldn't want to see bubbling in a vat. There were goblins in white lab coats, oversized pink gloves, yellow hard hats, and round black goggles stirring the vats, sniffing test samples, and chattering over mugs of brown sludge, which they sipped delicately.

And it reeked like dead fish and dog farts.

Gwen hastily tossed some red glitter and whispered, "Aerodynamic."

Now it reeked like dead fish, dog farts, and *roses*.

They went through a side exit and up a few flights of stairs to a door that read "CHIEF STENCH ENGINEER" in big green letters.

Tramplefungus knocked politely and let Gwen in.

The goblin behind the desk resembled a hairy wart trying to fit into a polo shirt two sizes too small.

"Ma'am, this is Gwen the Glitterwitch. She's here to rescue her brother."

"He's fifteen," Gwen added, remembering what the Mud Inspector said.

The wart eyed Gwen as she stamped some paperwork. "Not here. Teenage boy stench is seasonal. It's all about leftover tuna casserole and canine flatulence this month."

"Goblins took my big brother away. You're trying to turn him into a goblin!"

"See the Recruitment Office," the long hairs on her head quivered. "Tramplefungus, escort her out before she gets that flowery smell in the batch!"

Tramplefungus guided her back to the entrance, and she gave him the flypaper back.

"You'll want to take the Sewer Line to the central hub,"

he said, picking out little black flies and popping them in his mouth like raisins. "Then take the train to Goblinopolis. Dave runs the Recruitment Office."

"Dave?"

"Easier to recruit humans with a human," he explained. "They did a study on it. Very interesting read. Good luck!"

Gwen decided not to tell him he had twitchy fly legs stuck in his teeth.

* * *

"Adumbral!"

The golden glitter cupped in Gwen's palm transmogrified into lint-covered cough drops, which she handed to the goblin conductor. It counted out her change with tentacled fingers—three beetle shells and a lump of earwax—and let her off the train.

Gwen asked directions of a goblin who looked like a molting macaw on stilts, then was on her way.

The Recruitment Office squatted between a toenail consignment store and a pet rat groomer. When she walked in, a little bell tinkled above her head. It smelled like stargazer lilies and paper dust.

The human behind the desk appeared to be a rock star who had decided to be an accountant for a day. His hair was teased into a wild gold mane, his odd blue eyes darkened with kohl and smudged with pearly eyeshadow. But he wore a pair of khakis and a white dress shirt, his Oxfords shiny with polish. A nameplate on his neat desk simply read "Dave."

"Can I help you miss?" He asked.

Straightening her spine, Gwen said, "I'm Gwen the Glitterwitch. You stole my big brother Max and are trying to turn him into a goblin. I want him back, and not goblinified. He's my favorite brother, and I don't want him to go away."

Dave looked at her green witch's robes, the rainbow of glitter clinging to her hair, the pink spellbook, and her determined expression.

With a sigh, he turned to his metal filing cabinet and took out a manila folder. He flipped through the contents with black-nailed fingers and removed a sheet of paper with Max's photo, name, age, height, weight, level of maturity, and favorite song (which Gwen knew without looking was "Space Oddity").

"We can return him to the human world, but you're going to have to un-goblin him. The longest word you can find should work," Dave said, signing the release form and giving Max's file to a many-toothed goblin, who promptly ate it with a squirt of ketchup.

Dave got up, put on a trench coat, and took Gwen's hand gently. His fingers were long, white, and very warm.

"I'll walk you to the hospital. I know a shortcut."

* * *

Max was in a very white hospital bed with lots of machines beeping and whirring. Gwen and Dave stood in the doorway, watching a nurse in kitten-covered scrubs as she finished marking a clipboard at the foot of his bed and left.

"Go on, Gwen," Dave pressed against her back, guiding her to the bed.

Max's eyes fluttered open and he itched at the tube in his nose. He noticed her with a slightly baffled smile.

"What's up buttercup?" He rasped. "Haven't seen you in a while."

Gwen sniffled, fingers clutching the white sheet. Max reached over to squeeze her tiny, glitter-speckled hand.

"C'mon, G, don't cry. I'll be okay."

"I fought the goblins for you."

" ... the what?"

"Mom and Dad said you were bad, so the goblins were trying to take you away," she said, rubbing her tearing eyes. "So I went to the Goblin Kingdom and made them give you back. But you still got goblin bits in your leg and Dave said I had a magic spell—"

"Who's Dave?"

Gwen turned to point him out, only to find they were alone. The scent of lilies lingered in his absence.

"I have a magic spell that can save you," she said, opening her diary and turning to the very middle, where all good spells were. She pulled out her vial of eggplant-purple glitter. Her brother looked at the glitter, the book, then her.

"Let's have it then," Max said solemnly, eyes a little wet. "I don't want to be a goblin."

He helped her sound out the word, because it was too long for her.

Gwen scattered purple glitter over his goblinified leg and whispered, "Antidisestablishmentarianism."

It sparkled like amethyst under the fluorescent lights.

Max smiled wide and noogied her head. "I feel better already, G."

* * *

"My parents found me in my brother's hospital room. They were frantic and trying to figure out how I even got there. They scolded me and told me I wasn't a 'very good girl.' But I was pretty sure Dave wouldn't let the goblins try to take me …"

Dr. Jones trailed off, bringing her hand to the glitter-filled pendant at her throat. Ally's mother swiped her fingers under her eyes. Putting a sympathetic hand on Dr. Jones' arm, she murmured, "I'm sorry for your loss."

Dr. Jones startled and said quickly, "Oh! I'm sorry. Max survived. His leg had to be amputated, but he responded well to chemo. He's a physical therapist now and runs a surf clinic for local amputees."

They both looked a little embarrassed and returned to watching Ally's chest rise and fall.

"I can have him stop by, if you'd like," Dr. Jones offered. "The kids love him, and it's always nice to talk to someone who went through the same thing."

Ally's mother took her daughter's hand and smiled. "I think we'd like that ... but only if he brings glitter."

* * *

Dedicated to Michelley

Keys and a Caterpillar

Trine Jensegg

Alana died the night the moon turned red, and honestly she was relieved. The last few years had been hard. Harder than she'd let on. And although she had found the prospect of dying terrifying at first, she'd slowly come to accept it—and even look forward to it. She was old. Weary. And after so many months of fighting the illness, an ending began to sound like a blessing.

Which was why she felt rather cheated when she woke back up again. Even worse, she found herself in the dreariest place she'd ever seen. The room appeared to be some sort of an office. There were four desks along one drab, undecorated wall, but nothing else.

"How curious … ," she muttered to herself as she took in her surroundings. She stood in a line, but the other people in the room looked more like cardboard cut-outs than actual people, even when they moved. "I wonder what they are."

"They are people." The voice came from directly beneath her left ear.

"What the—?" Alana jumped, almost hitting herself in the head in the attempt to swat whatever was on her shoulder.

"Now, was that really necessary?" A blue caterpillar glared up at her from the floor.

"You?" The word was barely audible. "It can't be …"

"And yet it is."

Alana almost protested further, but just shook her head. There didn't seem to be a point.

"What is this place?" she asked, nodding at the cardboard people. "And what the hell are those?"

"I already told you." The caterpillar grumbled. "They're people. Just like you."

"But why do they look like that?"

"Ah." A strange look of understanding spread across the creature's face. "I'd almost forgotten. They only look strange to you. It's a new privacy feature, or so I'm told."

"Privacy feature?" Alana frowned. "Answer me, please … where am I?"

"Could you at least get me off this floor first?"

"Oh. Of course." She picked him up, trying to ignore the familiar ache in her old limbs. "I'm sorry."

"Ah, never mind that." The caterpillar shook his head, gesturing to the empty space between Alana and the desks. "Why not ask those questions of someone better able to answer them?"

The woman at the end of Alana's line looked like she wanted to make up for the room's drabness. Her clothes had so many different colors and patterns, it almost hurt to look at her. That and her overly bright smile made her look far more fake than the cardboards.

"Welcome to AfterCare!" the colorful woman chirped as Alana approached her desk. "Are you ready to make your choice?"

"Uhm …" Alana glanced anxiously at the caterpillar. "What … what am I choosing?"

"Well, that's entirely up to you." The woman beamed. "Like your Agent informed you, you have a choice of several different Afterlives. It must be exciting! But, I assure you, whatever you choose will be wonderful!"

Alana's heart sank.

"Agent—?" she whispered. "What agent?"

"You weren't contacted by an AfterCare agent?" The perky woman deflated.

"No … not that I know of?"

"Oh." The woman looked like she wanted to say something, but squared her shoulders and straightened her glasses. "I'm sorry for the inconvenience, madam. Let me just check your file, and we'll clear all this up."

Alana watched the woman turn to her computer. Her eyes darted back and forth as she read. At first she seemed only curious, but then her expression turned to a mix of horror and annoyance.

"That doesn't look promising," she muttered to the caterpillar.

"Indeed not," he replied.

"So ... now that we're just waiting, what are *you* doing here?" She flashed him a smile. "I was under the impression that imaginary friends were supposed to remain in one's childhood."

"That's usually the case. Most people stop having a need for us as they grow older."

"I've never been 'most people'." She winked at him.

"True." He smiled back. "You were always different."

Finally, the woman turned back to them. The perk and color had all drained out of her face.

"I'm so, so sorry. I—" She shook her head. "—I'm afraid there have been some mistakes made in the handling of your case."

"What does that mean?" Alana stared across the desk.

"Normally, whenever a human approaches their final days, an agent is sent to inform them of their rights, to comfort the person, and to help them select which path they want to follow in their afterlife. Sadly ..." The woman shook her head with a bitter look in her eyes. "Not every agent is particularly good at their job. The one you were assigned, I am sad to say, must have forgotten his duties. Again."

"Oh." Alana blinked. "I, uhm ... . So what happens now?"

The woman stared, and Alana could almost see gears turning in her eyes.

"Give me just one moment," the woman said, bouncing out of her chair and hurrying through a door behind her.

"Well, that was interesting." Alana mumbled. "Did you know this was going to happen?"

"Why would you ask such a thing?" The caterpillar looked oddly offended.

"Well ... why else would you be here?" Alana smiled, watching the caterpillar's face turn purple.

"I had my concerns," he finally admitted. "You always did seem to find yourself in awkward situations."

Alana just shrugged, looking at the cardboard people around her. He had a point.

The no-longer-perky woman finally returned, and Alana cautiously leaned against the desk again.

"I'm so sorry for the confusion, and I assure you that the agent in charge of your case will be severely reprimanded," the woman stated, failing to return to her earlier perky behavior. "In the meantime, we've come up with a solution to your problem."

"Oh. That's nice!"

"Yes." The woman smiled and nodded. "I've talked to the people in charge of AfterCare, and they all agreed that the best solution is to transfer you to the SDD."

"The SDD?" Alana frowned. "I'm sorry, but I have no idea what that is."

"The Sudden Death Department," the woman explained. "When a human dies in an accident, or by a sudden illness, there isn't time to send an agent. Those people are sent to the Sudden Death Department, to go through an interactive program that will inform them of their options. At the conclusion you're given the opportunity to choose your next path."

"Okay." Alana nodded. "And how do I get to this other department?"

"Just go through that door to your left."

"But there isn't any ..." Her complaints died out when she turned. Despite knowing with one hundred percent certainty that the wall had been completely blank only moments ago, it was impossible to deny the huge door in the middle of it.

"Oh. Okay then." She gave the woman a polite nod, and walked towards the door.

The new room looked more like what she'd expected from an afterlife. The room clearly had boundaries, and it felt like a circle, but there were no actual walls. Nor was there anything outside it. The only contents of the room were a fairly large circle of tables. Once she found herself in the middle of the circle, the door she'd come through disappeared. She frowned slightly, and turned her attention to the tables. As she approached, she discovered that each table held one single object.

"They are keys," she noted, leaning closer to look at one of them. "But what are they for?"

"There should be a sign," the caterpillar commented. "Look closer."

Alana walked around the table closest to her. Sure enough, there was an elaborate placard hanging on the side. She read it.

"Power? What does that even mean?" Alana looked at the caterpillar.

"I've heard of this place," the caterpillar said. "If I remember correctly, each of these keys represents a concept. Or a path, if you prefer. The one you choose will be the keystone your afterlife is based on."

"I see." She looked back down at the key and shrugged. "I've never been one to lust for power. I think I'll pass."

"Take your time," the caterpillar said. "I don't think we'll be disturbed here."

Alana nodded and continued walking. Just like the caterpillar predicted, each had an elaborate sign with a single word written on it. WEALTH. FAMILY. LOVE. That last one made her pause. Love. Wasn't that what life was supposed to be about? That's what all the films and novels had told her. She'd never been the romantic sort, but she still reached for the key. If nothing else, she wanted to examine the carvings on it. But the second she touched it, everything changed. The circular room was gone, and Alana found herself on an empty beach.

"So in my next life, I'll be surrounded by sand?" She raised a brow, glancing at the caterpillar on her shoulder. "I hate sand."

"Nasty stuff, I agree," the caterpillar grumbled.

Alana sighed, and walked towards the water, watching the sun as it slowly made its way towards the horizon. Despite her memories of finding sand everywhere for weeks after each trip to the beach, she had to admit that it was beautiful. The setting sun bathed everything in a soft orange glow, and the gently-salted wind recalled memories of sailing trips with her father. She'd forgotten how peaceful the sea breeze was.

"Alana." The caterpillar's voice brought her back from her memories. "We have company."

Surprised, Alana whirled around to see what he meant, almost dislocating her hip in the process. Sure enough, a person stood alone further down the beach, looking towards them. They were too far away to identify, so Alana drifted cautiously towards them. She'd only moved ten or so meters when her entire body froze.

"No," she whispered. "It can't be …"

She could see him now. Even from a distance there was no mistaking him for anyone else. She'd recognise that face anywhere. He looked exactly the same, as if the past fifty years had had no effect on him. As if his life had simply paused the second they parted. She walked faster, feeling younger with each step.

"I'm guessing you know that man?"

"I … yes." It came out as barely more than a whisper. "I mean, I did. But that was half a century ago."

It felt strange saying it, especially here. She didn't feel that old. Looking at him now, she could have sworn that she was still in her early twenties. He was just as beautiful as she remembered.

"Who is he?" the caterpillar asked softly.

"The one that got away." She sighed as memories flooded her mind. It took all her strength to look away from her old love. "We met in school. Many years ago. It was love at first sight. Or at least it was for me. We were inseparable."

"So what happened?"

"His father got sick, and he moved back home to help his mother take care things. We exchanged addresses." She turned her gaze back towards the man on the beach. "It was good at first, but we slowly slipped away from each other. With the distance, everything sort of faded. We never decided to stop writing each other; it just happened."

The man had almost made it over to them when Alana took a sudden step back.

"I want to go back to the tables." The words stumbled over each other as she rushed to get them out. "Now, before he gets here."

She took another step backwards, and cast a panicked glance at the caterpillar.

"Just close your eyes." He looked confused, but nodded.

In a blink, they were back in the circular room. Alana leaned heavily against the nearest table, afraid of what would happen if she let go. Her legs weren't as steady as they'd once been, and the sudden shift had unsettled her.

"Do you want to talk about it?" the caterpillar asked.

Alana started to shake her head, but hesitated. This caterpillar had been her closest friend once. He'd first appeared when she was four or five, and stayed with her all the way through her childhood. He'd told her the most marvelous stories of adventures he'd been on with other children. Sometimes that had been painful. Listening to the tales of other boys and girls like her, out on quests of their own, made her wonder if she'd ever have any.

"I was always a good listener," the caterpillar said, as if he could hear her thoughts. She just nodded.

"You were."

"Why did you want to come back here? For a moment there, you seemed so happy. Wasn't that what you wanted?"

"It might be." Alana sighed, feeling heavier than ever. "But I'm not certain yet. This whole concept—being allowed to select my own afterlife—I think I owe it to myself to at least consider other possibilities before I choose.

"That was wise of you." The caterpillar gave her a strangely proud look.

"Perhaps." Alana held a hand against her chest. Her heart was still beating wildly. "I just knew that if he made it over to us, if he touched me again, I'd never have the strength to let go."

It took her quite a few moments, but eventually she

returned to her task. Alana carefully inspected each table, each finely-carved sign. Some she rejected immediately. She'd never cared much for possessions or wealth, and sincerely doubted that she'd feel differently in the next life. Others made her pause. One was the beautifully adorned sign that read CAREER. She didn't even know why it stopped her. Growing up in the era she did, a grand career had never really been an option. Although her father had been kind enough to pay for school, she'd been expected to come back home and work in her father's bakery. And she'd been completely fine with this. She loved the bakery, always had. When her father passed away, it had been hers. And when she grew too old to take care of it by herself, her niece had taken over. The thought of having it any other way never occurred to her until right this moment. Standing there with the sign in her hand, she began to wonder. What if she'd been free to choose for herself? If she'd had any option in the world. Wouldn't that be a grand adventure? Her brows furrowed as her eyes turned to the key on the table. For some reason just thinking about it scared her.

"Well," she said, forcing herself to pick it up, "if this isn't the time to try new things, I don't know what is.

The office she found herself in looked nothing like the first one. This was the most marvelous place she'd ever set foot in. It had a giant window overlooking a magnificent park. The opposite wall was covered with shelves so tightly packed with books that she hardly knew where to look. But it was the massive desk in the middle of the room that truly drew her attention. She had to remind herself to continue breathing as she sat down behind it.

"My goodness," she said, inhaling excitedly as she looked over the items on the surface in front of her. "I believe I'm a professor!"

A grin spread across her wrinkly face as she examined the papers and books on the desk. They were about language and literature, theatre and music, philosophy and psychology. Every single thing she'd ever had an interest in learning, but never quite got around to. She started to open a book about

Norse mythology, when she suddenly remembered the situation she was in.

"Ah," she almost snorted. "I guess now is not the time to learn all of this."

"I would say no," the caterpillar agreed. "But this is the life you would have if you want it. This very office could be yours. You simply have to choose it."

"I know." Alana nodded, and pushed herself away from the desk. She walked over to the window. Was this what she wanted? The way this office made her feel, it would certainly seem so. How strange, that she'd never known how much she wanted to learn! Was that normal? For a person to get so tied to one life that she never even began to wonder what else was out there?

What else had she been denying? What else had she hidden from herself? Did every key in the circular room hide something she'd repressed? When she first arrived there, she'd simply thought they were stereotypes. That these were the same keys everyone was offered. Now she wasn't so sure. And if that were true, if all those keys led to something that made her feel like this ... how on earth could she choose only one?

"Oh, my old friend." She sighed and forced her eyes to shut out the view of the tempting office. "I'm starting to feel very, very confused."

Once more she had to lean against the table to keep upright. This time she didn't need to open her eyes to know they'd returned to the circular room. She could feel the difference in the air. The office had smelled wonderfully of old books and lilies. This room didn't smell of anything at all. Somehow that made her anxious. Did they do that on purpose, to try and make each key lead you to somewhere more pleasant than this place, to make them more tempting?

"Don't forget to breathe," the caterpillar said, patting her shoulder with one tiny hand. "I know this must be a bit ... much."

She snorted.

"That's quite the understatement, old friend." She shook

her head slightly, to force herself back into the moment. "Had I known dying would require such effort, I might have clung to life a bit longer."

"Yes, well, I'm sorry to say that particular ship's already sailed." The caterpillar chuckled. "Might I suggest you continue your quest for a new one?"

His words made her smile. She'd always longed for a quest, begged her imaginary friend to take her on one. And here she was, all these years later, on a quest of her own. And complaining about it. Her younger self would be so disappointed.

She took her time browsing the rest of the tables. It certainly seemed that each of them would lead to some exciting new life. And each one of those lives only promised further confusion at this point. Both of the two she had picked so far had led her to places she didn't want to leave.

"I'll pick just one more," she finally decided. "And then I'll choose."

"Well, then," the caterpillar replied. "Make your selection wisely."

She nodded, walking slowly around the tables. Part of her wanted to check every single one of the keys, to see all the lives she'd be passing up. But she kept her word. Finally, she found the one she wanted. APTITUDE. She looked at the key for a moment, considering. Then, once more, she held her breath and reached for it.

The view startled her. She was surrounded by mirrors, at least a hundred of them. They were huge, each easily fitting her entire image inside it. Cautiously, she walked towards the closest one, watching her familiar figure in it. But as she came closer, the image changed. The mirror no longer showed her as a feeble old woman in her faded clothes. The woman staring through the glass was undoubtedly Alana, only at the same time it wasn't. This woman was younger, and far more athletic that she'd ever seen herself. She held some sort of ribbons. A gymnast, perhaps? She shook her head slightly, and moved to the next mirror. In what world would she ever want to be a gymnast? There'd be far too little cake in that scenario. Her years in a bakery had done nothing to diminish her sweet tooth.

In the next mirror she looked to be around thirty or forty years old, wearing some kind of uniform. It looked like something military, or perhaps police? She didn't recognise its insignia.

"I'm guessing this is something similar to seeing myself as a professor." She mused.

"What do you mean?" The caterpillar leaned forward to get a better look at her uniform.

"I mean, this thing we're in didn't know what I wanted to be professor of, since I don't know myself, so it gave me a bit of everything." She gestured to the uniformed woman. "I suppose this is just meant to show me how I'd look in a military force. The uniform is just a symbol, since I have no idea what kind of force I would join."

"That does sound logical." The caterpillar nodded.

They walked in silence, gazing at one Alana after another. There were so many that the real Alana soon felt overwhelmed. She'd hoped that this final key she'd chosen would have offered her more. She'd hoped it would somehow give her something she wanted far more than the other two keys. But all this one granted was more questions. It only opened more paths for her to choose.

This one showed everything she could be if she set her mind to it; and as it turned out, that was quite a lot. Still, she searched every mirror, hoping that somewhere between all the Award-Winning-Novelist Alanas and Politician Alanas there might be an actual answer.

After what felt like an eternity she gave up. Her legs had grown tired from all the walking, and the closest thing she had to an answer was a version of herself wearing a fancy gown and a tiara.

"Sure." Alana snickered. "I'll just become a queen. That'll make a nice tale."

"Alana." The caterpillar shook his head. "I don't think you'll find your answer here."

"Neither do I." She sighed. "I was just hoping I might be

wrong."

Taking a deep, steadying breath, she closed her eyes once more, and returned to the circular room.

This time she didn't allow herself much time to calm down, but instead started pacing nervously back and forth across the room.

"What good has any of this done?" she groaned. "I'm no closer to knowing my afterlife now than when we came here!"

"You are, Alana. You just need to focus." The caterpillar patted her shoulder again. "Just think. When we arrived, you'd never imagined any afterlife at all. By now, you have seen at least two that you seemed truly passionate about. Remember that."

"You're right." Alana sighed. "Of course you're right. I'm just … really tired."

She stopped her pacing in the middle of the room, and took a good look around. Somehow it felt much smaller now than when they first arrived. Shouldn't it be the other way around? Now that she knew how many possibilities were hidden here? She just needed to think. To find the right key.

"Wait …" A thought finally emerged from the chaos. "You said that the key I choose will be the stone my afterlife will be built on. Right?"

"That's correct." The caterpillar nodded.

"So the key doesn't necessarily need to open a door?"

"I suppose not … but why does that matter?"

"It matters—" Alana grinned, "—because then it doesn't need to be an actual key at all!"

"What?"

"Tell me, please," she continued, "when I decide on a key, what do I do with it?"

"From what I've heard, you would simply say 'I choose' and then it would all be over."

"Excellent!" Alana smiled, and started looking around the room again. Finally, having seen what she needed, she reached to lift the caterpillar from her shoulder. She placed him gently on one of the tables. "Whatever happens next, my friend, I certainly hope to see you there."

"I assure you, Alana, you will." The caterpillar bowed.

Alana opened her mouth to say something more, but changed her mind. Instead she turned her back on the caterpillar and reached down to pick up something from the floor. Then, taking a deep breath, she held it out in front of her.

"This ... pebble—" a short laugh escaped her, "—is my key. I choose something new. Something different. Surprise me."

She had just enough time to turn around and smile at the caterpillar before everything ended.

Stardust, Always

Melon Farming

Carol Gyzander

"I helped Henrietta in her garden today, and then we went out to lunch, even though we were all dirty. So much fun in town—we were walking down the sidewalk arm in arm, two abreast, and laughing all the way." My mom beamed as she stood in the kitchen, recounting her day.

"Don't you mean … *three* abreast?" I smiled.

She groaned, and then laughed. "Okay, I stand corrected."

It was 1978. For several years at that point, humor had been our family's best method of coping with my mother's breast cancer and radicaal mastectomy. The cancer had invaded the lymph nodes, and the doctors gave her experimental chemotherapy, not even sure what to expect. Chemo works by trying to kill you and the cancer at the same time. They planned for the treatment to last maybe eighteen months, but after six months they decided the chemo had beat up her system so badly that it was probably enough.

I was home from college, and happy to see that she was done with chemo and back to some of her old activities, including helping the neighbors with their gardening. So when she looked down at her chest and her laughter came to an abrupt halt, I was a bit startled.

She recovered, hugged herself and gave a little laugh. "Well, then. That's interesting." Her voice was a bit brittle.

"What's up?"

"When I was helping Henrietta in her garden, we were bending over and preparing the rows for her vegetable garden."

"Okay. And …?"

"I, uh, seem to have dropped my prosthesis out of my

143

bra." She opened her arms and held them apart.

I couldn't help myself—my gaze went directly to her chest. Sure enough, she was lopsided—one half of her chest was flat. In those days, breast reconstruction was not as common as it is today, and my mom had opted to forego the surgery. I had never seen the prosthesis, but knew from her description that it was basically a breast shaped plastic bag of thick fluid that she tucked in her bra.

"Oh my God. You think it fell out—in Henrietta's back yard?" I was gaping at her.

Her eyes finally met mine. I couldn't help it and started to snicker. "What will she think when she finds it?"

One corner of her mouth twitched as she pictured her sturdy, no-nonsense German friend coming across the prosthesis in the garden. The twitch became a small smile, which grew broader as she considered the possible scenarios.

"Do you think she would return it? Maybe she'd put it in a little basket with some cookies and just, you know, drop it by the house."

I nodded my head. "Maybe she'll just do a ring and run. Leave it on the doorstep."

We shared a mental image of her stout friend puffing back across the street, hoping to get back in the house before we saw her. My snicker turned into a laugh and my mom couldn't help it. She started laughing, too.

"I bet she'll put a bow on it!" My mother was howling. Tears were running down our cheeks. It was several minutes before we calmed down enough to make serious consideration of what to do.

"I'm more than happy to go over there with you, Mom. Shall we call her first?"

Her smile faltered for a half a beat; then she shook her head. "No, let's just go on over. If we see her I can just say I left some tools over there. I mean, I don't really mind telling her, but I'd rather not if I don't have to. She'd just make a fuss."

She pulled a big sweatshirt over her head, and as I followed her out through the garage I saw her tuck a small trowel into the big front pocket as backup evidence. Smart woman.

The two of us strolled across the street, feeling quite conspicuous, and went around the back of Henrietta's house. As we approached the garden, I was impressed with the amount of land that they had prepared for planting—but then began to worry when I thought of all the digging and shoveling that they had done. And how many places it could have fallen out.

"Mom, I hope you guys didn't bury it. Or worse yet, puncture it."

"Oh my God. I surely hope not. I never want to have to go back to that shop again."

She shuddered. I had been away at college during her mastectomy and she had gone to the specialty store by herself to get fitted for the prosthesis. From what she had told me I knew that the saleswoman had been a complete idiot—had actually told her not to worry, because after a while the one remaining breast would apparently spread to the other side. "You'll just all even out, dear."

When I learned about this on my next visit home, my mom was still shaking with rage because, as a classic Southern lady, she had just smiled and nodded in response to this blatant misinformation from someone who was supposed to be a professional in her field. And she refused to let me go back over with her to talk to the woman. Didn't want to make a fuss.

Mom took my arm with renewed purpose, dragging me toward the garden, and pointed to the far side. "You start over there, and I'll start on this side. Just walk up and down the rows. Maybe we'll get lucky and find it on top of the soil."

As I walked across, I imagined that Henrietta was staring out her back window at us. I carefully avoided looking at the house. My head down, I walked up and down the rows staring at the ground, wondering what this thing actually looked like.

Suddenly, a glint of sunshine reflected off of something up ahead. I hurried over and squatted down, looking at a small plastic sack filled with fluid sitting on top of the dirt. It looked like a beached jellyfish. I poked it. It jiggled a bit.

I thought about what it must be like for my mother to get dressed every morning, half of her bra gaping and empty until she tucked in this blob, this plastic blob, and prepared to face the world. To pretend that she was intact—had never had a mastectomy. Deny the cancer. Smile and act like everything was all right. And the plastic would be pressed up against her skin on even the hottest day. No wonder it had slipped out while she had been doing sweaty work.

Tears threatened my eyes.

The humor had never made more sense than at that moment. I called out over my shoulder, "Hey, what did you say Henrietta was going to plant here?"

"Vegetables. Green beans, squash … why?"

"I think she started planting something else already. Come see."

Her footsteps approached from behind and I stayed crouched, hiding the object until she came around in front of me.

"Look, Mom. I think she already started planting melon seeds. It looks like she's growing you a new boob."

"*What?*"

She stared at the ground for a half a beat, and then burst out laughing for the second time that day.

"Shhhhh! She'll hear you! She'll think we're trying to pilfer her melons!" I was laughing along with her.

"Are you kidding? She's the one who pilfered MY melon! Do you think I should leave it here and let it grow bigger? Cantaloupe? Maybe a watermelon?"

"Nah, then you'll just be lopsided again. Let's harvest this baby and get the hell out of here."

My mom scooped up her blob, brushed off the dirt, and tucked it into the pocket of her sweatshirt. We linked arms and headed off to our own house, three abreast, and if Henrietta had seen us she never mentioned it.

* * *

Postscript: My mother experienced a second round of breast cancer twenty years later and again opted for a radical mastectomy. I asked her what it felt like to lose her second breast, and she replied that she wasn't concerned. Rather, she was happy to no longer have to wear—as she called it by then—"that damned thing" anymore. She again turned down the idea of reconstructive surgery and never wore a bra again, switching instead to a comfortable tank top under her clothes.

The cancer didn't get her. She passed from Alzheimer's over ten years after the second mastectomy.

* * *

Dedicated to my mother, Sally, who showed me how to grow in so many ways.

Stardust, Always

It's Just a Word

Sophia Diaz

I knew a man once,
who was brighter than the sun.
He laughed, he cried,
he smiled and frowned.
He was strong in his movement.
The world was such a brilliant place.

But one little word
changed the man
from the sun
to the darkness,
and the man I knew
was
slipping
away.

The harder I grasped,
the further he fell.
The more I reached,
the more distance came.

No matter what I did,
I couldn't stop it.
I held him.
I cried with him.
I loved him.

But time is your enemy.
The more it ticked,
the closer the end came.
But what can you do,
when there's no weapon to use,
to save the one you love?

Stardust, Always

You hold tighter.
You love stronger.
You cherish the 'always'.
You show them that cancer
is just a word,
and you'll defeat it.

A Bag Full of Stars

R.R. Virdi

If you wish upon a star, your dreams and desires will come true. For the stars are magic, and in them, the dust of men and women, and all their dreams. No one ever truly dies child. They become stars. Sitting—waiting—for someone to wish upon them. ~Grandma Ilis

Then I'll go find them, and bring you back a bag full stars. I'll make you better, Grandma. ~ Eela

Eela looked to the sky. It was a tapestry of black sequined with twinkling orbs far out of reach. She only hoped they weren't too far out of her grasp. She had made a promise. And promises were meant to be kept.

The ground in front of her flickered out of clarity. She blinked and cast a look over her shoulder. An oil lamp sputtered and waned under the wind. It's light struggled to illuminate the small cottage, much less the few feet in front of her.

She shut her eyes and breathed. "It's okay. I have them." Eela looked to the sky and repeated the mantra in her head, convincing herself the stars would be enough. Her fingers tightened around the empty sack of yarn.

It won't be empty when I'm done.

She exhaled and walked towards the forest, resisting the urge to look back to the lone cottage. Eela feared if she looked back, she wouldn't move on. And she couldn't be afraid.

The light from the cottage vanished as she passed its umbra. Her eyes struggled to adjust for a few moments. She pulled the edges of her carmine cloak tight around her. The simple action made her feel safer as the trees seemed to grow larger and closer. Their leafless braches, gnarled and crooked,

151

bowed under the gusts of wind. She clutched her bag tighter. It was as if the trees reached for her sack out of greed.

Her grandmother's voice rang strong through her head. *Remember, child, life and the forest have many tricks indeed. Never let them make you lose sight of your path and your dreams. Keep your head held high.*

It was good advice. Eela heeded it and turned her gaze towards the stars again. The trees dotted the edge of her vision, but the stars held most of it. She smiled and took in a breath. Settling herself, she moved on.

The path was long and she did not know how to catch a star. But she could see them. For now, that would have to do. She followed them.

Her eyes returned to the path ahead and trees appeared to shrink back to their previous positions. They no longer loomed over her as threats.

But for every danger that disappears in the forest, another takes its place.

Eela sucked in a breath as two glints of yellow peered at her from within the trees. She looked to the sky, then back, wondering if her constant star gazing made her see stars even in the forest. She was wrong. The twin orbs did not hold the light of wishes and dreams. They were hungry, and they stared without blinking.

Her lips shook. The air in her chest did the same. She couldn't bring her voice to leave her mouth. It stayed rooted in her throat. Eela swallowed, remembering why she traveled the forest at night.

A low growl rumbled in the thicket. Eela kept her eyes locked on the yellow orbs as she walked. They followed her step by step. Eela ran.

Her feet hammered against the soft earth. The cold air raced down her throat and lungs, drying them. She turned to look at the yellow eyes. They kept pace with her, seeming to blur into golden comets, hurtling through the trees. Eela glanced at the stars for courage and ran harder. The cold air felt like vines squeezing her insides tight. She ignored it and pressed on. When she turned to look again, the yellow eyes had vanished.

She gasped and came to a juddering halt. Her chest heaved as she whipped around, searching for her pursuer.

The trees snarled all around her. She spun in place, clutching her bag to her chest.

Something gray and large burst from the trees. It impacted the ground several feet before her, eyeing her.

Eela took a cautious step back, refusing to meet the wolf's eyes.

"How now, a child in the forest."

The air in her lungs froze. Her body followed. Eela licked her lips and thought hard. Grandmother did not teach her how to deal with talking wolves. She raised her eyes, staring into the wolf's.

Its mouth stretched, tongue lolling out the side. It looked like a smile—a hungry one. A ravenous gleam flickered through its eyes.

Eela swallowed the cold rock nestled in her throat. "You can speak?"

The wolf snorted and shook its head. "Of course; so can you."

Eela nodded.

"Why are you in the woods, child? It is dark, and dangerous things roam in the night." The wolf padded toward her.

Eela followed its slow movements, turning as the wolf circled her. She pressed her lips tight.

The wolf sniffed at the edge of her cloak. "Little girls should not be out when the hour is so late. Not in appetizing red cloaks. No, not at all."

Eela pulled her hood down and the cloak closer to her body. The wolf circled further around her. She moved with it, always keeping her eyes on the beast.

"My, what beautiful brown eyes you have, child."

Eela's voice was low and shook. "Thank you."

"They are big. Tell me, do you see me clearly?" The wolf sounded bemused.

"Yes. I see your yellow eyes glowing in the dark. And, I

see your sharp, hungry teeth."

The wolf's smile grew. "Is that all? What about a friend—a companion—in this dark place?"

Eela shivered and felt an invisible tug on her bag. "A friend?"

"What else?" The hungry light in the wolf's eyes grew. "Why else would I be here with you?"

"To eat me?" Eela regretted saying that.

The wolf huffed and shook its head violently. "Why would I do that?" There was an undertone in the wolf's voice that made Eela doubt its sincerity. "What, if I may ask, is in the bag?"

Eela blinked and paused. A voice of caution went through her mind, urging her not to show the wolf the contents of the bag. She pushed it aside. After all, there was no harm in showing an empty bag. With a roll of her wrists, she pushed the bag forward and flipped it inside out.

The wolf snorted, eyeing her askance. "It's empty?"

She nodded.

"Why do you carry an empty bag? No, let me guess. You're seeking something. You want to fill the bag with something precious—worthwhile enough to wander the forest at night—and bring it back."

She nodded again.

"And what are you seeking, little one?"

Eela shook her head. "It's a secret."

"Oh." The wolf stopped circling and padded a step closer. "I love secrets. Do tell."

She thought of her grandmother, and how she was without a clue on how to catch a star. "I'm searching for a star."

The wolf blinked. "The stars? Why, take your eyes off me, child, and look up, you will find your stars."

Eela did not think it was a good idea to take her eyes off the wolf. "I need to catch one, and put it in here." She pushed the bag toward the wolf a bit.

"Well, how fortuitous for you, youngling. I happen to know where the closest stars are. I can help you catch one."

The wolf moved to her side and pawed the ground. "Follow close and I will take you to your stars." The wolf's lips peeled back from its teeth. It was a macabre smile.

Eela's mind raced and tumbled. As many possibilities as there were stars crossed her mind. She came to a conclusion. The wolf might not be trustworthy, but her grandmother needed a star; she needed a cure. And Eela needed to be brave. So she decided that she would be.

After all, bravery is easier than it seems. And to be brave for someone else is even easier.

Eela nodded. "I will follow you. Help me find a star, please."

"But of course." The wolf lowered its head in a bow.

She ran to keep by the wolf as it sped off. It was a short lived run as the wolf veered and dove into the forest. Eela stumbled, waving her arms in circles to help keep her balance. She steadied herself and eyed the forest warily.

Yellow eyes stared back—waiting.

She swallowed and took a tentative step forward.

"Come, child."

Caution took hold of her. "I can't see in the forest at night."

"Ah, but I can." The wolf did not seem the least bit perturbed by her limited sight. "I shall be your eyes."

Or you'll take mine. Eela knew she couldn't wholly trust the wolf. And she knew she couldn't tarry. Grandmother was counting on her. She took another breath and slipped between the trees. Eela couldn't see it, but she felt the wolf smile. It was a cold thing that made her neck feel tight. An itch formed around her collar. She buried her fears, pushing them from her heart, down into the pit of her stomach.

The wolf's eyes blurred as he turned. "Follow closely. We would not want you to get lost, little one."

That's exactly what you want. Don't worry, I won't get lost. She looked up through the intertwining tree branches. Hanging motes of light flickered. She smiled. The stars were still there. They would guide her.

She chased the wolf, doing her best to keep it in sight.

Soon, the inevitable. No gray fur. No yellow eyes. No signs of her guide whatsoever. The trees seemed to stretch once again. They ran around her, growing tighter knit.

Eela shut her eyes and pictured the small cottage at the end of the forest—her home. She imagined the waning candlelight out front. The thought of losing that—her grandmother—galvanized her. Her fingers tightened around the bag and her heart calmed its staccato beat. She opened her eyes and found she wasn't alone anymore.

Six pairs of golden-yellow eyes stared back at her.

Her fingers flexed and scrunched the bag. *They won't take it from me*, she resolved.

A pair of eyes came closer. "I brought friends to help you—us."

Eela took a step back. "You were my guide." She kept her voice as neutral as possible.

The wolf's eyes looked like sinking stars in the night as it lowered its head in an awkward bow. "Alas, as shameful as it is to admit, I am lost." It turned its head to gesture at the rest of the pack. "You need a guide; and I, in turn, need guides of my own. Come, follow us."

A chorus of guttural huffing broke out among the wolves. It sounded like strained laughter.

The laughing wolves sent a cold lance down Eela's spine that struck her toes before bouncing back to settle in her throat as a frozen lump. "I think ..." Eela took another step back. A dry crack came from beneath her heel.

The wolves narrowed their eyes and prowled forward.

A ghostly figure came into view, lingering far behind the wolf pack. Eela's eyes widened to owlish proportions. The doe moved with eerie precision. As it moved, the edges of its body trailed a vaporous luminance. It was like the light that bled at the ends of stars.

"I think I have found a new guide." Eela pointed to the doe.

The wolves huffed and turned to follow where she pointed. Their ears stiffened as they saw the doe. They growled in unison and lowered to an aggressive posture.

Eela inhaled a slow breath. She remained statue-like as the wolves focused on the deer. The doe's ears twitched once. It knew the wolves had it in sight and didn't seem disturbed by the fact.

It bound into action, leaping through the forest. The wolves howled and set after in pursuit.

Eela exhaled. Her eyes ached as she scanned the trees. They felt tight and dry. Satisfied nothing dangerous hid in the trees, she took a step. No monsters came bounding out of the darkness. It encouraged her to take another, and another after that. She breathed out and a smile stretched across her face.

Just a test.

The wolves and danger had passed. Grandmother had warned her that the world liked to test those in pursuit of dreams and wishes. Eela felt proud she had weathered the danger well.

Faint, blue light, like a star on the ground, wove between the trees ahead. They stopped.

Eela gasped.

The spectral doe stood there, eyeing her.

Uncertain of how to respond, she fell back to another of grandmother's wisdoms. "Thank you." Gratitude was an important thing.

The doe bowed. It gave her a quizzical look. "Are you coming, child? The wolves won't be lost for long. They will catch your scent and come from you."

"What about your scent?"

The doe snorted and shook its head. "I do not carry one any longer."

Eela's face contorted into a puzzled mask.

"Are you coming?"

She shook her head and stayed rooted to the spot. "The last time I followed someone, I ended up here—alone—surrounded by wolves."

"That is why I came to save you. It's a rude thing to ignore a request from someone who has saved you." The doe's mouth spread in a manner that could have passed for an awkward smile.

Grandmother taught her to never be rude. Eela pressed her lips tight and thought for a moment. She weighed everything that had happened, what she wanted to happen, and what could possibly happen. The thoughts made her feel like a hive of bees buzzed through her head. She blinked and shook her head vigorously, clearing out the noise. "Where are you taking me?"

The doe tilted its head. "Where are you going?"

Eela raised her hand to the sky and pointed at a star. She trailed a finger from one heavenly orb to another.

The doe shook its head. "I do not understand."

"I need to catch a star."

Its mouth fell open. "Ah, I can help with that."

Eela's body tensed. "That's what the wolf said."

The doe did not respond.

She took a step towards the creature, hoping her sudden movement would not startle it. It remained stationary. Eela held out a calming hand as she approached. "You promise you can take me to a star?"

"Yes."

Eela's hand fell on the doe's neck. She suppressed the urge to inhale sharply. The doe was solid. She ran her hand down its back and patted it gently. "I trust you. Take me to find a star."

The doe set off at a slow pace, turning its head to ensure Eela followed. "Tell me, child, why do you seek a star?"

"To grant a wish." Eela paused before taking another step.

"What wish is that?"

She didn't want to answer the doe, but a torrent of thoughts overcame her. "My grandmother, is ill—dying—from something. Nothing we have tried works." She sniffed and shut her eyes to stop any tears. "I need a wish."

"Many have searched for stars, some have found them, less have had their wishes granted. What makes you think you deserve to have yours?" The doe's voice was level but Eela could hear something else in it. There were notes of subtle amusement.

"I need it."

"A simple enough answer. An honest one. Can I tell you something, child?"

Eela nodded.

"Your kind worries too much about death. Nothing ever truly dies."

Eela rocked back from the doe's words. "Nothing? What ... about you?"

"I am dead, but I am still here, am I not? I was part of the forest then. I am no different now. Out of body, yes. Out of mind, no. The forest remembers. So do I. Everything and everyone lives on in memory. As long as you remember the love for your grandmother, she will live on forever—always—in here." The doe touched its snout to Eela's chest.

She put a hand over her heart and met the doe's eyes. "Always?"

"Always," answered the doe in a voice that left Eela with no doubts.

"Thank you, but I still want to find a star. I will love her always. I will remember her always. But I made a promise, and I always keep my promises. I will catch a star. Please, Doe, take me to find one."

The doe paused and looked away from her. It stared off at nothing for countless moments before turning back to regard her. "Very well, follow me."

So she did.

Trees blurred into solid blankets of dull gray. The stars lost none of their vibrancy as the night grew. Clouds of purple and pink were trapped high above, bleeding out from the stars. The gassy mists floated by, painting quite the entrancing picture for Eela. She took is as a sign. She was on the right track.

"Run!"

Eela blinked, pausing to look around. "Sorry?"

The doe sped off with unnatural speed. "Run!"

She didn't need a third warning. Eela's heart beat like rain on metal. Her legs pumped, her cloak fluttered behind her as she covered ground. Yellow eyes hounded her in the distance.

"This way!" The doe's voice carried through the forest.

Eela watched a flash of light disappear to the right. She slowed her pace and followed after the doe, hoping it knew how to lose the wolves. An upturned root snagged her foot. A sharp *twang* went through her ankle, like the twig from earlier that had snapped in half. Eela staggered and yelped.

"Don't stop. Hurry!" The doe did not slow its pace.

Pain blossomed in her ankle. Fibers brushed against her lips as she moved the bag from her hand to her mouth. Eela bit down hard against the fabric. She gripped her ankle tight, ensured she could stand on it, and pulled the bag from her mouth. Eela gulped as the yellow eyes closed in. She ran.

A flash of ghostly blue and white grabbed her attention. The doe.

Eela cut between a pair of tight trees and winced as her ankle flared hot.

"Not much further. Run child."

She was trying.

Eela pushed the cold, biting wind away from her mind. She buried the pain. The tightness in her chest was thrown away. One thought dominated her mind. *Grandmother.*

The doe bounded around a large tree in two quick leaps and ran straight ahead.

Eela squinted in the tight. The trees grew closer ahead. Something lay beyond them.

The doe dove into them and out of sight.

Everything she pushed and buried away came crashing back. The pain. The fear. The exhaustion. Eela ran anyway, casting a terrified look over her shoulder.

More than yellow eyes came into view. Gleaming teeth with a singular purpose. The tips of snouts. And hungry eyes.

Eela strained her lungs and legs as hard she could. She reached the point where the doe had vanished, and came to a halt. The trees were too close for her to pass through.

"Jump, child!" The voice came from the other side.

Eela pressed her face to the trees, trying to peer through. She couldn't see a thing.

"Jump!"

She looked over her shoulder. The wolves grew closer.

"Jump!"

She did.

The trees bowed and bent, letting her slender form slip through. Bark groaned and cracked in protest of the movement. Eela spun and watched the trees snap back to their original positions. A *crack* filled her ears as something struck the other side of the tree hard. She heard a whimper followed by an agitated growl. A chorus of guttural sounds echoed from the other side. She exhaled and turned back.

Her eyes widened. The doe stood in front of a lake that seemed to mirror the color of the moon and stars. Vibrant, shimmering lights danced atop its surface. A boy, not much older than she, stood at the edge.

The doe met Eela's eyes and approached.

Eela looked to the trees then back to the doe. "How?"

"The world is open and willing to help those who follow their dreams and desires. Remember, those you love will live forever."

"Forever." Eela nodded her head.

The doe vanished like specks of dust in the wind.

She gasped.

"Why are you here?" The boy turned to give her the same look the doe had. His eyes were the same soft brown as hers. His complexion was ruddy and marred by forest earth. The same dirt stained his simple clothes. He stood barefoot, wriggling his toes in the ground.

"I'm here to find a star." Eela felt the truth was best. Grandmother always believed so.

The boy ran a hand through his unkempt black hair. He stared for a moment before speaking. "Why?"

Eela licked her lips. "My grandmother is dying. An illness. Nothing is working. Her body is failing."

He opened his mouth in a silent "ah."

She licked her lips and stood motionless in the silence.

"You came here for a wish." He eyed her carefully.

"Yes."

"Why? Many people have come here over the years. Many men and women have asked for wishes. Many of them have been denied. Why should you get yours?"

Eela didn't have a good answer, only an honest one. "I made a promise. Please."

The boy turned back to face the lake. "You don't want to lose her."

She shook her head, but he couldn't see it.

"You heard the doe, did you not? People pass on, but they remain with us forever. Why can't you let go?"

Again, Eela had no answer. All she had was her word. "I made a promise."

The boy said nothing.

"What do you know about the stars?"

He turned and flashed her a lopsided smile. "Everything." He waved a hand at the sky. "I know all their names. All their stories. When they were born. When they will die. And I know the ones who have fallen."

Eela blinked. "Fallen?"

"Some stars fall. Those are the ones who can grant your wish."

"Help me find one, please?" She took a step forward.

"If I help save your grandmother today, know that she will still pass eventually."

Moisture lined her lids. "I know, but not today. I want as much time with her as I can."

"Many people would likely want as much time as they could have. Life is like that. So are people. In each of us there is world, spreading out and creating ripples like this." He bent, picked up a stone and tossed it into the lake. Ripples spread out from it. "Like your grandmother. Ripples are always there. Her story, her love will be there too. Like the ripples, even when they are gone from sight, they still have an effect, they always linger. Always."

"Who are you, boy?"

His smile grew and he pointed to the stars. "One who fell to earth. I'm a man now. I wasn't always, but I was once."

She tilted her head. "I'm sorry?"

"We are all stories. When ours end here on earth, we become new ones." He pointed to the stars again. "Sometimes those stories change. Sometimes we remember this ..." He waved a hand to the forest. "Then we come back."

Eela held her breath.

"I'm what you've been looking for. I'm the one that can grant your wish. I'm a star."

She exhaled and took another step forward, spreading the bag open between her hands. "Please help me."

The boy pinched the lip of the bag between his first two fingers and thumb. "Of course."

Eela gasped as his skin glowed. His body broke like it was luminescent sand held together by nothing more than will. It filtered into the sack. Fire-like warmth radiated from it, filling her hands and, soon, the rest of her. She looked to the stars and smiled widely. Her fingers gripped the bag tight.

I promised, grandmother. I'm coming.

* * *

For Lacey. She knows why

Stardust, Always

Between the Masks

Kell Willsen

A life captured on camera, a distinctive voice;
personae by the dozens, constantly re-invented,
new parts to play, faces to wear, voices to use.
The masks go on, and the masks come off;
taking work seriously, but never myself.
My role: hero, villain, lover, lunatic;
waits in wardrobe when I go home.
Until this mask swallowed me whole.
Sans makeup or costume, I wear a face
that is me and not me, like many before.
Just another character, but not one
I can shrug off. All around me are
conscripted into this comedy.
Don't forget I'm still here,
beneath this final face.
When the lights go out,
there will be those who mourn
characters that were never real.
Each fan will have a favourite,
a face to be remembered fondly.
And there will be those, precious
and few, who will remember to
remember me **remember me** remember me

Stardust, Always

Adiós, El Amor Dulce

Suzanne Wdowik

The thing about piano is, there are so many styles of music and pieces in each style, that you can easily get stuck on one category and assume that you're the worst pianist in the world, because not only do you hate the pieces, but you can't play them for crap. But once you discover there are whole worlds just outside of the bubble you've created, you feel like the secrets of the universe have been revealed to you and the power of music is in your control.

Then again, you might start bouncing between these worlds and never land in one. Dabbling, but never committing. Seeing, but never understanding. Enjoying, but never finding the one that encourages you to be the person you never even knew you could be.

* * *

My first piano teacher moved away three years into my instruction. I missed playing with her dog in the backyard. My second piano teacher quit teaching to pursue another career. I missed her math books and hearing her daughter play. My third piano teacher … well, that's a topic that takes more than a simple phrase to accurately express.

Apparently two was enough for my brother, because he decided to quit piano at that point. I was at a crossroads. I'd never done piano lessons without my brother before. I wasn't sure it would even be possible to keep going without him. After all, I was the one following in his footsteps, not the other way around. Nevertheless, I went along with my mother's search for a new teacher. I got to select my third teacher from two choices she picked out. One was a middle-aged woman with dark brown hair cut short and neat like that lady from Misery (not that I knew any Stephen King at that age). The other was a nice old lady with a cute little dog and a warmly lit living room. I went with the second.

My nervous personality meant that my heart was always pounding when my mother pulled into the driveway of the little white house. I was afraid that I hadn't practiced enough, that I'd mess up, that I'd let my teacher down.

My teacher would always greet me with a wrinkled smile, let me pet her dog, and suggest I warm up my hands under warm running water if they were cold (which they almost always were).

We did scales and chords as warm-ups, then went right into my pieces. We jumped around a lot, trying to find what fit me best. I soon discovered my favorite composers. Dennis Alexander, Chopin. Lyrical music, the kind of stuff that tugs at your chest and makes your whole body tingle as if you were standing on top of a cliff looking down at the drop, pulling you down towards it but inexplicably also making you feel lighter than a leaf.

My brother came a few times to get music from her as well. She seemed to know exactly what he'd like, though she barely knew him. I heard him playing the jazzy pieces she gave him once or twice. Even now, it fills my heart to hear him play; we seem to be lacking in hobbies we share love for. My brother's love for the piano was the reason I started lessons in the first place.

One useful piano technique I learned from my new teacher's instruction—and immediately fell in love with—is the use of rubato. The Italian word literally translates to "robbed", which is a great way of thinking about it. Essentially, rubato allows a pianist to spend more time on one short section and make up for lost time by speeding up in another. It's this constant flow of give and take, a flow that is meant to conserve the overall tempo of the piece while allowing the pianist to linger on important parts.

Once I learned this, I immediately put it to use in all of my pieces so that I could take more time on the parts I liked and speed through the ones I didn't.

I quickly learned that that is not how rubato works.

Through practice and gentle coaxing and instruction and suggestions by my teacher, I learned that it's possible to add too much rubato. You can't tug and tear at a piece of music like a piece of plastic, lest you lose all sense of shape and direction. You need to pull it like taffy, carefully and strategically, letting the music push against you as you pull it, then releasing the tension and letting it carry you through. The music must swell to the point of highest emotional turmoil, then relax as the emotions burst forth, contemplating the aftermath of the climax.

I constantly tried to find this natural ebb and flow with all of my pieces, especially in a short, bittersweet song by Dennis Alexander that my teacher had me try. It was called *Adios, El Amor Dulce*, and from the limited Spanish skills I had at the time, I knew that it was something related to love and goodbyes, which were never a joyous combination. The cover of my copy has a couple—a young man and woman—holding each other and staring into each other's eyes (it's one of those artsy animated covers) as they stand on a bridge surrounded by snow.

My classmates had just started to get into dating and romance. I assumed I was a late bloomer, as that stuff never interested me. To this day, I have never gone on a date or even been interested in such a thing. So when my teacher explained that the love that Dennis Alexander had had to say goodbye to was his son (who had passed away a few years before the piece was written), I was both saddened by the story and filled with enough passion for the piece that I felt I could do it justice. Every time I'd open the piece, I'd look at the couple on the cover and smile to myself as if I had an inside joke with the author. *It's a different kind of love*, I'd think, *one that's no less important than the romantic kind everyone seems to be so obsessed about.*

The more I played *Adios, El Amor Dulce*, the more I felt in tune with the piece. I began to know it so well that I could let my mind wander and put my muscles and my emotions in charge of playing the piece. It was like I was losing control over the music, but that was okay because that was the only way for the music to be genuine. I learned to stop fighting it, instead letting it move me along with it like I was simply a conduit for the power it held.

I was told later by my mother that at the little recital of the four students my teacher instructed, my teacher sat with her eyes closed and nodded her head the whole time I was playing, letting the music carry her too. Everyone told me how beautiful it was and how beautifully I played it. All I knew was that I had taken the notes on a page, combined it with the emotions inside of me, and was somehow able to convey that to my audience. I felt like I had discovered a whole new form of communication, one that was more pure and honest than simple words.

* * *

A couple of years into my instruction, my mother broke the news to me. My teacher had lung cancer, and had had it for years, though she never smoked. She wasn't getting better. She wasn't sure how long she'd have. She hadn't told any of her students because she didn't want us to worry about her, but now we'd have to be prepared for times she'd have to cancel a lesson, or cancel lessons altogether.

My mind wandered back to the start of my lessons, frantically searching for years that weren't there. I'd only had her as my teacher for a couple of years; I couldn't lose her so soon.

Sooner than I'd anticipated, the number of days between my lessons grew longer. Sometime during the spring of that year, my teacher had to let all her students go. My mother told me she didn't have much time left, and that I should be prepared for the inevitable.

I remembered one of the first things she ever taught me. When playing the piano, she said, you had to dig into the keys like you were digging into clay. Using your whole body, you lean into the keyboard and shape the music the way you want it.

It makes you feel powerful, like you still have an important place in the world. Though the music carries you, you are the one who gives it the power to live.

The night that my mother came into my room quietly, like a ghost, I already knew. I lay face-down on my bed, face pushed into my pillow, feeling quite the opposite of powerful. Without a word, my mom sat down on the bed and hugged me. Though she made no sound for a minute, I knew she was crying. When she told me in a broken voice that my teacher had passed away, the emotion in me that had felt so detached from myself for months came out in a rush. I don't remember how long we lay there, or how I managed to get to sleep that night. I remember thinking that I'd never go to another piano lesson in my life.

The summer progressed, and I didn't even touch the keys of my piano. I was missing something in my life, and I thought that resuming my piano playing would emphasize that. I didn't take long, however, to realize that I missed more than my teacher. I missed what she had given me. I missed music. I missed how my entire body felt as I dug into a piece of music. Instead of keeping that part of my teacher alive, I was leaning backwards, on my heels instead of the balls of my feet, letting life happen to me instead of the other way around. If I really wanted to honor her memory and find that piece of myself again, I needed to grab life by the piano keys and play.

* * *

In memory of Mrs. Kretzmer

Stardust, Always

Five Years

Hayley Munro

"Earth is really dying, folks," the news guy said, his voice catching in his throat. "We have five years left until we're obliterated by the sun."

The six or so teenagers in the Starbucks cafe stared at the television in disbelief. It had been four days since the news went public, but people were still struggling to comprehend it, like it took all of their energy trying to forget about it so that when someone brought it up they had to take it in all over again.

Tommy, with his cellphone at his ear and his coat on his arm, watched the news anchor try and fail to conceal his tears. He watched the man's face contort and his eyes shut tight before he welcomed the weatherman in a cracking voice.

Da da-da dum-dum-dum.

He heard his heart, like the beat of a drum, over the sounds of the coffee shop and his mother's voice in his ear.

"Tommy? Tom? You still there?"

He snapped out of his trance. "Yeah, mum. Right here."

"Oh, well, good," she said, sounding quite pleased with herself. "You're coming home this weekend, right, sweetheart?"

He held the phone up with his shoulder as he pulled his coat on. "Yes, mum. I've told you twenty times already."

"Don't use that tone with me, Thomas. You may be nineteen, but I'm still your mother." She let out a shaky sigh. "Alright, honey. Drive safe. It's supposed to rain tonight."

"I will, Mum."

"I love you, Tommy."

"You, too," he said, and hung up.

Tommy hadn't cried yet. He hadn't done anything, really.

When he'd found out Monday night, watching the evening news, he didn't even react. His roommate, Alex, had been confused, swearing and crying over the phone to his girlfriend in disbelief. Tommy had merely sat, staring at the television, unable to move.

It was surprising he'd been able to move since.

"Leaving already, Tom? We've still got seven minutes until we close up."

Tommy turned around. "Gotta get home before traffic, boss. There's a rainstorm, apparently."

Charlie, the Starbucks manager, looked past Tommy, out the window. It had already started to drizzle.

"Well, it *is* Friday, after all," he smiled sadly. "Bet Hannah'll want me home early, on account of the baby and all."

"Should I tell Anna to close up?" Tommy asked.

"No, s'alright. I'll do it." He put a hand on Tommy's shoulder. "Be safe, kid."

Tommy nodded and thanked him.

He wished people would stop telling him to stay safe. Did it even matter at this point?

He stepped outside, into the rainy market square. Despite the oncoming storm, there were still tons of people out shopping. Ever since they'd made the announcement Monday, everyone had been out spending their life's savings on things they never would have bought had the world not been ending. Tommy couldn't remember the last time Starbucks had such good business.

He walked past a mother and her kids, who were all carrying tote bags full of food and supplies. One of the younger girls had dropped her bags on the sidewalk, and her mother was livid.

She grabbed her daughter by the shoulders and shook her, screaming, "Megan! Megan! No!"

One of the older kids, who looked about sixteen or seventeen, pulled his mother off of his sister while his other siblings stared in horror.

"Stop it, mum," he begged, hugging her hard so she

couldn't break free of him. "Stop it."

Megan was on the ground next to them, hugging her knees to her chest and crying.

Passersby walked around them without a second glance.

He heard the drumming of his heart again.

Da da-da dum-dum-dum.

"Oh, for chrissake!"

Tommy turned to see a man in soldier's uniform slam the door of his Cadillac. His left arm was in a sling. He stomped over to the front of his car and, swearing under his breath, popped the hood.

Tommy figured, from his arm, that he was having trouble starting the car. He considered going over to help him out, but he saw the man slam the hood down again and get back into the car. Tommy watched as the man lay his head against his steering wheel. The car started as he walked away.

Tommy's car was parked in front of the ice cream parlor. There was never good parking outside Starbucks, because of all the obnoxious teenagers who took it upon themselves to make the coffee shop their second home. He settled for parking a few blocks away.

He always liked the walk from work to his car. It was the one time of day he spent alone, and it gave him some time to think.

Lately, the only thing he could think about scared the living hell out of him.

By the time he reached his car, the rain was coming down so hard Tommy was surprised it didn't leave dents in the sidewalk. He reached into his coat pocket for his keys and, tremor in his unusually pale hand, tried to slide the key into the keyhole. A car drove past him, splashing him with water, and he dropped his keys into the puddle at his feet.

Tommy hadn't cried at all, up until then. Harder and faster than the rain, his tears were angrier than the mother's and more frustrated than the soldier's. Tommy was scared to death and he couldn't hide it from himself any longer.

He thought about his mother, miles away, huddled in her room. She was probably watching *I Love Lucy* reruns, trying to forget about how worried she was.

He thought about his boss, Charlie, whose wife was at home with their two-week-old baby.

He thought about the woman on the street, whose children would never grow up.

He thought about the soldier who broke his arm fighting for a future that didn't exist.

Tommy was nineteen. In four years he'd be twenty-four. That's the oldest he'd ever be.

He ran his hands through his hair and cried so hard he forgot where he was.

"Hey! Major Tom!" A voice called from the ice cream parlor. No one had called him that in years. "Are you alright?"

He looked up and saw Hermione, aproned, drinking a chocolate milkshake.

"D'you want one?" she asked, as if he were five and could be easily persuaded with ice cream. She motioned for him to follow her inside, and he did.

"Gosh," she said as he sat down at the counter. "I haven't seen you since high school." She walked behind the counter and took the lid off a blender. "How does chocolate sound?"

Tommy smiled. "You got anything else?"

"If by 'anything else' you mean different variants of chocolate, then yes. I can add extra chocolate syrup. And we might have some stale Oreos in the back." She laughed. "We're about to close up, so the strawberries are off-limits."

Tommy shrugged and took off his coat, laying it on the chair beside him. "Chocolate sounds good," he said. "So, you work here?"

Hermione tore the lid off of a tub of ice cream. "Nah, I just wear their aprons and steal their milkshakes." She dropped a scoop of vanilla into the blender. "What about you? You working?"

"You know the Starbucks a couple of blocks from here?"

"Jesus, really?" she laughed. "Why is this the first time I'm seeing you?"

He smiled and shrugged. "You like Starbucks?"

"Not particularly." she said. "That's probably why." She squirted a load of chocolate syrup into the blender and then put the lid back on. "Okay, cover your ears if you want to live."

Tommy laughed, but only a little.

Da da-da dum-dum-dum.

His heart was louder than the blender.

She turned it off and poured the milkshake into a glass, which she slid over to him. She leaned across the counter and handed him a straw. "It's on the house," she smiled. She went back and refilled her own glass. "So's mine."

"Thanks," Tommy said, taking a sip. "Hey, how's your mystery writing going? You got anything published yet?"

Hermione blushed. "I'm shocked you even remember that," she said, embarrassed. "I'm kind of just, I don't know, pooping out *Golden Age*-type stories right now. You know, curious murders in quaint, nonexistent English towns? Sending them to detective anthologies. I'll write bigger stuff when I'm out of college." She blew her hair out of her face. "What about you, Mr. Spaceman? Still set on working for NASA?"

Tommy shrugged. "I'm majoring in astrophysics."

"Vaat's gweat, Fom!" Hermione said through a mouthful of milkshake. "Sorry. I mean, that's great! You might actually get to go to space!"

"After umpteen years of school and pilot experience? Maybe." He ran a hand through his hair. *That's a habit that'll lead to premature balding,* he thought. "It's just all this, you know? We've only got so long."

Hermione grimaced, like it hurt her to think about it. It probably did. "I know, Tom." She reached across the counter and took his hand.

Tommy couldn't look her in the eye, so her looked at her arms instead. They were the same colour as the milkshake in his hands. He remembered how much he liked her in high school.

Da da-da dum-dum-dum.

"Uni is so hard, you know?" He was still staring at her

arms. "I've always thought, 'Hey, it'll be worth it in ten years.' But I don't even *have* ten years."

"Don't say that, Tom," she said, squeezing his hand.

"It's true though, isn't? None of us do! But, for some crazy reason, we pretend like we do, continuing with our everyday lives like nothing's happened. What's the point of going to school or going to work or *sleeping*, even, if we're all just counting down the days until we die?"

"Jesus, Tommy! Don't talk like that!"

"How else do you expect me to talk, Hermione? Look around you," he said, pointing outside. "Look at all these people. Tall, short, fat, skinny, nobody, somebody people. They're nothing more than dead men walking.

"We go to work. We go grocery shopping. We pay back our student loans. But it's all so pointless! Everything I've done my entire life seems so *pointless*. I mean, I should just quit school. I'll drop out. And I'll quit my job. I'm just going to die in five years, right? There's no sense in waiting it out!"

"That's so *stupid*, Tommy!" Hermione said, raising her voice. "You were never immortal. You were going to die someday—we all were. Death is inevitable."

"So isn't life just waiting for the inevitable to happen?"

"No!" she laughed, exasperated. "No, Tommy! You don't get it—there isn't a goddamn point to life. And even if there was, it'd be too crazy for us to comprehend. But that is *no* reason to stop living. Your life is what you make it, Tom, not what other people make it out to be! You say we're all waiting to die, but I'm not. I refuse to."

"What else can you do, Hermione?"

She ran a hand through her hair, frustrated. *Premature balding*, Tommy thought. "You *live*, Tommy. You enjoy life while it lasts. You dance, sing, and laugh like you'll never do it again. You do all the things you've always done, and all the things you've never done before. You read everything you can get your hands on. You wake up really early in the morning just to see the sunrise. You fall in love like it's the only thing you know how to do. You make memories. And you remember.

"Every morning I wake up and think of all of the things that are going to die with me: my mother, my brother, my dog, all of my short stories, rock-and-roll music, *The Catcher in the Rye,* elephants. My mind is like a warehouse nowadays. I have to cram in so many things to store everything in there. I feel like I'm going to vomit, like, *all of the time.*"

She laughed, and Tommy laughed too.

"But I'm living, Tommy. I spend most days either at school or making milkshakes to pay for school. I don't do it because I have to—I do it because I *want to.* Because I've always been waiting to die. Because it doesn't matter if I'm dead in a couple of years. It's everything I do while I'm alive that matters." She reached over and gave his hand another squeeze. "Because you matter, Tommy. Your life matters."

Tommy looked down at his milkshake, which had melted into a chocolatey soup. "Hey," he said, finally. "When does your shift end?"

"About twenty minutes ago," Hermione smiled.

"Do you, uh, need a ride home? Because my car is right outside."

"Next to the keys you dropped fifteen minutes ago?"

Tommy stood up and felt his pockets. "Crap."

She laughed. "That'd be nice, Tom."

They went outside, and it was raining so much Tommy could barely see his car. He felt around on the ground for his keys. "Great. Good. Not stolen." He slipped a little standing up, but Hermione caught him before he fell.

He coughed, embarrassed, and she laughed. "Hey, uh, Tommy?" Hermione said, still holding onto him. "Remember that letter you wrote? From high school?"

He did.

"I still have it, you know."

Tommy heard his heart again.

Da da-da dum-dum-dum.

She stepped closer to him. "You know, he and I, uh, we're not together anymore."

Da da-da dum-dum-dum.

He remembered how much he'd loved her in high

179

school.

"Hermione?" he said.

"Yes?" she said.

"It's raining quite a bit."

She looked up at the sky. "Quite a bit, yes."

They laughed.

Da da-da dum-dum-dum.

And then he leaned in and kissed her.

On the mouth, specifically.

And his heart did a guitar solo.

It was cold, and it rained, so he felt like an actor. He thought of his mom, and his family, and his home, and he was so ready to get back there. He thought of all the people he'd ever met: the fat, skinny, tall, short, nobody, and somebody people. He thought about how it didn't matter where they'd all be in five years.

All that mattered was now.

Because now he was kissing Hermione, and she was warm and soft and she tasted like chocolate ice cream. And she was kissing him back.

He thought about the only place he wanted to be in five years, and that was right here, with her.

When they finally broke apart, Tommy looked around. People were staring at them.

"Look at all these people," he said, running his hand through his hair. "I never thought I'd need so many people."

Da da-da dum-dum-dum.

* * *

A short story inspired by a David Bowie song of the same name
For Grandma.

The Metastatic Squatter

Kate Post

Your awareness goes on frequent vacations—
sabbaticals devoted to worrying
about bills, preschools, whether or not
you should have your tattoo artist etch
colorful denotations into each delicate skin cell of your arms.

The house sits empty
dishes in the sink, TV on, family dog
chewing the remote control.
The dog's the only one to notice the new guy.

He sinks into your couch, does a few dishes
tries to get the dog to stop growling at him,
answers your phones with "Hi there."
—typical house-sitter stuff.

By the time you get home—
turn on the lights,
try to see if you have been away long enough to smell your
own house,
realize he's been peeing all over the toilet seat,
letting the milk go bad, setting up coffee dates for you
with your ex who always smelled like another woman's
perfume—
it's a little late.

* * *

Dedicated to Liz, whose love and light know no boundaries

Stardust, Always

Faery Tale

Ashlee Hetherington

Her name's Faery. She earned it when she picked me up the last day of my freshman year.

"What did you do?" I screamed as I got into the car.

"Like it?" she grinned and ran her hand through her short hair.

"Totally!" I'd always been jealous of her full and curly hair, but this was so cool, so edgy. I didn't know anyone with hair so short. She didn't swat my hand away from her scalp as I played with it while we drove.

Having a sister twelve years older's pretty awesome. We were best friends, but she was also sort of a mom—or more like the cool mom you wish your real mom was. We spent a lot of time together and rarely fought. Our conversations went from postulating about the meaning of life to the plastic thing on the end of shoelaces, and why it was called an aglet. As a treat for surviving the school year, she took me to a local café and bought me a sugary blended coffee drink we wouldn't tell mom about, and got some complicated hot drink for herself.

She laughed, genuinely. The lines next to her eyes only showed up when she had a deep and hearty laugh. If those lines weren't there, I knew she was faking. Her freckles, aka "kisses from the sun" as our mom called them, made her look younger than she was.

"You look like a faery!" I blurted at her after we'd been sitting at the table for a while.

"Yeah?" She laughed and rolled her eyes. "Should I buy wings?"

"Duh. How else would you fly?" I scowled. "What a dumb question." I wanted my hair like hers. She was so cool. She was a faery.

Years later, at the same table with the same drinks, where she got her figurative faery wings she confessed her mortality to me.

"How long have you known?" I could tell she'd had the news and kept it from me.

"Two weeks," was all she said before taking a drink.

"Two we—" I swallowed the word before it caught in my throat and turned to a sob. I blinked to keep the tears in my eyes. I wanted to hate her. I couldn't look at her.

The condensation formed little beads, which slid down the plastic cup to the table and formed little pods. I fought so hard. Focused on the water. But I lost the fight and sobbed. She was quiet while I fell apart. I watched my tears mingle with the condensation from my cup on the table. She had cancer and would die from it—that was the only thing the doctor was sure of. But she wasn't crying. I felt her arms go around me, and she pulled my head to her, holding me tight while I sat there, unable to do anything but shake from the sobs. I closed my eyes again, gripping her arm in my hands, afraid to let her go.

* * *

"You know you don't have to do this, Baby Girl." She used her nickname for me more than my real name. She grabbed a box from the backseat.

"You're my sister." I furrowed my brows as I followed her to her apartment with a box of my own. I didn't mind moving in and couch surfing. "You want to move in with mom?" I laughed. "That fight was probably the most epic you've ever had."

"Whatever. It's not like I'm going to be some crotchety old woman or something." I knew she hated the lack of control and knowing she would have to depend on people more and more. She was going to have to watch things slip away. But she couldn't be on her own. "I finally got everything sorted with the lawyer for after I put a cork in it."

"Yeah? Did he laugh or look at you like you were claiming to be Metatron when you said you wanted to be shoved into a wine bottle and chucked into the sea?"

"A little, but then he said he's had clients with weirder requests. For once I'm in the normal category."

"Have you found a bottle yet?" I asked when she opened the door.

"Yup. We're gonna drink it right now." She set the box down on the floor and danced to the kitchen. She had two glasses and an unopened bottle.

Part of why I was there was to make sure she didn't do stupid shit. "Should you be drinking?" I hated having to act like her mother, but she was on a lot of medications.

She looked at me with the most annoyed glare she'd ever had. I could hardly see the blue of her eyes between her nearly closed lashes. She forced an empty glass into my hand, then poured wine into hers. I followed her to the balcony. She had it set up for a night of lounging and wine drinking, with two chairs and fuzzy blankets. I grabbed the bottle and poured a glass. I decided not to let the night devolve into a fight over how many of the meds she was taking didn't mix with alcohol, or how bad the cold was for her already compromised immune system. How could I, at twenty-two, boss her and her thirty-four years around? Especially when she was already stubborn and telling her what to do was as productive as reading with your eyes closed.

"What should we drink to?" she asked. I shrugged. "Hmm." She bit her lip and looked to the right.

"Can't we just drink like we usually do?" I took a large and undignified gulp. Massive faux pas with wine people.

"You're so difficult." She rolled her eyes and took a drink.

"We never toast. Why start? They all sound lame. Like some cliché saying the obvious." She glared again. I grinned. She was really upset, though. "OK." I had to compromise a little. "To kicking cancer's ass and looking beautiful, dahling." I held out my glass. We clinked and laughed and drank.

By the time the third bottle was open, all responsibility

and concept of time had disappeared. The sun wasn't far from peeking into the living room and blinding our hungover eyes.

* * *

It was one of the first days I was allowed to play outside; the rain had finally stopped after three months in six year old kid time, in real time it was only three days. As a kid, it was like I was an only child because most of my first memories don't really include my sister actually living with us. She was already grown-up and out of the house when I was six. On this particular day I put on a dress—the only dress I had. I didn't bother putting shoes on; they were unnecessary and cumbersome. I ran around the yard with my dog in tow. I ran in large circles, around the tree, lay in the flowerbed, and got up and did it again.

"What are you doing?" My sister's laugh danced on the breeze as she got out of her car and walked into the front yard. She stood over me, looking down at me as I lay amongst the flowers. I grinned up at her.

"It's okay," I whispered to the flower nearest my ear. "She can know, she won't tell."

"Are you talking to the flowers?" she asked me.

"Well ... " I thought about lying, but decided I could trust her. "No, I'm talking to the faeries."

"Faeries? Here in the yard? Wow, you're lucky. You know, only magical little girls get to talk to them. They don't talk to just anyone, especially old people like me." She seemed jealous of me.

I realized that maybe I shouldn't have said anything. What if she told my mom or someone and they tried to get the faeries to talk to them?

" I won't tell anyone." She smiled.

"Promise? If you do, they'll have to find a new home." I stared up and waited.

"I promise," she vowed. I considered her promise and decided it worthy.

I nodded once and promptly listened to the flower.

"What are they saying?" she asked in a whisper as she bent down slightly and hovered over me.

"They say they like you."

"Really? If they're your friends I'm sure they're cool. I'm gonna go talk to mom. I'll come back and we can talk to the faeries some more, okay Baby Girl?"

I simply smiled and she went inside. When she came back outside, she did as she said she would and sat with me in the garden while I told her what the faeries had to say.

* * *

I woke to the sound of the world ending. The thin walls shook from the booming and zooming of lasers, torpedoes, explosions, a complicated sci-fi score, and fake space heroes fighting real bad aliens on a quest of the galaxy.

Of all of the middle of the night wake ups, this was, by far, the most frustrating. It wasn't a hand shaking me because she didn't want to sleep alone; it wasn't her voice asking me to get the meds I had locked up because she was in a lot of pain. This was a jarring, obnoxious noise that I couldn't sleep through. I used to love that movie.

It was an odd sight. She was propped up, surrounded with pillows and the necessary remotes to watch DVDs. She had her cracker stash out and water bottles littered the bed. I couldn't believe how different she looked, and so fast, too. Two hours ago, I sat next to her while she threw up for what felt like hours. I always wondered how she had anything to throw up because she wasn't really eating anything. She couldn't seem to get her hunger up—side effects of the chemo.

"What are you doing?" I growled at her.

"Watching a movie," she replied, looking at me like I was an idiot for asking. I should have known what she was doing.

"Do you realize it's 3:00 AM? I can't sleep with space ships firing, screaming and—"

"Watch it with me, it's almost over." She smiled. I was tempted. I was responsible for introducing her to a lot of her favorite movies and shows, but I had responsibilities, as much as I hated them.

"I have to get up in the morning. Work, you know what that is, right?" I left the doorway, "Turn it down!" I ordered as I walked back to the living room.

I plopped down on the couch and looked at the coffee table. Smiling faces and large print stared back: "Surviving Cancer,"How to Talk About Cancer,"So, You've Got Cancer ..." It seemed the only one missing was "Cancer for Dummies." All those stupid pamphlets and brochures full of grinning people, written by the most patient people in existence, written by people who made optimists look like pessimists. The survival stories. The happy endings. The promise that it would be difficult, but it wasn't impossible with positivity and perseverance. Difficult? Understatement of the century. They didn't say *how* hard it would be. They lied. They fluffed it, and made it seem doable. It was all but impossible to remain sane. And they lied about there being a "happy ending." There was no "happy ending" for this cancer case.

I missed a sound sleep. I missed my bed. I missed my space. I hated my life. I grabbed the cancer bullshit that littered the table and, before I could stop myself, I ripped it all to bits. The carpet looked like a Picasso painting; part of an eye there, a bit of cheek here, a corner of a smile atop an ear. It wasn't enough. I wanted to destroy something else. I wanted to destroy something the same way my life was being destroyed. I slipped my shoes on and grabbed my sweatshirt.

I let the door close behind me, blocking out the good guys saving their alien friends, and left to clear my head.

* * *

She would load the squeaky shopping cart up with things she didn't need and couldn't afford. I'd sneak by and pull out what I could, making the employees hate me, I'm sure. I'd just tuck the mascara, the fifth shampoo, the piggy bank, the high heels she couldn't wear on random shelves. She wouldn't notice items missing. We called it chemo-brain. When we'd get the register, I'd have to pay the hundred bucks. A couple days later, I'd return the items we didn't need. To return them, I had to go through her things.

"What are you doing?" She hadn't started showering, though the shower was on. Crap.

"I was just looking for something." I smiled up from the floor.

"Those are new." She pointed to the pants with a tag next to me. Then she saw two shoe boxes.

"They won't fit you."

"I was going to return them. We need the money and you aren't wearing them." I could have lied, but I felt guilty with outright lying.

"You can't just return my stuff."

"Well, I paid for it, and you don't have the money to pay me back. I have to pay the bills."

"You don't have to do anything!" She grabbed her purse from the coffee table. "You're not my keeper!" Her shoulder slammed into mine as she barreled to the door.

"Apparently I am," I barked, as she flung open the door and started down the stairs. I watched while she continued to the sidewalk. When I couldn't see her anymore, I went inside for my keys and cell. I kept a block between us. At least she had shoes on this time. Her hand next to her ear let me know she was on her phone. Her gait was steady and faster than I thought she'd be, but she teetered closer to the zooming traffic more than I liked. My cell started buzzing in my hoodie pocket. The new text message icon showed up on top of the screen.

"You hit her?" the text from mom made me gawk at the flailing arms of my sister still ahead of me.

"Unbelievable!" I spat to my phone and shoved it back into my pocket without texting back.

Fifteen minutes passed before I saw my mom's car drive

by and she pulled over between the two of us.

"I did not hit her," I growled into the window.

"I know. What happened?"

"She got mad because I told her I was going to return some stuff we couldn't afford. Just go get her. She can stay with you tonight."

"We'll talk later, see if she wants to stay longer and give you a break."

"Whatever." I turned and headed back the way I'd come from. I looked back and saw them drive off. I went home and finished going through her room for things to return them.

* * *

One year, three months, and five days passed in varying degrees since her diagnosis. At times it felt longer, and other times it seemed like she had just started treatment. Her days were unpredictable. Weeks of absolute horror were sometimes followed by days when we could almost forget she was dying. We functioned on the tails of a bell-curve, always in the extremes.

"It's for you!" She yelled from the kitchen. The phone was in her outstretched hand when I got there.

"Hello?" I said to the caller and went into the living room.

"How is she doing?" my aunt asked in a hushed voice.

"Fine, you just talked to her. You didn't ask her?" I questioned, as I walked onto the balcony.

"I did. I just wanted to know how things *really* are."

"They are what she says they are. She's having a pretty good few weeks." I replied and sat. How long it would last, no one knew. I hated the good days. They left me wondering if it would be the end soon. I was left trying to figure out just how many more she'd have. How long until we were left with only bad days?

"Well, that is good news." My aunt's voice was full of a hope and a happiness that I envied.

"Yeah. Things are looking really good if she keeps up. She's eating and everything," I explained.

"I'll stop by this weekend," she said, reminding me that it was time for her to bring her version of giving me a break: pre-cooked food. It did make things easier. I declined everyone's offers to have her stay with them for the weekend because I couldn't entertain the idea of not being there if she needed me. I didn't feel like anyone would do the job right. Everyone eventually stopped offering to take her off my hands, but they still brought food by, as my aunt was doing. We wouldn't complain because we both hated cleaning the mess up after cooking.

* * *

I said goodbye to my sister twice.

The first time was when I found her lifeless body in bed while Metatron turned a baseball bat into a fish. She looked like the sister I knew—peaceful and loving. She didn't have the weight of a war she'd never declared crushing her soul or body anymore. But she wasn't *in* there. She wasn't the same. Despite knowing she wasn't there, I couldn't bring myself to leave her side.

The second time I said goodbye was when my mom and I threw her into the middle of the Pacific, sending her back to where she came from, where we all came from.

The tears stopped falling as I wrapped my arms around my waist, hugging myself. The salty air whipped around my face, sending my hair fluttering.

I closed my eyes and rocked with the waves.

Stardust, Always

Finding Things After You're Gone

Rachel A. Brune

"The physical world waits for me, but I do not embrace it—for somewhere there's a long-lost dream, and I am off to chase it."

—Jennifer Brune, 1985-2012

I rummaged through your closet without much hope of finding what I was looking for. There wasn't much left, and others had found it all before I came home.

My eyes passed over the basket more than once, because it was falling apart and I didn't know it was yours. I didn't know you made things out of yarn and needles. Just one more thing I didn't know.

I didn't know, when I came home, wondering if you had a chance to read the story I started—the one we were going to write together—that the time was already past when we could have started something we would finish. Do you remember how we raced to finish our first books? The bet we made— that you collected? I forget what movie we went to see. I forget a lot these days. But I remember how you looked at the paper I handed you and how you set it to the side.

So I took the basket and the yarn and the needles and brought it downstairs. Because you left so quickly, and there were so many things I didn't know, but if I finished this project, then maybe I, too, would be part of that secret life.

Did you know, the day before you left, that I had never met the sisters who came, fluttering around your bed like crows in the snow? They carried the Eucharist and they told me they had been on this journey with you. It was a journey of which I had only glimpses, postcards sent from a relative who remembers you even when you don't write back all the time.

You were patterning a rainbow, rows of colors and textures, and I stared at it until I put it away. Maybe you were smiling at me, when you put our story away. Maybe it was only ever my story, a comfort for me when I couldn't find a piece of you to take with me. Memory's a tricky thing.

* * *

Reading that book you sent me, I found these artifacts of you: veterinarian appointment slip for a dog who died before you did; your name in your handwriting on the frontispiece; unfolded silver gum wrapper. They marked your place and I re-read the words your eyes had cast over, and reveled in the uncharted territory beyond.

I found in the pile of mail on my desk a birthday card you wrote. Was it the chemistry-set neurons that forgot to fire, forgot to send me this memento until it brought only pain and memory instead of congratulations?

But you did not leave me your shade. I found her sitting, perched on the corner of the hutch in the living room, listening to music I hadn't forgotten to turn off.

It was an obscure album from an obscure band from the '90s. We had listened to them together, when I had an old car and a new license and every trip to the A&P was an adventure together.

And sometimes we would put some dollars together, and there would be a movie and a long, late drive through the Jersey night, while we sang to Bon Jovi—loud, with all the windows down.

There was freedom and the promise of freedom, and I would light the way and you would hold the flame.

I stood in the dark of the living room for a long time, hoping these memories would drift away, recognizing in them the unfinished heat that comes in the wake of incomplete mourning.

You turned to me then, and the night left holes in your form, held together with shadows and the punk rock chords that fell like a lullaby around us.

Stardust, Always

Final Curtain Call

Amanda Parker Adams

Standing in the wings, waiting for my cue. The curtains have seen better days. The boards creak with every step someone takes. Dad said they always did that. You always knew where you were by the creak of the boards. The podium, which I told them not to put out there as I'm too short to stand behind it and see over the edge, stands in the middle, near the apron of the stage. The footlights are at varying stages of burnout. One or two are completely out, but they won't be replacing them. No need.

One last time. I heard the audience settle. Gus, the stage manager, broke from his usual serious demeanor to try telling me we had a packed house. I knew what that excited face meant. I covered my face with my hands, trying to not mess with the headset mic dad bought for me to have my hands free for readings.

"I don't want to know, Gus. You know I don't like to know how packed it is."

I'd rather speak to an empty house. I pulled my hands away as he chuckled.

"Hey, Gus, why the podium? I asked for no podium."

"Sorry, luv. I can have the boys remove it, or maybe move it to the side."

"Thanks, Gus. I don't want to be a burden to you and the guys."

"No burden, really. Everything will be gone soon, including my job. I thought of retiring a few years ago, but I didn't want to train someone new. I knew the boss wasn't doing well. I knew the kids wouldn't want to keep this place up either. The writing was on the wall even then. I figured I'd stick around." He waved the two stagehands over, "Hey boys, can ya move the podium over to the side of the stage. Miss Jamie don' want it."

They walked out on stage and slid it off stage. He headed back to his post with the mic.

"We jus' hoped more speakers would show up."

They're all gone now. Lately the stage has been used for community events, but the owner died and his kids were even less interested in running a theater than I am standing on a stage. It's been hemorrhaging money since Mr. Ackerman died nearly two years ago. No repairs or anything done. The roof started leaking over the dressing rooms, so most of them were of no use. Gus did the best he could managing the place. Mr. Ackerman put provisions in his will to provide for Gus to be paid until his own death if he outlived his boss. Gus is one of those stubborn old men who just refuses to go quietly. He's pushing eighty and is still going like he's twenty-five. This theater has been his life. The kids tried contesting the provision for Gus, but the magistrate wouldn't budge. Ackerman was respected in the community; his kids, not as much. Not at all, really.

We also tried to get the theatre on the registry of historic buildings, but no luck. Too much damage. We fought for a year, but the kids were adamant. They aren't much younger than I am. Yet, they never saw the history of it. All they saw was a big fat cheque for the land. Even Mr. Ackerman tried the registry himself when he was diagnosed with cancer, but the process is slow and he never lived to hear the answer.

To me, it feels as if the building chose to die when Mr. Ackerman passed. A theater is a living, breathing place. If these walls could speak, the stories it could tell would make the plays performed in it pale in comparison. Dad regaled us as we got older with all the bawdy tales of conceit, deception, greed, cheating and antics from behind the curtain. Things you didn't let the public or little kids know about.

Gus peeked out at the audience. The front of house manager, who was volunteering her time for this one last event, let him know on his headset that the doors were closed and everyone was inside. He dimmed the lights and got on the mic.

"Welcome to the Old Tram Theatre." The audience applauded. They recognized that voice. Gus -was- this theatre. I fear he may not bother for much longer after this weekend himself. He started working here for Mr. Ackerman's father when he was barely eighteen. He worked his way up, devoted to the Ackermans and the Tram. This was his home, his heart and soul. I don't think he'll know what to do with retirement. "Please welcome to the stage, for one last night to share her stories with us, Miss Jamie Courtenay!"

I took a deep breath and walked out on stage.

"Welcome everyone," I said after the applause died down. "As you likely know, my father was Richard Courtenay." Another round of applause. If the night was going to be like this, we weren't going to get out of here until after midnight. "Thank you. I have to admit something: while my father was a sucker for the spotlight, I am not. I'm probably more nervous being up here than a first time drama student. My father walked these boards for many years. He said many of the greats of his time had as well. I only knew their names, heard their voices. Legendary musicians performed between play runs, equally legendary actors stood on these boards right where I am now. So many have graced this stage at some point in the decades. My father performed in a play with Alan Rickman. He was still young at the time and Rickman was doing more film work. He still returned to the stage from time to time. My father returned more often.

"I was never the theatrical one in the family, but with my father being in the spotlight so much, I grew up around it. When my first book came out, I did a reading or two here. My first reading here had more people backstage than in the audience. Dad's career had waned a bit, so our name didn't mean as much. He got a movie gig with Alan, playing his sidekick. Then people remembered.

"My uncle worked these boards as well, although he never moved past stage work like my father. He was content with the simple things. He didn't seek fame. He was content with just getting by. My father never understood that mindset.

He wanted his name on the marquee. He never quite made top billing on screen, but he was a star here and at home.

"Come Monday, this old building will be reduced to a pile of bricks, steel, and wood. While the building will be gone, the memories will not. They will live on in all of us. I grew up here, spending hours in my father's dressing room doing my homework and minding my younger siblings. They were all too chicken to come up here tonight, so they're sitting out there with you, hiding from the spotlight."

My eyes adjusted to the lights and I was finally able to see faces. I almost wish I hadn't. The house was packed. As packed as it could be. The balcony was deemed unsafe to be occupied while we were planning this one last hurrah. We could only seat people on the main floor. I swear I saw- no. It must be the lights playing tricks on my eyes.

"My dad worked with many people on this stage as he earned his stripes as an actor. He used to say you could always tell where you were on the stage by the squeaks of the boards. We tested him after he retired from film. We brought him here, with the permission of Mr. Ackerman and Gus, who was amused by this claim. After years of his bragging, we blindfolded him and brought him out on stage. Sure enough, whenever we asked him where he was as I led him around, he was deadly accurate. Down to how many feet from the apron of the stage. He knew these boards better than anyone around. Except possibly Gus, who is hiding backstage. You know his voice, but he never shows his face when there's an audience. In all of my years, never once." I turned to look for him, but he was sitting quietly in his chair. I motioned for him to come out, but he didn't respond. "I guess he's still playing shy. He's nearly eighty and has been here since he was eighteen. This theatre has been his whole life, and a large part of my own.

"While I grew up here, my calling was elsewhere. Dad wanted me to follow in his footsteps, but I was never comfortable on stage or in front of a camera. Never my thing, really. I preferred creating the tales for others to tell. Thus, I began to write one act plays for my siblings, who were more theatrically inclined than I when we were younger. They performed what I wrote on evenings when our father wasn't working. Then I began to weave more intricate stories that turned into books. As his star waned, mine brightened, and then when people made the connection, his career had a second wind, with a little help from Alan. I've been writing since I was ten, but published since I was twenty. In our planning for tonight, we chose to share a peek the archives and pull out recordings of rehearsals and performances. So enjoy the memories."

I stepped aside near the apron and watched as the screen came down further upstage and began to show old footage going as far back as the 1970's. The building was older than that, but portable video cameras were a little easier to manage by then. After an hour of video clips, the screen darkened and the stage lights came back up.

"A decade ago, cancer claimed my father. The same kind that took his friend and mentor, Alan Rickman. We got to say goodbye, but it still was never enough time. There never feels like there is enough time. I was in Australia when I got the call. I had just gotten off the stage from a reading in Adelaide. He was gone. Just like so many others. The stories this building could tell if it talked. But the memories stay with us all. I thank you all for coming tonight. May you keep the love of theater alive for generations to come. The legacy of The Old Tram needs to live on in us."

The applause died down as I vanished into the tired wings for the last time. The boys were trying to wake Gus. Once I got offstage and my mic was off, I checked his pulse. Nothing. I rushed back out onto the stage. The lights were down and house lights up, so I was able to look for my siblings. One of my brothers is a doctor, but I knew in my heart it would be no use. He was gone. He was the heart of this theater, and so it's only right. I just never got to say goodbye. As I scanned the bustling audience below, my attention returned to the balcony.

It was dark up there so I saw very little. I did see faces. Faces I knew. Rickman, O'Toole, Lee, Gielgud, Harris,

Olivier, my old man, uncle George, and many others who walked these boards in the lifetime of the building. Then off to the side, I saw Gus. They each began to look a little more solid, yet not quite there. I could see they were all smiling. They blew me kisses and took their final bows, then vanished for the final curtain call.

Twenty-Six

Paula Hayward

Twenty-six. There is still a bit of invincibility left in you at that age. I had it and then I did not. It was winter, I was sick, normal sick stuff. I went to the doctor when a swollen lymph node in my neck stayed swollen for several weeks. I expected antibiotics; I got a biopsy instead. Then came those dreaded words: "You have cancer." Details are fuzzy now years later; I cannot remember if it was a biopsy then the diagnosis or if the diagnosis came after the surgery to remove the entire lymph node. It does not matter, I still had cancer.

This was during the early nineties and I didn't have a cell phone. I drove around after the doctor's visit, found a pay phone, and called my then husband. The whirlwind began. I used to cringe when I told people I was a cancer survivor. My cancer was caught early, stage 1A. My cancer had a high cure rate, Hodgkin's Disease, now called Hodgkin's Lymphoma. My cancer. That is not something you want to stick on your goals list at twenty-six. World travel, decent job, good friends, cancer. Nope, but there it was, not something you could put off until the right time. There is no right time for cancer, cancer chooses, you do not.

My treatment ran from December, the first doctor's appointment, to June, my final radiation treatment, and included two surgeries and six weeks of radiation. I continued to work. In fact, there was some joy in coming into work at ten-thirty after my morning radiation treatment. I actually got to sleep in for an extra half hour. As a non-morning person that extra half hour was bliss.

By June my chest and neck looked like a lobster and felt like the worst sunburn ever. Wearing a bra to work was like torture, so I switched to camisoles. There were people at work who did not know I was going through treatment. A few years after my diagnosis a co-worker developed cancer. Another co-worker remarked how he had never met a cancer survivor as he spoke out about what he considered her impending doom. I stuck out my hand and introduced myself, even though we had worked together for years. He did not know. That was one of the first times I felt like a survivor.

Calling yourself a survivor is hard. It took me years to claim it entirely. For one, my cancer was caught early. My cancer was also a mild form, at least that was what I was told at the time—high cure rate with a good chance of long-term survival. Those thoughts made me feel sequestered from other cancer victims. Cancer victims, not sure I like that term. Maybe it is all right, but cancer is like getting picked up from your everyday life and being placed in the middle of a battlefield unarmed and unprepared. Suddenly, you have leaders on horses telling you what to do—the copious amount of doctors you see, using words that you do not understand. They are trying to explain while the enemy approaches, their screaming ringing in your ears.

I hated sitting in the oncologist's office. No one was smiling, so many people were losing their hair. The atmosphere was surreal, like the waiting room for Death. There were support groups available, yet I never went. That may be my one regret. I had family support and lots of friends ensuring my mind stayed positive. To attend a support group would have been inviting the negative, a peering into the Death that I knew I would not see. How arrogant. My friends were great, my family was too. But as the years have rolled on, there is a certain grief I feel that they cannot understand. They were not in the battle. They do not have my scars. They cannot know the stories I need to share. I have no kindred spirits from my time of cancer, no one with which to swap stories.

Because I only had radiation and not chemo, I only lost the hair that was in the direct path of radiation. I did not shave my armpits for two years, that was nice. The path of radiation was to the back of my jawline, so I lost only the very back lower portion of my hair. I hate my thick, curly, unruly hair. It has always been a pain. I had already cut it short, but the day it came out in clumps in the shower, I started to cry. It was another part of the battle, one where I felt weakened. But, I survived.

Arrogantly, perhaps a way to cope with my own brush with Death, I started to see cancer as something that people could beat in this modern era. My co-worker returned after her treatment. Other people who I knew had cancer were surviving. It was a glorious few years. Then someone I knew died from cancer. It felt like a punch in the gut. As I took off the blinders, I found that other people were dying from cancer. An actor died of Hodgkin's Lymphoma. That one got to me, because surely he had enough connections to receive good treatment. Hodgkin's Lymphoma was supposed to be "good" cancer, right? Cancer crept closer to home as I watched the ambulance wheel out my neighbor for the final time, a victim of cancer. My arrogance had been completely stripped away.

There are long term side effects to treatment as well. Twenty years, you would think after twenty years of surviving you would just get a gold star and a cookie. No. My thyroid stopped working; I knew that would happen. The mounted oncologists screaming at me in the midst of the battle had warned me. The earaches are a pain, the broken molars are no fun, and the scar tissue that ruined my once flat abs is an ongoing object lesson in vanity.

I had an appointment with a new general practitioner late last year. We did not really hit it off, and in his report he wrote I was ambivalent about my chronic health problems. Maybe I am simply not afraid. Twenty-two years out and I now have a slight heart murmur, possibly due to the radiation. I have an upcoming appointment to find out why. With a heavy sigh, I will follow through. There is no putting the armor away, yet the screaming is not so frightening now.

When you hear about someone dying from cancer, you realize that we are not invincible, even those we hold in high esteem, those that we love, and those that we admire. When you hear about someone dying from the type of cancer you survived, it forces you to stop and ponder your life, your death, and what could have been.

My son arrived a few years after my treatment, born via C-section as my previous surgery created issues with my labor. I had a life after cancer. I am still having a life. I started college at age forty-six, and my divorce was final at forty-seven. At forty-eight, my son started going to the same college I attend, and my dad died, not cancer but from a host of chronic health issues. Life continues as does Death. There is still a probability that cancer will ultimately kill me. Secondary cancers and life threatening long-term side effects happen.

Today, I am not unarmed and I am not unprepared. Right now, I watch from the sidelines peering onto the crowded battlefield, trying to cheer on those in the fight. The arrogance is gone, replaced by an empathetic stubbornness. An anger at the injustice of cancer rises up when I hear about its continued carnage. I am forty-eight and I am not invincible. I am human, I am mortal. I am a cancer survivor who is—even now, twenty-two years later—still in the process of surviving

The Storyteller

Becca Bachlott

"And it's a human need to be told stories. The more we are governed by idiots and have no control of our destinies, the more we need to tell stories to each other about who we are, why we are, where we come from, and what might be possible."—Alan Rickman

Esmeralda stared wide eyed at the very large beast that stood before her and readied her sword, grasping it tightly. Her blue eyes gleamed when the sunlight hit them as did her heavy piece of fired steel. The dragon huffed and puffed. She knew she should have been scared because the monster was fierce, but she wasn't. Somewhere deep inside she knew she could beat him. She just had to believe in herself.

The beast charged at her and she braced herself for impact. The dragon was at least 10 times her size but she wouldn't back down now. She hadn't come all this way to just walk away. She stood bravely in front of him even though her knees began to quake beneath her. The beast came at her and she thrust her sword swiftly just as he lunged at her.

The dragon shrieked and hissed. She sensed he was trying to use his fire breathing ability. Unfortunately, she stabbed the poor creature right in the throat. He wouldn't breathe fire now or ever again. Sadness kindled in her heart as she stood there watching him struggle to cope with his fate. She knew he would have killed her without hesitation but she could still feel tears well up like a spring behind her eyes.

They were bittersweet tears, joyful because the battle was finally over but also full of sadness. Her whole life had been about preparing to battle this fearsome creature. He'd tortured and terrorized her small village for hundreds maybe even thousands of years. Any child born, rich or poor, boy or girl, learned how to fight in hopes that one day one of them would defeat him. Now that it was finally done, she wondered who she was without him.

When she'd told her family of her plan, they tried their best to convince her to let someone else do it. She knew her family believed in her. Mother had always encouraged her to do whatever she wanted to do. Father never made her feel insignificant for being the only girl amongst four brothers. She knew their fears were because they didn't want to lose her.

She gazed into the dragon's misty yellow eyes one last time. She saw something there besides pain within them. His eyes seemed to be pleading with her for mercy. As she gently stroked his cheek, she pulled out the sword and thrust it once more finally finishing him off.

"Fair thee well, my dragon. You died honorably. You will not be forgotten."

She returned to the village with his head as proof of her victory. The villagers all rejoiced and cheered her name that evening. She'd never truly wanted to be a hero, she'd only wanted to feel safe in her own home. She just needed the chance to be able to live her life without fear and sadness. As they all continued to cheer and celebrate, she took in a deep breath and silently rejoiced in her victory.

After that day, the legend of Esmeralda continued to spread across continents and generations. Today she's remembered as the hero who defeated the undefeatable monster. And she lived happily ever after.

The End

David Foster closed the book slowly. He gazed over at his daughter Laurel who was lying in her hospital bed at St. Jude's Children's Hospital.

"Daddy, can you read me another one? Maybe we can read the one about the starman this time."

"You should really get some rest sweetheart. I can read you the story about Major Tom tomorrow. I promise."

"Daddy, when I grow up, I want to be brave and strong just like Esmeralda."

"Oh sweetie, you already are. I am so proud of how strong you are. Now try to get some sleep."

"Goodnight, Daddy."

"Goodnight Laurel."

David leaned over and planted a light kiss on her cheek, then sat and watched as she drifted off to sleep. He often sat at her hospital bed and wondered what she dreamt about. Tonight, he hoped that she was dreaming that cancer was a big yellow-eyed monster and that she was a brave knight beating him. He also hoped that once she won she would never forget how he had impacted her life. Her spirit was a bright and shining beacon of hope in a time when everything seemed dark and futile. The doctors had told him and his wife that the chemo was working. It looked like she'd make it through. The entire staff had labeled her as a fighter and he knew they were right. He sat the book on the table next to her bed, leaving it there to comfort her. If she woke up in the middle of the night, she would reach for the book and read it to herself.

He longed for the moment that he might be able to finally take her home and tell her these stories from her bedroom. Until then, he'd settle for the next evening when he could open up another book and tell her more about heroes and dragons, space men and mysterious planets yet to be discovered. David knew how they helped take her mind off of everything that was happening to her. For his part, they somehow always left him with a feeling of calm. Heroes always win and in his eyes Laurel was the biggest and best super hero of them all.

* * *

For Jana Adams and Brenna Hunter

Stardust, Always

Check Ignition

Tony Hillier

Bowie, the creative knife
who cut through generations
dizzy with Ziggy we were awestruck

Ground Control to major cancer
Ground Control to major cancer
ha ha ha ha ha ha
I'm a little cell and you can't catch me
ha ha ha ha ha ha

Bowie held our hand
at work, rest and play
with his Life on Mars
He never Sold us the World
he gave us a new world

New World that questioned the Establishment
put the Establishment in the dock
found it wanting
found the Establishment guilty

He has left us, not with guilt
but with gauntlet thrown down
so we can choose to use
our Bowie-knife of creativity
to make Changes for a fairer
more beautiful world.
Check ignition.

Ground control of carcinogenics
Ground control of carcinogenics
Ground control of carcinogenics

No pressure. Heroes here. Let's dance.
Let's Dance with the China Girl
in the street, in the Vic[1],
off the walls, on the ceiling.
Let's dance, let's dance in our hearts.

---

[1]This poem was first performed at The Victoria music venue, Swindon.

He Wasn't Sick in April

Georgette Frey

The phone ringing at 7:15 on my only day off woke me up quickly but not fast enough to catch the call. "Shit, what did I do now?" I mumbled as I looked at the screen. I immediately tried to call my dad back as my boyfriend, Joe, asked what was wrong. When he answered he sounded out of breath and I could tell he was in the truck. "What's wrong and where are you?" I asked before he could say more than hello.

I couldn't make out much of what he was saying as he wheezed and gasped while telling me to meet him at home. Work had sent him home. He couldn't breathe and refused to go to the hospital by ambulance because he didn't want to leave his truck and wanted to be at home. I was dressed and told Joe to do the same before I ended the call. My daughter heard the noise and came out dressed. By 7:25 we were at his house waiting for him to show.

My daughter and step-mom, Donna, rode with me while Joe helped my dad to the passenger side of his truck and drove him to the hospital. This was only the second time he had been to the emergency room in his life, and we were not letting him out of it. He was a large man and we all thought heart attack, they run in our family and he had had a quiet one at some point in the past. Being pliant was a new thing, and his being agreeable to seeing a doctor and not driving himself the rest of the way worried me more than his labored breathing. The men beat us to the hospital and my boyfriend helped the security guards get my dad into the emergency room where they wheeled him into triage right away. When we arrived, my stepmother and I completed his registration. When the woman asked for his co-pay I told her we would pay if he were discharged; our policy covered hospital stays completely without the co-pay and I knew they were not going to send him home.

Once he was settled in a room, he called me back. He had driven the whole way home in fear that he would stop breathing. He had been going fast enough on the highway that the governor on the truck shut him down twice. For the first time in my life I yelled at my father; I asked him, "What would have happened if he wrecked." His reply was that Donna "Would be well taken care of." I lost it. I asked. "What about the family of four he could have killed and the lawsuits she would face from his carelessness?" He admitted he never thought of any of that, another first. I told him he should have stayed put, or taken an ambulance. Joe and I could have taken my step-mom to Pittsburgh. We worked for the same company, getting the truck would not have been an issue.

We stayed through shift change and late in the day, he was taken to the cardiac unit with congestive heart failure. I answered all of the admitting nurse's questions and we had brought all of his pills so that his medication regime was properly documented. Everyone went home to eat and let him rest.

Two days later he called me from the hospital the kidney doctor had just left, "We need to talk."

"I'll be up as soon as we put the groceries away." I was two blocks from home and told my boyfriend, "It's cancer."

"Is that what he said?"

"No, he's not going to tell me has cancer over the fucking phone. I heard it in his voice. "

Within the hour, he was telling me the same thing. He didn't remember what it was; he just knew it was a blood cancer and not leukemia. He knew it was rare and the only reason they caught it was because one of the hospitalists had seen it before. I found a nurse and had her look at his charts. They were already deferring more to me than to my father and his wife. I had never heard of it either, Kappa Light Chain Amlyoidosis. Thank the gods for Google and a friend who is a cancer researcher. I found a YouTube video that explained it and then ran my understanding past my friend who said I had it pretty well down. His bone marrow was shooting off disfigured amyloids and they were clogging his organs up. It started with his kidneys, which was putting an even greater burden on his heart and lungs. It could not be cured but with luck it could be contained. They told him he had from weeks to up to five years. He wanted to see my teenagers finish high school. He agreed to chemotherapy but not dialysis; he had seen what that does to people and he didn't want to go through it.

Once he was home, we alternated between specialist appointments. My step-mom took him to one in Pittsburgh but that didn't turn out so well. She got lost in the parking garage. Her nerves combined with never having driven into the city were problematic. He didn't want anyone else to know beyond my uncle and us. My cousins didn't know, although I did tell my mom. I kept both of our jobs updated and became fairly friendly with the head of HR in the company we both worked for. I made the calls, had papers signed and returned them on the days he was too weak.

We went on vacation for one week in July to Washington D.C. when he only had a chemo appointment; it was at the local hospital so my step-mom could take him. While he was gone, my uncle came over and made extra steps so he could get in and out of the house more readily and made a step to help him get in and out of the truck.

When he couldn't wear his shoes anymore because of his feet swelling he had another first: sandals. We found hiking style ones in his size online and called the store to hold them for us. His hair was getting long because he couldn't go see his barber and wouldn't tell any of the hairdressers in the family that he was sick. I teased him and said I was going to start playing Jimi Hendrix and The Grateful Dead instead of Rush Limbaugh in his truck. He laughed.

He made one chemotherapy appointment and then ended up back in the hospital. He couldn't get up or walk without assistance. I had never been more thankful that my boyfriend is disabled and is home all the time because he was able to help my dad get around. The next purchase was a stair glide and a lift chair. He used the stair glide once. The lift chair wasn't used because he ended up in the hospital, yet again. The nurse in the emergency department was taking blood, but not with the normal sized containers, these were HUGE. I asked him why, and he replied, "His blood is being cultured and sent back to the Cleveland Clinic." Google came to my aid again. I didn't say a word to my stepmother when we were in the room together. The nurse was wonderful and by what questions he didn't answer, I knew my idea was right; infection.

They moved him back to the cardiac ward. I was looking to see if my cousin was on duty so I could ask questions and know I was getting a straight answer but she was off. The head nurse came in and told us it was only a temporary room and, he was being moved again. They were just cleaning the newer room.

The new room was a pressurized room to keep him from getting additional infections. He had picked it up either there or the cancer center and he was septic. That's when they both understood that it was serious, and he wasn't going to get the five years. I called work and had my daughter take my step-mom's phone and call her mother. I figured she needed as many people as possible. I called off and my boss gave me grief over it. I then called HR and got put on partial Family and Medical Leave of Absence. When my boss called me back I told her that I was covered and if she had an issue she could call the office and hung up. While I was in the family waiting room making calls and my step-mom found a place to hide to cry, my father's kidney doctor tried to push something on my dad that he had made clear he didn't want; a visit from another doctor that had made a poor decision earlier with my father's care.

The doctor said, "But he's a nice guy."

"I'm sure the Queen of England is nice too, but we don't want her here either," my daughter told him. The doctor stopped pushing.

That evening dysphasia started; he couldn't swallow his

pills or his dinner. We got the nurse. She was young and was upset when he couldn't choke on command for her. Then she said, "I have sick patients to care for." Earlier we had tried to review his care with her and she insisted she knew everything that she needed from his file.

"When did a hospital based blood born infection that is keeping him from chemo mean he isn't sick?" my daughter snapped.

When the nurse asked why he was doing chemo my daughter almost put her through both doors. Luckily my boyfriend and step-aunt were between the two. At that point, I found the doctor, told him I thought she was overwhelmed with her caseload and needed to be replaced immediately for her safety. The next nurse was lovely. We took my step-mom to dinner and went home hoping to get some sleep.

It was after midnight. I was in the shower when the phone rang. It rang once and stopped. It was my father's cell number. I immediately dialed back. The nurse answered, "He is being taken to intensive care. His blood pressure dropped, but he won't let me tell how low." She handed him the phone.

"We're getting dressed and will be right up." I told him. He said not to but I asked if he had called my step-mom, when he said 'yes' I told him we were coming, I didn't want her alone if something more happened.

We stayed with him until nearly dawn; my nurse step-aunts were coming up in a few hours to sit with us and to ensure we understood everything. I started notifying more family. They had put him on medication to raise his blood pressure, but it didn't go back to normal.

The ICU was wonderful; we had family in and out all day long for the next few days. There were even some calls at the nurse's station for me when people couldn't get through on cell phones or via Facebook. There was only one other patient on the floor, so the nurses said they didn't mind and they were glad that family came and were pleasant, because too often there is fighting amongst family. I had made it clear that anyone who started crap would not be happy. At one point between his room and the waiting area there were over twenty of us. My cousins were working on making arrangements to come home and join us.

The dysphasia was getting worse so the medication that they could not do via IV was crushed and put into applesauce. He was missing some of his favorite foods and I knew that he couldn't eat them so we worked around it. Joe got him a milkshake from his favorite restaurant and I bought lemon-filled doughnuts from a bakery and fed him the filling since he couldn't eat by himself readily. Straws became difficult as well so my daughter stuck a few together for him so it was long enough. Despite my daughter's foot phobia, she spent hours rubbing his feet for him because they hurt from the swelling.

He knew he was dying and started making final arrangements. The doctor called a hospice. I called my mom and her dad. My step-dad brought my mom up to say goodbye. It took pestering neighbors, but my aunt had someone get a hold of my grandfather and he called the nurse's station to say goodbye, that's when he told me he had cancer too. My parents had divorced over twenty years before, but what did it matter now? One of my mom's brothers brought my son up so I didn't have to leave to go get him. My dad wanted to go home to be with his cats and wife. When the doctor and caseworker tried to ask me what I wanted I kept referring them back to him, he was still very aware. I was simply there to make sure they complied with what he wanted. Hospice ordered a bed for him at home; my boyfriend and uncle went to the house to turn the dining room into his bedroom. He was told to leave via ambulance because we wouldn't be able to get him into a regular vehicle and they would have to stop his medication. He understood. I was the last to leave his room. I told him it was ok if he didn't make it to the house.

My father was always a big man, the cancer made it worse from fluid retention. It took eight people to get him in, but he made it home. The hospice nurse came and we set up the chair and television to be handy for her. My daughter stayed the night with my step-mom and some of the other family. Joe and I went home, but didn't sleep.

Family arrived en masse on Monday. My mother's one niece showed, as did some cousins that had never been to the house before. His boss was there all day as was a co-worker's husband. It didn't matter what side of the extended family they were on, people showed. The guy next door had been my brother's best friend and had lost both of his parents stopped by. He couldn't even talk because he was so upset. My dad asked if he was okay and John completely lost it. Young men who were next door to family showed up as did some of my friends, including one who had within the year lost both of her parents and step-father to cancer. One cousin had a red-eye flight and didn't leave my father's side from the time she showed up until her mother made her go back to their house. She had been up for 48 hours, her sister, brother and youngest nephew were en route, but got caught in city traffic.

We called his priest repeatedly to get there, he was in the driveway when at shortly after 4 p.m. on a Monday in August, my father stopped fighting. My cousins didn't make it, though I had his body held until they did. My youngest cousin never got a chance to tell my brother goodbye, never made it to the funeral, but my brother was buried with pictures of them and a letter. I wasn't allowing that to happen to him again.

Taking him out to the funeral home down the street was a spectacle. There was a fire truck, four ambulances and two police cruisers. The firemen and police all know me, as did half the people driving past to stare at the scene. I heard a few people in their cars say, "That's Eric Frey's house." Some I waved to, some I waved to with only one finger.

At one point, I yelled to the gawkers, "Haven't you ever seen a dead body before?"

Cancer harms more than just the patient: families hurt, emergency personal are faced with raw emotions of families splintering before their eyes, and doctors have to admit that they failed.

My father's PCP's last words to me when I called him were, "He wasn't sick in April, I swear it."

Sometimes, with some people, cancer rocks the world.

Stardust, Always

The Cost

Tucker McCallahan

"Oh my God! It's like walking onto the set of *Evil Dead*!"

"The original or that shitty remake?"

"Either. Wow. Is there a trapdoor that leads to the basement?"

"It's called a root cellar." I dropped my bags onto the dirty floor and gave my two companions a tired glare.

"Scary." Tina flipped a light switch and jumped when it worked. Light flooded the main room of my grandparents' cabin. She gazed around. "And this is your idea of relaxation?"

"No." I stretched and went to open a window. "I wanted to come alone, remember?"

"Uh huh." Rick strode through the room, one hand pulling the large cooler and the other dragging his suitcase. "You're not well enough to be alone."

"Thanks for the reminder, Captain Buzzkill."

"Be nice." Tina's hand trailed across my shoulders as she headed for the door. "We love you, remember?"

I said nothing. Rick, Tina and I had lived as a trio for over twenty years. As much as I loved and appreciated them, since my diagnosis their constant presence had gotten smothering. In seconds, Rick returned and went right back outside to help Tina unload the rest of our gear. Standing there alone, the depression I couldn't seem to shake rose up and owned me. Nothing was worse than waiting to die, and lately, that's all I'd been doing. This trip, coming up to the mountains, was supposed to make me feel better.

So far it wasn't working.

We devoted the next few hours to making the cabin habitable. Nobody had used it since my grandmother died, so we had twenty years' worth of dust, dirt, and rodent droppings to dislodge. My energy flagged after less than an hour, and Tina sent me outside to get some fresh air while she beat an area rug like it had personally offended her.

The view of the mountains was spectacular. The cabin was far enough into the foothills to be considered remote, but civilization was only about an hour away. As I stared down into the far valley, I realized what had been pristine land when I was a child was now covered with houses.

It made me feel old.

I walked around the cabin, intending to enter through the back door. As a kid, I'd loved this place. My memories of it were full of fun, adventure, and magic. Now I noticed the gutter had rotted off the roof, and the forest had encroached to crowd up against the back of the cabin. The clearing I had played in was gone, consumed by multiflora rose shrubs. I shuddered. Getting through that bramble of thorns would require a flamethrower at this point.

I went back inside. Tina chattered at me, but I ignored her. I went to the bedroom I'd slept in as a kid and uncovered the tiny twin bed. The old mattress stank like mold and felt damp to my hands.

"I inflated an air mattress in the other bedroom, babe. Why don't you go lie down in there and I'll get this room set up?"

Rick stood in the doorway, a roll of duct tape around his wrist and a Dewalt cordless drill in his hand. He'd taken his button-down off and wore a plain white T-shirt that already showed his perspiration. He was everything a healthy man in his mid-forties should be, and I hated him just a little bit for that. I forced out a thank you and went to what had always been my grandparents' room.

I didn't think I'd be able to sleep surrounded by the scent of decay and memories of dead relatives, but surprisingly enough, I drifted off quickly, birdsong and the hum of Rick's drill in my ears.

* * * *

"Wake up, sleepyhead."

I blinked and rolled to find Tina leaning over me.

"Hey." My mouth was bone dry. "What time is it?"

"Four-thirty. Why don't you get up and help me make dinner?"

I climbed off the high-rise air mattress with Tina's help. My left shoulder hurt. The damn port they'd put in for chemo always ached if I slept on my side. I caught a glimpse of my reflection as we walked through the hallway to the kitchen and ran my hands through my hair; the back was sticking straight up. Tina giggled at me.

"I liked the bedhead."

"Oh yeah, I'm a stud."

"Always." She kissed me and I caught her around the waist to return it properly. Her lips curved against mine and I smiled reflexively. "There's a smile." One hand stroked my cheek. "We've missed those."

"I know I haven't been that much fun lately."

Tina settled against my chest and wrapped her arms around me. Hugging her back was pure instinct. She smelled like Downey fabric softener and Rick's cologne; she smelled like home.

"Alex?"

"Mmm hmm?"

"You've been amazing. Rick and I–"

"Oh no." I pulled away from her and shook my head. "We're not getting all deep and emotional without alcohol."

"You're not supposed to drink!"

"You're not supposed to like being between two guys, but Rick and I don't complain." I smirked as she blushed a hot shade of scarlet.

"Damn!" Tina spun and stomped into the kitchen, but she was smiling. She pointed imperiously at the veggies on the counter. "Make the salad."

"Where's Rick?"

"He went hunting."

"He's hunting *alone*?" I leaned my hip against the counter and waved the paring knife for emphasis. "He doesn't know

223

these woods!"

"Calm down, Grizzly Adams. He's got his cell." Tina chuckled. "He doesn't want pasta tonight, and I told him if he wanted something else he'd have to go kill it himself."

"Mornings are the best time to hunt around here."

"Well, when he comes back empty-handed, you can razz him mercilessly about his lack of knowledge and skill."

We managed to light a burner on the gas stove without setting the cabin on fire. Tina sautéed slices of zucchini for the pasta sauce while I cut up cucumber and tomato. Before we knew it, dinner was ready and the sun was dropping toward the horizon.

Rick was nowhere to be found.

Tina stood between the cabin and the SUV, her phone held aloft as she sent yet another text message.

"Service sucks here!"

"Do you know which way he went?"

I sat on the edge of the sagging porch and loaded the clips for my Beretta. The M9A3 was new, and I'd never fired it anywhere but at a range. Vivid memories of my grandfather shooting coyotes from this porch played through my mind as I loaded the gun and slipped the spare clips into my pocket.

"No. Over there?" Tina waved her phone toward the thick woods that crowded the cabin. "Do you think he's ignoring me?"

"He's probably not getting the texts."

"I don't think you should go looking for him."

"And if he fell or sprained an ankle, and he's sitting out there waiting for help?"

Tina chewed her lip. I could almost hear her thoughts. She was worried I wasn't well enough to go tramping around the woods, and she was right. I didn't have the stamina for it, and the sun was sinking.

"I'll go with you," she said.

"What if he makes it back to the house?"

"We'll leave a note."

"Tina, have you ever gone hiking?"

"No."

"It's getting dark. You'll slow me down."

"But—"

"Look. If I don't go now, I'll run out of daylight before I run out of energy."

She dashed over to the SUV and grabbed a huge roadside flashlight. I slid the gun into its holster and took the light from her.

"I won't be gone long."

"Alex ... what happens if you don't find him?"

"You drive out of here, and as soon as you get a good cell signal, you call the cops."

"OK." Tina wrapped her arms around her torso. If she kept gnawing on her lip she was going to make it bleed. "Go."

I slipped the light into my backpack and brushed my lips over Tina's. I had no idea what Rick took with him when he left; Tina hadn't paid attention. I wouldn't have gone anywhere without a first-aid kit, matches, water, and a good knife, but I'd spent every summer here for over a decade. Most of the wildlife was harmless, but we had cougars, coyotes, foxes, rattlesnakes, and copperheads that weren't so innocuous. I'd grown up with a healthy respect for wild animals.

I walked straight into the trees, checking the setting sun as I went. I really didn't have much time before I'd be walking blind, and a sense of urgency propelled me forward. Rick agreed to this trip because of me. A pang of guilt hit. I hoped like hell he wasn't hurt.

Forty-five minutes later, twilight had fallen. I needed to turn back. My lungs burned from the thin mountain air. My lower back and thighs were on fire, too. I stopped where I was and swung my backpack off. Cracking open a bottle of water, I popped a pain pill. I capped the bottle and was zipping the pack when the sound of running water filtered through the rest of the forest noises. I'd made it to the creek.

As a kid, I'd traced the creek up and down the mountain. I could follow it through the woods to the clearing that wasn't clear anymore, and then make it back to the cabin. The idea of skirting an entire field of brambles and thorns didn't thrill me, but it was better than walking blind in absolute darkness. Heartened that I had physical landmarks to guide me back, I headed for the water.

I almost tripped over Rick.

My guts surged up into my throat. He wasn't hurt; he was dead. I knelt, swallowing the bile and blinking back tears, and pulled the big flashlight from my backpack. I looked him over, trying not to touch him. He was very pale. Blood had leaked from two rips in his throat and pooled under him.

Staring at the injury, the image of a cougar sprang into my mind. Cougars used their big paws and claws to trip their prey, and then held it down while delivering a kill-bite to the throat that usually broke the neck. They had massive fangs and a jaw powerful enough to drag down elk and moose.

I shone the light around. The forest floor was clear of drag marks, and no trees had any scrapes from claws. Rick's rifle lay on the ground not two feet away. I forced myself to shine the light on my dead lover again. He had no other injuries, not even to his hands. If the animal was hungry, there would've been flesh missing. If Rick had surprised it or run from it, he would've been clawed up.

My stomach rolled over as I stared at Rick so pale and still. The coppery scent of blood shot up my nose, and acid surged up my throat. The burn didn't cover the horrible smell. I choked and coughed, but having my mouth open only made it all worse. An owl hoot split the silence like a scream. My grief morphed into fear. Full darkness had fallen. Hungry cougar, spooked cougar, feral cougar–I'd take D, none of the above.

Looping the light's carry strap over my arm, I shrugged the backpack up onto my shoulders and picked out the edge of the creek. I needed to get back to the cabin. Tina would fall apart over this; we'd been preparing for my death, not Rick's. We had to call the county sheriff. We'd have to tell Rick's parents and his brother. I wept as I walked, guilt, grief, and anger snarled in my head.

Hiking back took forever. When the glow of the cabin's electric lights finally appeared in front of me, relief spread through me like an antidote. I found a burst of energy I didn't know I possessed, made it to the porch, and stopped.

The front door was wide open.

Fear flooded my mouth with an awful bitterness. The sweat down my back and over my forehead suddenly felt ice cold. I drew the Beretta, thumbed off the safety, and moved through the doorway.

The living room was a mess. The coffee table looked like kindling. A standing lamp lay on its side, shade askew, bare bulb spilling light across the floor.

Tina lay on the floor. At first I couldn't make sense of what I saw. My brain needed time to put the puzzle together. Something whip-cord thin crouched behind Tina as if holding her in an embrace. I blinked several times. Its mouth pressed to her throat, and as I brought the gun up, it glanced up at me. Blood smeared its lips and chin—Tina's blood.

"Let her go."

It ignored me, lowering its face back to wounds identical to the ones I'd seen on Rick.

"I will shoot. Let her go."

When the creature continued to ignore me, I took aim and fired. My bullet hit its shoulder, punched through, and ended up in the hallway wall behind it. The flesh knit together as I watched. The thing stared at me, sucking harder at Tina's neck. I emptied my clip into it, but every hole I created healed with eerily beautiful efficiency.

I reloaded. I didn't know what else to do. This thing had no fear; not of me, the noise, or the gun. I'd just chambered a fresh round when it let go of Tina. She slid out of its arms onto the floor with a dull thud.

"Save your bullets."

I froze. Its voice was musical. In the time it took me to blink, Tina's blood disappeared from its mouth. I couldn't tell if it was male or female, and it didn't really matter. Its beauty was hypnotic; I couldn't tear my eyes away.

"You aren't in any danger." Large spherical eyes tilted up to think about those words, and as it smiled, fangs glistened from between its lips. "Well, not danger from me anyway."

"You just killed my family. I think I'm pretty much fucked."

"I don't know what that means."

"It means I don't believe you."

"I do not require your belief." It gazed at me, its nostrils flaring as it inhaled. "You are ... wrong."

"What?"

"Wrong." It stretched slowly, its lithe body undulating like a serpent despite having arms and legs. "Unwell."

"I have cancer."

"You are unfit for feeding."

That struck me as funny. This thing was telling me the same thing I'd been telling myself for months: I wasn't good for anything. The adrenaline I'd been operating on ran out. Fatigue and hysteria swallowed me. I backed up against the wall beside the open door, gun up. I tried not to choke on my laughter as I slid down to sit on the floor.

The androgynous creature stood and approached me.

"You are dying."

"Yes." I struggled to get a good breath. "So it doesn't matter whether you want to eat me or not."

The thing sank down beside me and touched my face with a slender finger.

"Do you wish to die?"

"No."

"If you could live forever, would you wish it?"

"What's the catch?"

"I do not understand."

"What's the price for living forever?" I glanced at Tina, silent and still. "Nothing good comes without a cost."

"True." It regarded me with interest. "You presume living forever would be good."

"Better than dying."

"You presume death would be bad." Its gaze followed mine and landed on Tina. "She enjoyed our communion."

"Doesn't look like it. Looks like she fought like hell."

"Some fight." It shrugged. "Some do not."

"Guess that depends on how badly they want to live."

It gazed into my eyes and my pulse sped. It had no iris, just solid green eyes with vertical pupils like a snake. Its voice came out in a sibilant whisper.

"How badly do you want to live?"

That was the question I asked myself repeatedly over the last year. Every time I went for radiation, every time I had a chemo drip, every time I begged off doing something because I felt like crap, I asked myself if it was worth it–if I wanted to work so hard to beat the disease that might win anyway.

I had my answer, finally.

"Bad enough to fight for it."

"Why?"

"Nothing good comes without a cost."

"You would fight for such a small amount of life."

"Yes."

"You would wish to live forever then?"

I thought about it. If I was willing to fight for my life now, what would I do to live forever, to never face death? But even as I thought the question, my brain clicked on and I voiced my answer.

"I don't want to watch any more people I love die."

"Are their deaths more important than a stranger's passing?"

I blinked. Good question.

"To me, yes, but to the universe, I suppose not."

"The universe?"

"You know." I waved my hands around wildly, the Beretta still clutched in one. "Life. The universe. Everything."

"I do not understand."

"You don't spend much time around people, do you?"

"For many years I lived among men." It sat back on its haunches and studied me. "In another land, across the water. Things were different then."

A long uncomfortable silence passed. I didn't like the way it stared at me, unblinking and contemplative.

"You never told me the price for immortality," I said.

"You would not pay it."

"I'd have to kill people, wouldn't I?"

"All living things must feed."

Cool fingers stroked my face. Its touch was soothing, almost lulling, though my heart beat so fast it seemed to stutter and trip. The creature both attracted and terrified me.

"You could join me," it said. "Live free; go where you choose; do what you choose."

"What about family?" I asked. My chest ached and I tried not to look at Tina. "Lovers? Children?"

"The families of multitudes will live within you."

"Because I killed them."

"Their lives will sustain you."

Despite the depression I'd suffered for months, this wasn't a difficult choice at all. I didn't want to die, but I certainly didn't want to spend eternity eating people alive, like cancer. I shook my head, never breaking eye contact with the strange creature.

"No."

"Then I shall leave you to your slow death."

It rose with uncanny grace and walked out the open door into the night. I trembled so hard against the wall I smacked my head and hurt my back. The relief of surviving was almost as strong as the guilt of it. I made myself take slow, even breaths and tried to slow my fluttering heart.

An arm snagged me from around the edge of the door.

I went sailing backwards as the creature yanked me through the doorway. Arms like steel bands crushed me again a bony chest and cut off my yelp. Scorching breath seared my throat. I fought like a madman, but the creature's strength was absolute. A shriek hit my eardrums like shards of glass. The fingernails on one of its hands grew into talons, and with one stab, it pierced my throat.

All the heat flowed out of me. I shivered uncontrollably, clutching at the thing. Dizziness swept over me and I reeled. Pleasure coursed through me like a morphine injection. I floated in perfection and had no desire to move. I was going to drown in bliss.

Its face appeared in front of me, hovering like an apparition.

"Why?" I whispered.

"It's what I do."

Using a talon, it sliced its wrist and pressed it to my lips. Unable to resist, I lapped at the liquid rushing into my mouth to the irresistibly sweet song of its laughter.

"What *we* do now. Together. Forever."

* * *

Inspired by Whitley Strieber's novel and the David Bowie film, "The Hunger," as well as my partner's struggle with cancer.

Stardust, Always

A Passing Peace

Diana Hudson

I don't know where I am. I don't know how I got here. All I can remember is being led here by an almost non-corporeal being. She entered this stone maze with me but, as the entrance closed behind us, she vanished, leaving only trailing words.

"Find your way to the garden. Find your way to peace."

Peace is not a word I have been familiar with for a long time. The past few years were torment. Torment and pain for myself and everyone I loved. This seemed to be no different, but if there is truly peace in the center of this maze, then I will find it. I am not the kind of person to just give up.

My first order of business is to assess where I am—besides a maze; that part is pretty obvious. It is cold and the walls are chiseled stone. I only have two directions to choose from, right or left. I evaluate both directions. They look the same, no discernible distinctions, except I am drawn to the left. It is almost like fate is telling me this is the way I need to go. I turn and walk down the long corridor. There are no openings nor way to see what may lay beyond the confines of this wall. I reach out and touch the stone on the inside wall, a slight vibration emanates from the wall and I can feel it pass through my body. It reminds me of the energy from a tuning fork. The stone I'm touching begins to move and vibrate, as do some of the surrounding stones. When they attune themselves to the same frequency, the section opens up into a doorway, presenting a new corridor.

Once I pass through the threshold, the old passageway is sealed off. It seems that whatever path I take, I have no way of returning to a past option. So I have to make sure that my choices are something I can live with, so to speak.

* * *

This new corridor has a different atmosphere about it. It feels lighter, almost childlike. I remember playing as a child with my friends. Playing in the creek, catching frogs until the sun went down and hearing my mother's voice calling me to come inside and get cleaned up for dinner. A tear slips down my cheek. That was a long time ago but it's as fresh as if it were yesterday. I walk further down, wiping the tear from my face, knowing my family have long since passed. The further I walk, the more the air changes. It's almost aging the further I go. I come upon an area where a choice has to be made: straight or right. I examine each area very carefully. They all look the same but the feelings that emanate from each direction are vastly different.

The feeling I get from the corridor straight in front of me is as if it was suffocating. The area to the left feels strange, like a flushing heat. I don't like this feeling so I turn away and opt to go down the corridor on the right. The moment I walk a few feet in, the path behind me seals. As I walk, I see images in my mind of a family trip to the beach when I was barely a teenager. As I recall these events, I hear a voice that sounds like it was coming from nearby but from nowhere at the same time.

"As you recount this family trip, remember the choice you made. The path that went straight was the sailing trip with your friends you wanted to go on instead. That trip ended in disaster and you lost one of your friends. Had you gone, you would not have survived. You chose right to go with your family. Continue on; I am sorry for your loss."

I walk along, pondering those words. What other choices could have led me astray? I try to take a deep breath, but am hindered by the quality of air around me. I cough, trying to catch my breath. I recover when I feel a pressure on my right shoulder and someone holding my left hand. I felt comfort, something I haven't felt in a long time. It was time to progress.

The next section I come upon is a dead end with only two doors. One is old and made of the same stone as the walls surrounding me. The other is wood and looks out of place. I place my hand on the wood and try to suss out the emotions coming from it, but I get nothing. I do the same with the stone door with the same outcome. So, I have to make a blind choice. I close my eyes and try to feel a draw toward one door or the other and lean in towards the wooden one. Reaching out, I push it open.

The cold air hits me like a ton of bricks. It is cold and the smell of chemicals to create a sterile environment is overpowering. The cleanliness is everywhere, disinfectant and antiseptic that made everything sterile, burning my eyes. I know I am in a hospital. I had felt this sting to my senses before. That's when I remember being sixteen and in a car accident. I remember the pain and fear I felt. The list of injuries I had were extensive but I fully recovered in time. This is when that same floating voice comes to me again.

"This was a fixed point. You would have ended up here regardless of the door you chose. This was part of your fate. Some things in life are a learning experience and are meant to be. They will not be any different than what is meant to happen. This was one of those moments in your life. Continue on."

Those haunting words make me uncomfortable for some reason. While I can't understand the reason for this, I am beginning to lose faith that everything is going to be okay. However, somewhere deep inside me, I am sure I will find a new meaning to my faith somewhere, within this labyrinth of my past. Continuing down the long passage, I begin to get that prickling of your hair when you know something bad is coming. That's when I see the opening to the left side. I think about just passing it and continuing on this path but I know that isn't the answer. I was told I had to make peace, so I turn left.

I am again in a hospital, this time sitting beside a bed. I am only eighteen and I have to say goodbye to my grandfather. I don't understand why; I just know that I will no longer have him to go fishing with and to play chess with. My heart sinks as I recall when we were told he was gone. Now, everything is clear. He had lung cancer from all the labor he did as a young man working in some deplorable conditions that would never be allowed in today's time.

* * *

I compose myself and continue on. This corridor is long and chilly. I don't feel completely whole. I feel sick. I can't understand why I am feeling this way when I hadn't been this way earlier. The further I go, the more I lose energy and I have to push myself to the opening that I almost overlook on the right. When I turn and see the path behind me close, I understand why I feel so unwell. It's how I felt in this memory. I am in a doctor's office and I can see the look on his face as he reads over my chart. He lets out an exasperated breath as he tries to find the words that will ultimately change my life forever. He looks at me with despair and torment in his eyes. Then those chilling words come.

"I'm sorry, but your tests came back positive. You have cancer. We can try to treat it aggressively and we are hopeful for remission."

I continue, seeing the times I went in for a treatment regimen of pills and chemo. My hair slowly thins and, before long, is gone. I see the weight loss as if it happened overnight. I watch my body go through these changes in a blink of an eye instead of the years it actually took. I see myself back in the office and the doctor sitting across from me again. He looks over test results and paperwork from everything I had been through trying to battle for my life.

"None of the treatments are reducing the cancer cells. I am sorry, so sorry, but the only thing we can do is make you comfortable." He hands me the paperwork for hospice care. I will have to give up and leave my family and go into a hospice care facility or I can remain in my home with my family until the last possible moments. I don't want to be a burden to my family but I am not ready to leave them yet.

I stop and lean back against the wall, sliding down to sit with my knees against my chest, my head buried in my arms. I can't fully comprehend what is going on and why I am seeing this. I hear the same ethereal voice. It is calming to me at this point in time.

"You have seen the good times, and the bad times, and the times to say goodbye. You have seen your circle of life. Everything begins, and everything comes to an end. It's nature; it's life. Do you understand this now?"

I stifle back more tears and say, "I understand now. This is my time. This is my time to end this life and begin anew."

"You are correct. You are almost to the garden and your peace."

I gather myself together and stand. I walk forward and out of this memory. There, before me on the left, is an opening to a small patio-like area. I walk inside and stand as the exit vanishes yet again. This seems to be a reflective area. I can smell a garden, but there are no doors or openings in this circular chamber of the labyrinth. I have to figure out how to get out of here. I walk the circumference of the room, running my fingers along the stone walls. This time there are no vibrations nor does anything even attempt to open. When I turn back to the center, a small fountain has formed.

I walk over to it and, as I gaze into the falling water, I am surrounded by a sense that I know everything has a reason. I can see the whole of my life playing within the droplets of water as they fall. I was not perfect, as I much suspect no one really is. I can see that I made a life for myself and for my family. But as I watch myself grow older and older, I realize that I lived a full and meaningful life. I had friends and family who loved me and physical possessions didn't mean anything anymore. It is all about the love I feel at this moment. The soft voice approaches me once again.

"Do you understand now?"

Pondering the question, I answer the best I can. "I believe I do. You said I had to find peace. I have found peace within my life that I did the best I could. That should account for something. I know I was not always the best person, but I loved and was loved in return. I am not ready to go yet though. I have so much more I can accomplish."

"You have done what you were supposed to do. You lived a long and loving life. You have generations of family and one life that is just beginning. You are not missing any of it."

I think about what the voice just said and it hits me so hard, that last statement makes things so clear. "You mean, my granddaughter, she's pregnant?"

"She is. She will have a beautiful little girl who will grow to become someone special all because of the stories told of your life. When one life ends, one life begins."

For the first time, I truly understand. "I'm ready." I speak those words with such commitment that it surprises even myself.

In the blink of an eye, a passage appears in front of me, leading down me to the opening of a completely different area. It is as if I'm standing in a botanical garden, smells abounding and flowers blooming bright. Fruit hangs from the trees. I know I have found the peace I have been searching for. I have made it. However, I know my journey is not quite over just yet. A young woman, dressed completely in white, appears. Her long dress flows within a breeze only she can feel because, to me, not a breath is stirring.

"You have found peace. Your time is almost up. I think you already know what is happening."

I purse my lips and look to the woman, as I realize just who she is. "I do. You are the angel here to guide me to death."

"In a way. I am here help you find the peace within your life to be able to pass in solace. For you are not dead yet. You still have one important thing left to do. Say goodbye. Then you will meet the angel who will guide you from this life to the next. You may take your time, just know that your body grows weaker, but your family is all by your side."

I am ready. Not ready to leave them, not ready to have to miss the future and the time with the baby that is still growing. I am ready because I know it is my time and I will see my family again in the next life. I know and I am comfortable in that knowledge.

"I am ready. Can you take me to them?" I prepare myself for the complete change in reality. The woman leans in and kissed my cheek.

Everything around me fades into nothingness. I can hear everything within the darkness, some are loud sounds and others are soft words that I can't quite make out. My eyes flutter and shocking bright light floods into my vision.

I can hear the voices of my family more clearly now, yelling for the nurse because my eyes are open. It takes me a moment to realize that I am lying in a bed, my bed. I feel the familiar sounds and smells around me, I am home. I see everyone around me, tears in their eyes and smiles on their faces. It pains me to know that those smiles are going to be short-lived.

I try to speak, my voice raspy. "I love you all. Just know that I am happy and I found my peace with everything and within my life. I will be okay. My sweet, beautiful granddaughter, can you come here and take my hand?"

Her young hand slides into my withered hand. "You have the light of this world within you. You take care of that baby now, you hear."

Her face looks shocked, "How, how did you know? I only found out yesterday."

"An angel told me." I hold her, our last hug in this life.

I look to the corner of the room and see another beautiful, ethereal woman, this time dressed in a black, flowing dress, and I know my time is up. I whisper, "I'm ready."

As she comes closer, her beauty shines down upon me and the last thing I ever feel is her lips against mine.

I can only say one last thing as I feel my essence pull away, "Always remember me. I love you all."

I can hear the echo of everyone in the room as the night creeps in. "Always"

One last time I hear the voices of the two beautiful

angels as they speak as one. "For now you are within the stars, free to be the starlight in the sky to watch over your loved ones, until you meet again."

* * *

In memory of my father, Michael Hudson, who passed shortly after surgery to become cancer-free, and my grandfather, Lloyd White, who passed from prostate cancer. This is also dedicated to my cousin, Beth Birchfield, who is fighting her battle bravely and refuses to give up.

For My Father

Andrew Barber

Part One—Before
December 18 2010

I was sleeping
When Mum called.
My first thought was that someone had died.
I was half right.
Someone was dying.

It's only been a couple of months
Since you said you had prostate cancer
And I almost cheered.
Apart from skin cancer,
The prostate form has the highest survival rates.
If you have to have any,
At least have one that can be cured.

Then came the news
That, like the human race itself,
It had spread and colonised.
It insinuated itself into the bones,
Commuting around their rigid infrastructure
Like a subway map,
And targeting the liver,
Where it got much more aggressive.

And now you know you're dying,
But you don't know when,
Father, mother, other son
Entering into a pact of voluntary unknowing
Because, as my brother said,
You would count down your days
Like an advent calendar.

Do you have days, weeks, months?
Only the doctors know
And they have been banned from speaking.

Whatever you have is not enough,
Not enough for me to say
What I should have been saying all along,
Thanking you for all you have taught me.

You gave me the joy of music,
The music of maths,
The logic with which I try to understand the world.

I didn't thank you because
I was proud and stubborn
And thought I'd learnt these things myself.

But it was your genes that gave me
The chance to do so,
Your songs I listened to when I was growing up,
Your impregnable numeracy that propelled me through
my career.

Thank you Dad
A thousand times, thank you.

Part Two—After
January 28 2011
9:00 AM

Mum rang again,
This time in tears.
It was done.

The oncological mystery tour was over.
The music had stopped
While the fat lady was still dressing as a Valkyrie.

There were no last words:
In a final insult to a life spent talking,
Morphine absorbed the power of speech.

By the end, even the lungs were ravaged.
All soft tissue between the groin and the clavicle
Bore the taint of the invasion.

Cancer patients are not resuscitated,
Apparently.
One strike and you're out.

One struck
And my father died.

And what struck me immediately
Was the regret,
The total lack of opportunities
To talk to you again,
Discussing steam trains and cricket,
Not because I wanted to -

Because it was worth it
To hear the enthusiasm in your voice,
Nostalgic for a time
That we cared about
The same things.

Stardust, Always

I wish I wasn't an atheist.
I'd love to believe in your soul
Ascending to heaven
Like soot from a candle
When your light went out.
I know all that will remain
Is the ash from your immolated husk
And the memories of you.

But they are immortal
And I'm not the only one to have them.

* * *

Dedicated to Alan Francis Barber'

Always Stardust

Joshua L. Cejka

Three important men occupied the reception area outside the doors of The Prince's office. The first two were the sort you would expect: confident and well groomed, they stood shifting their excellent shoes under themselves as though the world should take note and be impressed. Staring with an equal measure of judgment and approval at the decor, they juggled the sheafs of official looking papers in their subtle and elegant portfolios. Recognizing that a pretty woman was also present, the two men tried, in vain, to position themselves in the room such that the still fetching eyes of the no longer young receptionist, Ms. Archer, would gravitate to them. When they noticed the stumps where her first two fingers should have been, they quickly turned away to measure themselves against the third man.

When he'd come in, Mrs. Archer put her hands to her mouth but a smile leaked through the vacancy where her fingers should have been. He jauntily doffed his shocking green hat at her and smiled back. Had the other men been slightly less concerned with radiating seriousness and gravity, they might have noticed an entire conversation passing between the ridiculous looking fop and the pretty receptionist. It ended with questioning eyes bouncing over the two of them and back at Ms. Archer. She shrugged a little. He dropped himself on the mauve couch with an insouciance that suggested he was prepared to wait comfortably till the end of time if need be.

In those few minutes they shared the space, it became clear that the two standing men were less than duly impressed with the man on the couch. They nudged each other as he pulled a battered notebook from a pocket. They stifled an impolite giggle as he began to hum. He paid them no mind, jotting carefully with a pen that appeared to have been made by the finest dwarven craftsmen. One of the men shrugged at the other and then relaxed into the important business they were to conduct.

"I'm a little worried, Jarry."

"About what?"

"That he won't see how critical this is. He's already shown a willingness to ..."

"If you're talking about the Elves and the Dwarves again ... "

"Of course I am, Jarry. Not just permitting them passage. That would have been understandable. Kind. Compassionate even, But to permit them to stay ..."

"Completely different, Carl. Anyone with a brain can see the dangers involved. He is not a stupid man."

"But does he take it seriously? As seriously as he should?"

"These are vampires. Werewolves. Even if some of them have forsworn human blood in the name of their heathen religion ... it's in their nature. You can't change the stripes on a pig. He knows this." Jarry, clearly the politician of the two, maneuvered his cravat a little around his throat. "But I think you're right. We should start with the religious angle."

"Really? I was just going to say we should start with the political angle. The will of the people and all that."

The man in the green glanced at Carl's strange head gear. It looked like a very nice ceramic bowl on his head. He raised his eyebrow at Mrs. Archer who nodded thin-lipped in response.

A priest.

The slight movement of the Green Man drew Jarry's attention. He swiveled his shoulders to allow himself a disinterested glance at the green man, which immediately became a much more interested glance.

The man in the green was now in blue. Brilliant orange hair flared from his skull and a flicker of lightning shot from the orange to his perfect chin. The man looked up at them as though the politicians glance was interrupting his concentration on his humming.

"The religious argument is more inscrutable." The Politician regained his practiced indifference and turned back to the door.

"What's inscrutable mean?"

"Formidable. Harder to refute. It's difficult to turn down appeals to the greater good when couched in religion."

"Yes, Jarry, but I think the political ... the will of the people ..."

"The Prince is a politician, Carl. Politicians are skilled in maneuvering around populist proposals. Trust me."

The Priest in his satin vanilla hassock shifted from one foot to the other. Had he looked, he might have seen the smile Mrs. Archer and the man now in blue shared.

"If you say so ..."

"It's the best way to go, Carl. He can't resist the ... ummm ... logic of a religious appeal."

"And we have the will of the people to fall back on ..."

"Exactly so."

The man now in blue, hummed a little more. The notes suggested just a hint of warning. Mrs. Archer stifled a giggle and stood up from behind the desk, went around it and placed her three fingers on the door.

"Gentlemen, The Prince will see you now." The doors must have weighed a ton but she flung them open as though they were made of paper. Then she stood aside and gestured with the disfigured hand.

"Remember, Carl—this is important. We cannot fail."

"Critical." Carl nodded.

"It has been a pleasure, Ms. Archer," Jarry muttered as she let the door close behind them.

There was a brief chortle of shared laughter they could hear behind them as the door slowly closed.

"It certainly will be, Councilman Dingle." She smiled through the thinning crack. He utterly failed to read it accurately.

The priest stole one last look as the bright light of the doorway diminished to a sliver. The man on the couch, still humming and writing, had now turned silver. He was grinning at them and waving. The priest could see his teeth. Then the door closed them in.

***

It seemed a mile from the door to the desk behind which sat The Prince. Between them, a vast green carpet which followed the angular walls to a blunted point just before the desk. Both men, standing on the broad edge of it, were forced to consider the distance and how it narrowed like a throat, and how its rich colors and thick shag seemed capable of hiding alligators. This far away, The Prince was a distant black smudge blotting out the sun seeping in the windows behind him. They heard the skritching of his pen on parchment like nails raking a nearby chalkboard.

No one knew where he'd come from. Because they were distantly aware that they had a King, they were marginally familiar with the concept of princes, but until he'd actually shown up alone with only the royal retinue and a missive with the Kings Mark they'd never believed they would actually see one.

And now here he sat. Princes were supposed to be young wastrels, spending the king's coin and getting into trouble. The city had prepared for a certain amount of rapaciousness. Instead, they got an older gentleman who wasted no time for even a coronation celebration. He simply got to work.

Aside from the scratching, the silence in the room was huge and solid. Both men knew that they couldn't even risk a whisper without it getting funneled straight down the throat of the space and into the ears of The Prince. They could only clash their suddenly nervous gazes and take a step.

Men of their type prided themselves on their ability to gird up their masculinity even in the face of sense and reason. They were transfixed in the faith of their own importance. If there was something they paid attention to, it immediately made it important. What they fixated on was deemed worthy of fixating on. Yet here they were, facing down the maw of the office, seeing for the first time—it seemed—at what actual industry and work looked like. It looked like work. Papers, petitions, and reports were everywhere. Silently, they agreed their way was better. To be perceived as serious and business-minded was much better than actually being serious and business-minded.

They took a step, and then another, quickly accomplishing the distance, noses slightly raised as though keeping their eyes from investigating the green at their feet in case it actually did hold alligators. Somewhere, a clock ticked away quietly, marking the soft sounds of their feet shuffling along. By the time they reached the desk, their failing confidence and quaking self possession had their feet moving nearly at a run.

The Prince didn't look up, even when they nearly skittered into the desk. His pen skritched again and finished with a flourish. The two men waited, hearing their own heavy breathing.

The Prince waved the freshly inked paper in the air for a moment, and then laid the page on a teetering pile with an arm that swam through the air with graceful menace. Then he sat back and allowed the imposing chair to absorb him as he placed his elbow on the arm and laid his finger along his cheek. His eyes did their best to gently skewer the men before him.

"Gentlemen." His voice was like a vat of butter, and the words came out as patient and forgiving as an octopus about to drink the body of a clam.

"Your worship." Jarry adjusted his tie. He'd worn it to impress. It was brilliant blue silk, but he had to admit he didn't like the way The Prince looked at it: like he was trying to calculate how long it would take him to use it to choke the life out of him.

"My liege ...," Carl gasped.

The Prince waited.

He looked like a man who could muster who could watch mountains grind themselves to desert, but once his patience had finally worn thin, his vengeance would appear like the aftermath of a huge turkey dinner, languorously slipping one into a lovely pool of oblivion.

"You are the assemblyman for Whitedoe Bay?" The Prince pulled a scrap of paper from the pile on his left and dropped it in front of him as though it had recently been used in a public bathroom.

Jarry nodded.

"Yes, My liege."

"The people call it Widow's Bay, do they not?"

"The jealous and petty do, My Lord."

The Prince said nothing, but pulled another piece of paper from the left of the desk and again dropped it in front of him.

"And you are the High Priest of Pudding, Lord Emberton ... known to friends and family as ... Carl."

"Yes sir. You may call me Carl, if you wish."

The Prince's eyes flashed at him like a rattlesnake bite, the brow arching quickly and then settling back to rest like a feather falling.

"I've had the opportunity ... ," He lingered on 'opportunity' as though it tasted like curdled carriage grease, "of perusing your proposals ..."

"Then you are aware of how vital they are to the safety and security of everyone." Jarry smiled and nodded, not knowing what else to do.

"As you can see they're well considered and well vetted by both the religious congregation and the constituents ..."

"Of Widow's Bay." The Prince finished with a sliver of a smile so thin you could cut yourself with it if you weren't careful.

"You object to my proposal to give shelter to the supernatural populations fleeing the purges of Nobresk?"

Jarry and Carl shared a quick look.

"Not ... object ... per se, sir ..."

"I'm sure your reasoning was sound and compassionate, it's just that ..."

"Given the religious sentiment ..."

"And the will of the people ..."

"We feel it is too hasty to bring them into the fold, as it

were."

Carl tittered a little.

"Thus the proposals ..."

"Which, actually, should help facilitate your compassionate plan."

The Prince pinched one of the papers between his fingers and held it at arm's length as though it stank.

"If I am correct, you would have me confiscate farm land to the north, erect large enclosures, keep the refugees in those enclosures ..."

"Only until such time as they can be assimilated and take in the gospel of pudding."

"The People of White Doe are uncomfortable with the prospect of Vampires and Werewolves wandering among them, eating their food ..."

"Dating their teenaged daughters ...," the Prince finished.

"Exactly so, My Liege. And spreading their heinous, violent religion ..."

The Prince dropped the sheet again. It hit an air pocket and drifted to the floor without him even shifting his eyes to it. His body drifted to the other side of the chair and he stared at the Priest.

"Tell me, Minister, which orthodoxy would you preach: Vanilla or Chocolate?"

Carl took a step back.

"Vanilla, of course. Chocolate is heretical, as you very well know."

"Yes. You've illustrated that quite well, with all the corpses lined along the Kingsway."

He tapped his chin with a long finger.

"And the people of Widow's Bay support your proposal?"

"As you can see, we have over 500 signatures."

"They wouldn't all be drawn from your congregation would they, Minister?"

"I don't see how that would be relevant, My Liege."

"You really don't do you?" The Prince tapped his chin again as he stared at them. Neither of the men particularly liked the gaze. It felt piercing.

"Well, gentlemen. I appreciate your coming. I will review this proposal with as much consideration as it is due. Now," He smiled. They relaxed a little, surprised at the brightness in it.

"I have a task for each of you. Minister ..."

"Could you at least give some consideration to their wearing some sort of identifying mark?" Jarry had to interject, and instantly regretted it.

"I will deliberate upon the wisdom of all of your proposals, Assemblyman. For the good of the province, as you say. Now then, as I said, I have charges for both of you."

The Prince spoke slowly, each word fattening like a droplet before escaping his lips.

"Councilman, here at City Hall we have a few pets in the basement. The children love them. I was wondering if I could ask you to feed them today? I'm afraid our usual pet handler had a nasty on the job accident yesterday and will be unable to adequately perform his duties."

Jarry didn't much like the idea, feeling it was beneath the dignity of an elected dignitary. But there was no saying no to The Prince.

"I'd be delighted, My Liege."

"Excellent. Mrs. Archer will show you the way."

"What shall I feed them?"

"I'm quite sure you'll find something suitable. Mrs. Archer knows what they like."

The Prince turned to look at Carl but somehow it felt more like he was being pulled into view.

"Minister, as you know, there is a great forest near the lakes to the west. A population of Pudding-less men have taken up residence in that forest and I believe they are in need of the gospel of Pudding. I hoped you would take up a mission there."

"I will dispatch a priest forthwith."

"I believe it would show The People more consideration if you yourself took up the ministry there. To show your extreme faith in their conversion, as it were."

Carl tipped his weight to his other foot, suddenly feeling heavy.

"You do mean, sir, the Black Band?"

"I don't know what they call themselves, Minister. Entrepreneurial sort from what I understand."

Carl would have called them bandits, but not in the presence of the Prince.

"It will be done, my liege. As you know—everyone loves pudding." He swallowed his own words and found them bitter.

"Indeed." The Prince smiled and shoveled another paper from the pile. Without another word he took up his pen again. Iron gray hair enclosed his face. The men stood a moment more until they realized they'd just been dismissed.

The man formerly in green, formerly with lightning streaking across his face, passed them as they crossed the great green carpet again. He flung himself on a couch as the door closed.

"You enjoy that far too much. Why didn't you simply execute them?" He was in green again, but this time it was more of an emerald.

"I thought I had." The Prince sighed into his papers.

"I mean in a formal sense ... a princely sense."

"Far too messy. Executions send a statement. This is much cleaner."

The Duke, whose hair had gone a spiky white, lolled his head over the sumptuous arm of the couch to get a better look.

"Sometimes I worry about you."

The Prince gave him his best forebearingly innocent look and shrugged.

"Some days I worry about me too."

"Well ... I suppose it's easier than the old days." He noticed the large axe on the wall crossed with an ornate long rifle with silver elven inlays along the stock.

" ... I see you've kept them, just in case."

"You would think one of the petitioners would have noticed them before now. Not a single one."

The Duke fished inside the emerald cloak. Improbably drawing a full sized guitar from a pocket, he began to pluck it before the clothing changed again to rustic browns and fine leather.

"Can't you do something about that?" The Prince glared at him.

The Duke stopped plucking for a moment to pick at the fine leather waistcoat that had appeared on him.

"It's a curse, Alan. You aren't supposed to 'do something' about a curse except live with it." The Duke grinned.

"It's irritating."

"It has its uses. I didn't have to become a prince for one."

The Prince gave him an impatient look that suggested he didn't believe a word of it, but the Duke failed to notice as he tuned his guitar. Single notes filled the room, instantly robbing it of some of its gloom.

"Alright. It's true. I just prefer *not* to do anything about it. Kaedi looks nice. Haven't seen her in forever."

"It's Mrs. Archer now. She's taken up knife throwing."

"How is she?"

"As deadly as ever. You should see her with a pistol. She doesn't appreciate the noise though."

The Prince raked his fingers through the curtain of iron hair at his friend. The massive chair no longer absorbed him as he flung one leg up on the desk. The Duke's smile melted as his friend let out all the air that seemed to be supporting him.

"It's that bad is it?"

"What have you heard? Did you see Loony?" The Prince tapped. The Duke tried to ignore the heavy and impatient sadness that crowded around his friend like a third person in the room.

"Yes. I saw him."

"And?"

The Duke held out an open hand and shrugged before returning to twisting the pegs on the guitar.

"He says it's not a question of Ether."

"I thought as much."

"It's a problem of Stardust. You know how the Elves are ... particularly the shaggy northern ones: all riddles."

"What did he say?"

"The stardust in her body has fallen out of alignment. The body wars against itself ..."

"So the Wizards are wrong. As usual. Did he have a cure?"

"She needs a Prophet."

"Don't we all." The Prince muttered. He was not a man to fidget but he couldn't help to shovel around bits of stray paper into slightly less disorganized piles.

"'Prophets set right what is wrong in the stars.'"

"Did he have any brilliant insights where we might find one fairly quickly?"

The Duke didn't answer. His fingers flashed out a trilling deep cascade of notes that stirred vivid memories in both men. The notes slowed to a long sustain that collapsed gently into silence.

"How is she?"

"Dying, David. And she knows it." The curtain of hair fell in front of his face for a moment. He pushed it back and David could see fresh wetness on his friends cheek. "She keeps her spirits up. And the rest of the ward."

"So, like her mother then?"

The Prince choked on a memory that perked up one corner of his mouth.

"She tells them stories of us."

"She knows then."

"Of course she does, she's her mothers daughter. But she keeps our secrets well. All of our secrets."

"Have you told her?"

"Why? What would be the point in knowing?"

"There's the truth and then there's Truth, Alan. Sometimes you can see truth. Sometimes you need to feel it."

"You have been spending too much time with the Elves. You're starting to talk like them."

"You've chosen your exile, i've chosen mine."

"Damnable Bards. You always think you can change the world with music."

"Because we can. Damn you warriors, always thinking you can change the world by acting bravely."

"If only you could sing her out of this with a song."

"If only." His fingers played the strings again, starting strong and fast but diminishing with sudden hopelessness. "And if only this was something you could swing an axe or shoot at ..."

The music continued still, little notes plucked on strings that swelled and filled the space, finding their feet and standing up. The Duke kept at it, entranced by his own sound until he heard another noise that didn't belong.

"I can't lose her again, David."

The Duke stopped the music with a gentle rap on the guitar body. His oldest living friend cradled his stubbled chin in his hand. He stared at the desk and the papers in front of him as though they were a million miles away and made of dust. It was hard not to see how old he looked and how time had done what hordes of enemies couldn't. He wondered if that was how he looked? A ridiculous old man in clothes that couldn't stay the same from moment to moment?

"You remember that time in the Caves?" The Duke started when he'd found his voice. A slight smile cracked The Prince's face.

"With the Dragon?"

"With the Dragon. I was down to my last charge, you were barely able to keep your arms up ..."

The Prince's smile widened, the memory shining in his eyes now.

"Who would have thought that would work?"

"She did. I don't know if she really thought it would. But she just decided 'no one's tried this before' and went ahead and did it."

"She could talk a—" His tongue tripped trying to find an apt metaphor but discovered the reality of what she'd done outstripped all hyperbole. "Well ... she did it."

"There was never a moment where all was lost, Alan. There still isn't. We'll find a way."

The Prince nodded as though he wanted to believe it but couldn't.

"Time to be heroes again?" He smiled weakly.

"It's always time to be heroes, my friend. We've worn many faces for so many people ... .Might as well put that one back on and see if it still fits." The Duke's suit rippled and became black with a simple white cravat. He shifted his icy blue hair back and tried to smile.

"I'm not sure that role fits anymore."

The Duke searched his friend's collapsed form and his blanched face.

"It was always an act, Alan. You just didn't know you were playing it. We lose the things we can't afford to. That's how Life teaches us how to live ... and when it comes to it, how to die."

"When did you become such a philosopher?" The Prince smiled. It was a weak smile, crammed with years and distance, but it was seeded with good memories. The Duke took it, held it for a moment in his eyes and then ventured to ask.

"Can I see her?"

The dark black of the Prince's form shot from his chair and he clasped his friends arm, pulling him effortlessly to his feet. The Duke had long ago forgotten how strong he was.

"Of course. When was the last time?"

"It was before she fell ill. She was very little. Barely a baby."

"You've been gone far too long, David. We're far too old and have far too few friends left to keep up appearances for proprieties sake."

The Duke, standing, raised an eyebrow at his friend.

"People will talk. They might be mostly stupid, but even stupid people put things together some time or other." The Duke slung his guitar on his back and shrugged. "Could be a bit dangerous."

"Then I guess we'll be heroes again, if just for today." The smile didn't quite reach his eyes, but it was trying and that was better than nothing.

***

The Duke stifled a smirk watching the nurses on the ward recoil from his friend and push their tiny, emaciated charges out of the way of his sweeping black cloak. They had no idea who he was. Not really. All they saw was The Prince: the formidable source of dread. The children—so small and sunken, their eyes darkened with sleepless nights full of pain—grinned broadly and pulled away from the nurses, trying to get a better look at the dignitaries drifting through their midst. The Duke let his coat turn a yellow spotted with red dots. Elegant tails flowed out behind him. He could control it, a little, here and there. He shot a mischievous grin to a little girl with no hair clinging to a door frame.

Alan knew the way. As so often with him, the way cleared ahead of him but this time it was more from fear than reverence. He took a left and strode quickly on until the blue speckled tiles ran into a very large man in a doctors costume. The 'doctor' brought a fist to his chest and bowed.

"Sir."

"How is she today, Captain?" The captain's eyes drifted over to the comical Duke in his red and yellow coat, lingering for a moment on the neck of the guitar peeking out from behind his back.

"Well, My Liege. She's been telling stories this morning and practicin' her 'spells'."

The Captain opened the door to the room. A clot of children in hospital gowns mobbed around a bed in the center of which sat a girl, a smile cocked up one side of her face heading for her slightly pointed ears. She saw them in the doorway and grinned. It was the same smile David remembered—the one he hadn't seen in ten years. He stopped in his tracks, his breath gone as though the Captain had knocked it out of him. Without knowing it, he clutched the door frame and wondered why his knees suddenly left him.

It was like seeing a ghost.

"Dear Gods, Alan ..." He flung the name out without

meaning to and felt the Captain shoot his Prince a curious look.

"I know." The Prince said, grasping his friends arm.

"She ..." He couldn't continue. The girl looked at the two of them, her grin widening and becoming toothy and her eyes brightening even through the shadows surrounding them. The bright copper hair wasn't there—just a round dome of pale terminating at the slightly pointed ears and there was a weariness on her sunken cheeks but there was no mistaking those features.

"My Prince!" She called from the clot of children who all scattered like mice. The girl dumped herself off the expansive bed and shot her way over to them, enclosing The Prince in arms that were far too frail. They only held enough strength to hold his friend together. "I was just telling them of Alan at The River. The way he battled the elemental with nothing but a rock."

"Don't forget the elven wizard who helped," he reminded her with a smile that betrayed only a trace of the fear and pain he felt.

"Of course not. Nor David's song. The one that stopped the waters."

"That he never missed an opportunity to remind them of."

The girl glanced around the big black form. She seemed tiny next to the Prince.

"And who is this, a new guest?"

"This is my friend."

The Duke let his coat turn a deep purple and go longer still, flowing around his boots.

"The White Duke!" She said, her grin brightening even further. "You never told me you knew him." She held out a tiny hand. The Duke choked on a tear as he reached for it. He knew his eyes were like diamonds and no song could stop those waters.

"Duke. This is my charge, Lily."

"Charmed." He said, meaning it more deeply than she could ever know.

"Did you know my mother too?"

The waters came full force now as though every sad song he knew burst forth and all the magic they held dropped around him. It was powerful magic.

"I did, my dear."

Good gods, Alan, He thought. *If ever there was a time to be a hero* ... He looked into the girls smoky jade eyes and saw so much of the past and far too much of the present. He'd seen his friend be brave in the darkest places. He'd seen things he couldn't put into song. But only he knew, in that moment, what sort of courage he'd been ekeing out for the past few years.

This time we have to win. He thought. This is what is important.

A rough hand, used to the hilt of a weapon, grasped his, unseen between them. It clenched harder than he remembered. Was it still strong enough?

"Come on then, Duke. Give us a song."

What song could he give? What could be done for a ward full of children? And the big world outside full of important men making big decisions ... The Prince, his friend, pretending to be one of them ... What the hells was all of that to a ward full of children?

Music could save the world. He had faith in that. But Alan was right too ... acting brave was the same thing as real bravery. He pulled the guitar off his back and began to play.

Eventually, he found words to go with it.

Diagnostic

Zoé Perrenoud

One day
last year
it came so fast
we heard you
put a use-by date
on all those unlived promises

we speak without
a care

Today
right now
and far too quick
we watch you
leave before the end
to all those unknown afterlives

you slip beyond
our reach

Some day
sometime
but not too soon
we'll meet you
on the other side
of all those unshared memories

that sever us

       from you

Oubliette

Lacey D. Sutton

I have never been in a crash before, and I have no memory of being in this one. One moment there was a wall of white headed towards me. I blinked and there was bright sunlight streaming through cracks in the snow that covered the windshield. The plasticized metal mesh of a deflated airbag pooled in my lap and a sharp, burning smell filled the car.

David Bowie still crooned from the car's stereo, from the mix CD my sister had given me.

As the pain sweeps through
Makes no sense for you
Every thrill has gone
Wasn't too much fun
At all
But I'll be there for yoooooooou-o-hoooo
As the world falls down

Falling...

That's right. I had been trying to eject the disc when ... when whatever happened. I exhaled and struggled to draw in the next through the anguish that flared through my chest. My eyes filled with tears and my mind filled with shock.

A muffled sound slowly penetrated my awareness. After a moment I identified it as knocking at the driver-side window. I turned my head and other parts of my body screamed their distress at me. The snow that covered the front of the car did not obscure the entire side window. Through the fogged, icy glass, I swear I saw a familiar face.

"Sandy?" I croaked and fumbled for the door handle.

Snow cascaded onto my arm as I pushed open the creaking door and I jerked back, then bit down against the renewed agony. The light was blinding, stabbing my eyes as I squinted out at the scene outside my car.

Sometime in the past few minutes the sun must have broken into the grey winter day, but something was off about the colors. A world that should have been pale blues and blacks was yellow-whites, golds and greens. The scene blurred and wavered, and I closed my eyes to block out a vision that made no sense.

"Hit my head ... harder than I thought ..." Rubbing my aching forehead, I looked for the person I had glimpsed through the window, then felt like smacking my head again. It must have been my own reflection. Sandy and I had always been mistaken for twins, even though we had been born four years apart. Seeing her here was impossible. I'd been on the way to her funeral, after all.

I leaned my aching body back in the seat, struggling to breathe normally, to think normally, to do anything that could be considered normal in this situation.

So, I did what any normal person would: I passed out.

* * *

Feverish and sticky, I drifted back into consciousness. Childhood memories of napping in the sun washed over me, but it had to be in the near-negatives outside. Was the heater finally working? I fumbled at the scarf wound tight around my throat without success. The taste of bitter butter attacked my tongue as I used my teeth to pull off my gloves. This time I pulled the scarf loose. The skin underneath was slick with sweat, and I waited for the freezing outside air to bring relief.

Instead, a warm breeze caressed my neck, carrying with it the scent of dried grass and sweet meadow flowers. At my back was not stained fabric and cracked vinyl, but hard dirt. Sitting up ... turned out to be very stupid.

I spent the next few minutes flat on my back listening to

the grass rustle and reassessing the situation. My pounding head said this was no dream, but I was lying prone in the middle of a field. It was as hot as mid-August, even though it was January. It had to be a dream.

Speculation was getting me nowhere, and the headache was subsiding. I rolled onto my stomach and pushed up with a grunt.

The field's expanse was broken only by clumps of trees and, in the distance, a river that looked just like the Susquehanna. By that, I mean it was wide and muddy-green. So, like most rivers on Earth. My ice-encrusted car, Rustbucket, was nowhere to be seen, nor was any snow. Nor was the road, telephone lines, nor other sign of human civilization. Where the heck was I?

"Hello." A small face popped up in front of mine, brown eyes framed by thick black lashes and a deathly-white mask.

My response was a garbled shriek as I scrabbled away from the creature.

Distance let me get a good look at the ... child? Not with the muscles that rippled on his sweat-streaked chest. Definitely not a child. PC terms spun through my head, but none of them applied to the person still crouched down in the flattened grass.

I had gone to high school with a "little person," although Carol preferred the term dwarf, being a huge Tolkien fan. This individual was not a dwarf in either the medical or the fantasy sense. He was beardless, with a hooked nose. White and black paint striped down his seamless face, but from his neck to his leather pants, his skin was the brown of unfired pottery. His hair was long and dark brown, slicked back, with feathers sticking up in a clump from a top-knot.

He stood, returning my stare. He had to tilt his head back quite a ways—he was roughly three feet tall, but perfectly proportional to a fully grown adult man. Like someone had used a shrink-ray on a powwow dancer.

"W ... who are you?"

I had managed to stop myself from saying "What are you," only because it took long enough to get my mouth to

265

work that some of my wits returned. I noticed the hatchet hanging from his belt, his loin cloth, and the quiver slung across his back. The reason why the image of a powwow dancer had crossed my mind made sudden sense—the last time I had seen someone dressed like this it had been on a high school field-trip to an Iroquois celebration. Only they had worn a lot more clothes. I considered that, then decided who was I to complain?

"I am Jogah. Are you lost?"

That word sparked across my brain, recalling the legends my father had told me of tiny people who had helped the Tuscarora. Of tiny people who had helped lost children of the tribe, which is what I certainly seemed to be. 'Jogah' had answered my unspoken question without my asking it.

I took a deep breath. When in fairyland, do what the fairies do, I guess.

"Pleased to meet you, Drum Dancer, and—" I looked around, as grasshoppers sang and the golden stalks bent in errant breezes, "—and I am very, very lost. Where am I?"

"Not too far from my home, if you require hospitality." The small man coughed and gestured at the ground. With a blink I realized he was inviting me to sit. To be honest, I was surprised I hadn't collapsed yet. My limbs felt heavy. The adrenaline that had propelled me to my feet drained, leaving a dizzying void in its place. I sat down with a thump, black lace dress pooling around my legs. Wincing at my clumsiness, I waited for a surge of pain. Surprise made me straighten with a gasp. All my injuries from the accident were healed.

Then the truth sunk in. So ... not fairyland. This was Heaven. It wasn't at all what I expected. Had I hit my head that hard, even with the airbag? Because I was pretty sure that you couldn't die from a few aches and pains.

Jogah waited, as patient as if there was no time here. From this perspective, I could appreciate a physique that looked ripped from the cover of a romance novel. So he was a very buff, very hot, Native American angel. If he'd only been taller, I'm sure there would have been heavenly choirs singing.

"Er, that's sweet, but can you be more specific? Really,

where is this place?"

"On the banks of the Susquehanna, in a territory that was lost to the English years before. Are you from the town?" Brown eyes narrowed, and then blinked. "Or are you with that other woman?"

"The Susquehanna runs through Heaven? Wait ... woman? What woman? Did she look like me?" I tugged at my chestnut hair, disheveled strands straggling around my face.

"In hair and height, yes. In clothing, no. Are you searching for her?"

My throat tightened, and I had to gulp before I could answer. "Yes. Very much. Can you tell me where she went?"

Jogah pointed behind me. I turned and then nearly fell backwards. Moments before it had been a tree-encircled field. Now a wall of golden stone rose behind me, with trees peeking over the top like a walled garden.

"What is *that*?" I looked left and right. The wall stretched as far as I could see in all directions. Right behind me gaped the sole entrance, framed by boxy columns, but there was no garden inside. The only thing visible through the opening was another wall. Walking towards it, I saw that the inner wall formed a corridor with the outer one, a corridor that ran in both directions from the entrance.

"That is the place lost people go."

Awareness dawned. A labyrinth. Heaven had recreated my favorite childhood movie, the one that Sandy and I had play acted so many times in a field much like the one behind me. I got a little excited at the thought of adventure, but there was also a knot of frustration. I would have to hunt for Sandy through the freaking Labyrinth. Why hadn't she waited for me? So typical of Miss Selfish Sandy.

I thought about turning around and following the hunk to his house. It's not like I had been the one to send my sister to the Demon King. As far as I could tell, she made that trade herself. Frustration transmuted into anger as I glared at the entrance.

"That's where my sister ... I mean the other woman went?"

Jogah nodded. "When last I saw her. She is family, you say? I hope you find each other." He gave a little wave and turned.

I took a moment to appreciate that neither the breechcloth nor the leather chaps had a seat to them. Then it occurred to me that he was leaving.

"Wait! Can you guide me? Do you know how to navigate the labyrinth?" The jogah was no goblin, but I wasn't going to quibble right now over Heaven's interpretation of an 80's movie.

He glanced back at me, eyes wide like I was insane. "I am not lost, girl. Farewell."

I watched him walk into the grass, so distracted I could barely appreciate the sight. I was alone, bereft, in a strange place. Oh, yeah, and dead apparently. This was not the storybook quest I'd hoped for as a kid.

I was also frying under the sweltering summer sun. Stripping off my quilted down coat, I dropped it onto the dirt. That didn't help. I was covered with sweat under my heavy velvet and lace dress. It had been the only black, semi-formal thing in my closet and, well … I hadn't intended to die and end up in the Summer Lands today. At least I was wearing clean underwear. I considered tearing off the sleeves, then hesitated. The weather in the Labyrinth might be different. I compromised by putting my hair up, re-fastening the butterfly clasp into the bun.

My fingers lingered on the enamel wings, remembering when Sandy had given it to me during our trip to Tijuana. I would never have gone there without her coaxing me. I bit my lip and closed my eyes, thinking of her as I stepped forward through the break in the towering walls.

There was nothing under my descending foot. With a scream, I pitched forward into darkness.

* * *

"I HATE YOU I HATE YOU I HATE YOU!" I rasped

as I pounded bloody fists on the slime-encrusted walls of the oubliette. I didn't know who I was yelling at, just that I had been screaming for hours. Well, except for those twenty minutes where I'd explored the circular dungeon, groping hands failing to find any doors or windows, and the thirty minutes where I had just cried. It had begun with the typical pleas for help, but around the time I had shredded my last intact nail, my shouts had descended into incoherent raging.

Maybe it was directed at the black void that was all I could see above me. Maybe it was toward the stones that had killed my manicure, or the stupidity of going looking for adventure. Or the insanity of *dying* on my way to a memorial.

No. It was none of those things. I knew exactly what I hated with so much passion that I had reduced my vocal cords to shreds. Or should I say who.

I hate you, Sandy. Why ... why did you leave me?

Numbness washed over me, a blanket of dead emotions snuffing my anger. I rested my overheated head against the damp rock. It took an effort of will to not thump it until my forehead bled like my hands. I welcomed the numbness I was done with my fury, done with being scared and with being in pain. I couldn't deal with it anymore.

An oubliette is a place to put anyone you wanted to forget. Could it also be a place to learn *how* to forget?

Some stubborn part of my soul couldn't let go of my sister's betrayal, last in a string of them. Even discounting all she had done in life, Sandy had been at the car, had been spotted by Jogah. Why hadn't she waited for me? Why had she taken off? Again.

"How could you leave me behind, Sandy?" My croaking whisper hissed around my prison, finding no more release than I had.

"I'm not leaving you behind, silly!" The voice came from the darkness above me, light and laughing. "I'm scouting the path!"

My breath caught as my head jerked up. A tan arm was stretched towards me, out of the dense black miasma. Light shone from her skin, like the hazy glow in old Polaroid pictures.

Memories. Skiing in deep, virgin snow, made effortless by following in Sandy's tracks. Long hikes shrunken by all the shortcuts only Sandy knew. The countless bits of wisdom and advice, passed down by a sister four years older than I. She had done everything before I could, had made all the mistakes, and by doing so had laid the path to let me ski smoothly through life.

Her hand unfurled, a dusky rose of hope.

With grimy and blood-smeared palms, I let go of my anger and reached for rescue.

* * *

After the deep gloom, it took a minute for my eyes to adjust. A circle of blue sky came into focus, bordered by golden stalks of grass. I was again on my back in the field where I started. I knew where I was, not by having to look around, but by a stomach-lurching recognition. I wasn't here by accident.

"I know this day. This is the day you told me Dad died."

Sandy squeezed the hand she still held, like she had that summer afternoon nearly a decade ago. She had dropped by the park where I was hanging out with friends and convinced me to go for a walk with her instead. We ended up here, in the field where we had dreamed together of goblins and bravery. She and I had lain down among the blades of grass ... and Sandy had broken my world.

She, Mom and Dad had been so positive, had spun the trials of Dad's cancer into funny stories that could be laughed off. I knew he was in treatment, I knew he was ill, but ... I guess with the naiveté of a teenager I hadn't ever thought that my strong, amazing father could be taken down so quickly by a few aggressive cells.

It still hurt that no one had prepared me, letting reality shatter my delusions, and the ground to fall out from under me.

That had been the summer I turned seventeen. The next year I applied for colleges as far away from her as I could get. The University of San Diego had fit that requirement nicely.

"Why did you do it to me again, Sandy? Why did you lie to me—to my face—about what was going on with you?" My words scorched my raw throat. I couldn't yell; I couldn't argue. All I could do was ask the questions that had gone unanswered in life.

"Because there was nothing that could be done, Merri."

I turned my head to look at her. She was young and healthy—her hair the mid-back length it had been before chemo made it fall out. The yellow work t-shirt from the bar just emphasizing the glow to her skin.

"There was nothing anyone could do. When I got the diagnosis the first time, I was so scared I didn't know what to do. So I did everything the doctors told me, and begged you to come back, and fought it. We thought I beat it too, didn't we?" Her lips curved in that smile she made when she got the joke before me.

"By the time they found the tumors hidden in my spine, they were spreading too fast. The doctors told me all they could do was knock them back, give me months maybe instead of weeks." She squeezed my hand. "I was done being sick, and done being scared. Do you get that? I just ... I didn't want anyone else to be sick or scared for me either."

"You mean you gave up." Now I was getting angry again. I didn't get it. I didn't understand not telling me or Mom about how fast we were going to lose her. It didn't make any sense at all.

Wait, no. There was the night I stopped by the old house and Mom had been crying. And the strain around her eyes in the days that followed. So it had just been me again, left to be blind-sided by losing a sister I was just beginning to trust.

Something squeezed my other hand, and a deep voice said, "Nah, she didn't give up, honey. She just ... got realistic."

I jerked my head to the left and saw the jogah laying there, looking up at the sky. He was adult human-sized, and even though his face was still covered in paint, at this distance and in profile, it was unmistakable.

"DAD?" I squeaked. Oh. My. God. I'd ogled my own dad's ass. If I wasn't already dead, I would be begging someone up there to take me.

Dad had been a fireman. I knew he had to be buff to do that, but ... I ran that train of thought off the rails. Where was the mental bleach when you needed it?

"Why the heck are you a jogah?"

His chuckle was as deep and rich as I remembered it. "I guess you could say I always want to help people."

An understatement. He'd lived for his job. And died for it too. He'd been one of the first responders on 9-11, had worked tirelessly at the site for days trying to find anyone to rescue, and had volunteered for body retrieval when it became clear that rescue wasn't a possibility. He had come home, night after night, covered in dust and dirt, had showered just long enough to wash off a layer or two, and then collapsed into bed so he could do it again the next day, until the job was done. Life had gone back to normal for a while after that. Until he developed a cough that just wouldn't go away. We'd moved to Binghamton my sophomore year, back to where my grandparents and Sandy lived, so they could look after us kids while my mom looked after my dad.

"You weren't that helpful to me earlier! Why didn't you say something?"

"What could I have said? 'Hi, I'm really short, but I'm your dead father?'" Again the chuckle. "Nah, honey. I couldn't do that. I just had to send you after Sandy, and trust that everything would get straightened out after that."

"Yah, that worked out so well." But his chuckle was infectious, and the three of us started laughing. It was just us, family, together on a beautiful summer day. Healing.

"So, what now? Is there something fun that dead people get up to in the evenings? Vampire clubs? Cemetery tours? Canasta?

"You're not dead, Merri." Sandy sounded amused, and tapped the bridge of my nose. "In fact, it's time for you to wake up. Just do me a favor, OK? Don't walk in my footsteps this time."

* * *

"Oh good, she's waking up. Ms. Dodge, please stay still. We're nearly done."

There was a muffled knocking sound, and I opened my eyes enough to see white. Was I still in my car? I was chilled, but not cold. Still, the need to shiver swept over me. I managed to suppress it–less willpower and more fear of injury.

The knocking stopped and the woman said, "All finished. We'll take her back to her room now, Mrs. Dodge. The doctor will be in soon with the results, but now that she's waking up, it hopefully will be all good news."

There was a pressure on my hand, and I realized it was being held.

"Mom?"

"Yes, Merri, I'm here. You scared us!" She was being cheerful in that brittle way that had become habitual over the past year.

"God, Mom, I'm sorry. I thought I was going to be late, and the car hit ice or something and spun out, and ..." Fingers pressed to my lips stopped my croaking.

"That's OK, Merri. You're awake and it'll all be OK now."

"Please, ma'am. We have to get her onto the stretcher."

My hand was released. With an odd, floating sensation, the board I was strapped onto lifted and swung onto a stretcher.

I was trundled down a wide hallway, white squares of ceiling tiles flashing overhead. The stretcher was pushed through a curtain "door" and into a room filled with beeping and swishing sounds. With the expertise of much practice, I was moved onto a standard hospital bed. The nurse hooked me up to machines, which began to chime to my own rhythm. I tried to relax but, damn, I hated hospitals.

Mom did, too, and she got talkative when she was trying to ignore the bad the world kept inflicting on us. She told me about the first part of the memorial, before she had been pulled away on learning that her only living daughter was found unresponsive in a car halfway to Endwell.

They had decorated the old bar with yellow and lilac bunting, like it had been a birthday party instead of a memorial. There had been some nice speeches, a lot by old regular customers, and some by friends who had stuck around the area.

"I thought ... I thought you had decided not to come, after all," Mom said. She wasn't looking at me, but down at the hand she had regained possession of. "You were so angry at her. At me—"

"Not you, Mom," I couldn't let her think that. "Never you. Just ... don't leave me out anymore. OK?"

"Promise, honey," she flashed her tired smile at me and looked over the bed.

"Ms. Dodge, Mrs. Dodge." A man in a white lab coat, stethoscope obscuring his name badge, walked towards my bed. "I have good news, and some other news." He didn't pause to ask which we preferred to hear first, plunging on. "The good news is that the CT-scan didn't show any internal damage, so your head injuries are just superficial. No lasting harm from your little incident."

He flipped a printed photo out of a folder, and for a second it looked like a face peeking through a foggy window. Then I recognized it as a partial cross-section of a skull—mine, if I had to guess.

"The other news is that the CT showed a small mass in one of your ethmoid sinuses." His finger tapped a nearly invisible white dot on the photo. "Our technician is looking more closely at it, but from the shape it could be cancerous. It is very small, confined, and relatively easy to access. We will schedule a biopsy, and we can talk about further treatment options after that. But all-in-all, I would say that it was very fortunate that we found it when we did. Tumors like these can be quite aggressive. You must have a guardian angel looking out for you."

My mother's hand tightened vise-like around my own, but with a floating sense of release, I breathed out.

"I think I might have two, Doctor."

* * *

For Pat and Dawn, who showed me how to face death. For Sher and Linda, who showed me how to survive. And for you readers, fighting cancer along with us.

Stardust, Always

The Big C

Debbie Manber Kupfer

A lump, there can't be a lump. I lay in bed looking up at the ceiling. The mosquito was back, taunting me from its position high up on the light fixture. I knew as soon as I turned off the light it would be at me again, the little vampire. I'd read somewhere once that only the pregnant female mosquitos bite, that they needed the blood for their young. I supposed as a mother I was supposed to feel compassion for the little bloodsuckers.

Benign, I suppose it could be benign. I had breastfed for a million years (well, seven actually). Wasn't that supposed to count for something? I was vegetarian (unlike that insidious mosquito). Never smoked. Exercised, almost daily. Made all the healthy choices. I was forty-seven years old—too young for cancer.

The house was too quiet. My mother was probably asleep. The loud radio or television background music was gone, never to return. That had been my father, you see, who had always needed a soundtrack to his life. If I'd been my mum I would have wanted to keep the music in his memory, but she seemed to prefer the silence. I didn't like the silence. In the silence I was forced to think.

I looked over at the large black suitcase lying on the floor by my bed, all packed and ready to go. I'd already been too scared to sleep, even before the mosquito and the lump. My father had always been able to wake up without alarm clocks, so there weren't any in this house. My mum, who had always been an early riser, thanks to my dad, was now getting up later and later each day. I wondered what she would do after I'd gone. In just a few hours the taxi would arrive to take me back to the airport. I'd been here for six weeks ever since

I'd received that fateful phone call in the middle of the night.

My father had been sick, in and out of the hospital for months, his sugar levels spiking and dipping. I'd talked to relatives. "Should I come out?" "No, there's no need. You take care of your own family. Your dad will be fine."

It had been a brutal winter in St. Louis and the months had been filled with petty disasters. First, our refrigerator had died. Then the new one could not be delivered because of the layer of ice that wouldn't shift from our driveway. In truth, it would have been nice to escape to warmer climes for a while.

The week before he died was the last time I talked to my dad. He made me smile. He was sharing his hospital room with another man of about the same age and temperament. "And you know what?" he said. "He has a wife who nags him just like mine."

The flight out for the funeral was relentless, sleeping and eating impossible. I looked around the crowded cabin wondering how all these people could be carrying on with their lives when my father was gone. I felt sick to my stomach. Never had the words "Welcome to Israel" felt so wrong.

My mother seemed so small and vulnerable when I hugged her. I couldn't imagine her living without my dad. They had been married for forty-nine years.

At the funeral I gazed at the small form of my father wrapped in a prayer shawl and clung to my mother. During the week of shiva, the customary time of Jewish mourning, I met countless friends and relatives who had known my dad. Sometimes I would find myself on the verge of a smile, and then I would remember.

I stayed in Karmiel at my parents' house for six weeks. At five weeks we returned to the cemetery and placed a stone on his grave. I'd requested Theodor Herzl's words be etched in the granite: "If you will it, it is no dream." My dad had finally achieved his dream, had moved to Israel for his retirement years. The only downside was that his only daughter and grandchildren lived thousands of miles away in St. Louis.

As I lay looking up at the ceiling, one saving thought came to me. At least my dad would never know about my cancer. Because as the mosquito buzzed waiting to feast on me, I knew without a doubt it was cancer, and I was terrified.

After no more than a few minutes of snatched sleep, the early morning taxi arrived to take me back to the airport. I hugged my mum and briefly wondered if I would see her again. *No, mustn't think like that.* But I couldn't help myself, the fear had taken control.

The taxi driver knew my parents and scolded me for leaving my mother alone. When I explained I had children and a husband in St. Louis he said, "So bring them here, or take her with you. She shouldn't be on her own." Wish it was that easy.

In any case, my mum was happy in Israel. In Karmiel she was surrounded by friends in a way that was never true for her in London. Ironic, really, when she'd never wanted to come to Israel in the first place. That had been my father's dream.

The dread built up over the next few days. I returned to my family in St. Louis, but I told no one about the lump, just quietly scheduled my annual gyno check-up and mammogram, which I was due for in any case. I wouldn't tell anyone unless it was cancer, after all, why worry them?

But my fear shone through and my husband guessed. He tried to reassure me, of course, but I knew better. The mammogram found nothing, but a diagnostic ultrasound revealed not one, but two lumps.

The fear felt like a boulder centered in the pit of my stomach as the staff at the Breast Center scheduled me for a biopsy just a few days later.

"But don't worry, dear. It's just a precaution. Most lumps are benign."

The sheer terror I felt at that point outstripped worry by about a hundredfold. I'd seen those brave bald women on the TV and in the grocery store. I could never be one of those women. I was naturally a wuss. Hell, I hated needles so much I'd never even had my ears pierced.

Yet, as would become my mantra in the next few months, it's amazing what you can get used to. Somehow I got through the biopsy. Over the next few days I jumped every time the phone rang. I imagined myself bald and breastless. I cried, the terror building inside me like a nuclear bomb waiting to explode.

And then the call came. A message on the answer-phone. "Can you please call the Breast Center?" It still could be nothing, right? They could be calling to say I was okay. But if that was the case wouldn't they just leave a message?

I was shaking when I called the office. I kept messing up the phone number and having to start again. By the time the nurse came on the line I was so worked up I could barely make sense of what she was telling me. Yes, there were two lumps. Yes, they were cancerous. But I should feel lucky, they were of the slow-forming kind that was easier to treat.

Lucky? How could I possibly feel lucky? I desperately wished I could backspace the time to last summer before everything had gone bad. Last summer I'd taken my daughter to London. We'd met up with my parents there. My dad considered it his last hurrah. We'd tried to convince him otherwise. You'll have plenty of future holidays. No, he said, this is it. He was right.

Despite wanting to move to Israel, my dad loved London, as do I. It was wonderful sharing those few weeks with my parents and my daughter. Wonderful for her to spend time with her grandparents. As I sat listening to the Cancer Center nurse on the other end of the phone, I desperately wished I could go back to that summer and stay there.

At the end of the call the nurse told me I needed to come in as soon as possible to talk about treatment. If it was so slow growing, I thought, why the rush? Because it wasn't slow growing, was it? There had been no lump six weeks before and now there were two. The nurse was trying to make me feel better. It wasn't working.

My husband came to the appointment with me. It was a good thing, too, because at least he was able to listen to what they said, take notes, ask questions. I could do none of that. The fear had taken hold. Choices, apparently I had choices, maybe. It would depend on another test—a breast MRI which would determine if the two lumps were linked together. If they were I might be able to get away with chemotherapy, a lumpectomy, and radiation. If not, I would have to have a mastectomy.

"Mastectomy"—the word terrified me, more than anything else. The thought of losing a part of my body was my deepest fear and I was being forced to confront it. It did no good to talk of reconstructive surgery and success rates. I would not be myself anymore, would not be whole.

The Cancer Center nurse was young and flighty, reminding me more of a kindergarten teacher than a medical professional. She talked flippantly of women who chose to be flat-chested, like it was no big deal. Maybe for her, so young that all this was merely an abstraction. Yes, I would have the MRI. I would see if I could save my breast.

In the MRI machine I felt like I was suffocating and had to stop to use my inhaler for my asthma. The sounds of the machine pounded in my brain. *Let it have a good result, let it have a good result.*

In the meantime I'd told my kids, told my mother. My mum was very calm when she heard the news and I realized I was right. My father would have panicked. She would take my cancer in her stride, never once believing in anything but a healthy outcome.

The results of the MRI came back. Yes, the two lumps were linked. "That means we can try the chemo first, right? We can see if we can shrink them down; that's what you said, right?" I pleaded with the doctor, begging him to take my side.

"Yes, we can try," he said, "but we can't promise anything?"

We went to a different doctor, to get a second opinion. The second doctor wanted me to schedule a mastectomy immediately. "We're talking about life and death here," he said, holding my hand and looking into my eyes. He was very young and to me he seemed terrifying. Aren't doctors supposed to reassure you? Not put the fear of God in you?

I returned to the first Cancer Center. "I'll take my chance with the chemo."

They scheduled me to have a port put in. It would make the chemo easier, so I wouldn't end up like a pincushion. I was glad of that. My fear of needles was partly born from the fact that I have bad veins. During my two pregnancies I dreaded the blood tests. The nurses inevitably had to stick me over and over until they got it right.

Directly after the operation to put in the port I went down to the Cancer Center for my first chemotherapy. I still felt groggy and strange from the surgery, but the Cancer Center was a surprisingly cheerful place, and I wondered at the good spirits of the other patients around the room, chatting with their friends and family, reading, eating, watching TV. Very few looked sick, but there were tell-tale signs that all was not as it seemed, including a few of those ubiquitous bald brave women and some wearing hats, scarves, or wigs. How could they be so relaxed, when they all had some kind of cancer, when I was still terrified and groggy from the surgery?

My husband stayed with me for that first treatment and then I was sent home with a bundle of pills for the nausea that had yet to set in. The smiling nurses, ever optimistic, assured me that it wouldn't be so bad, that the drugs would take the edge off the nausea. I dread to think what it used to be like, before those little white pills.

Within a few hours of leaving the Cancer Center the nausea began. Waves and waves of it—I dry retched over and over again—the medication apparently acted like Dramamine—something I remember taking as a kid when my parents hadn't wanted me to throw up on a long bus journey. Yes, the drug stops you throwing up, but doesn't stop you feeling sick. That feeling stays with you all through the miserable journey.

The nausea after my first chemo was about a thousand times worse than anything I'd experienced before. I stayed up most of the night, crying and retching, my head pounding so hard, I thought a malicious witch had put a curse on me.

"I don't think I can do this," I repeated to myself over and over again. "I'm not going to survive this. How can I carry on? What about my kids, my life? It's not fair, it's not fair. Why me?"

The next day wasn't much better. The headaches continued, pounding migraine-like pains that gave me no peace and responded to no painkillers. I called the Cancer Center. "No, headaches were not a normal side effect of chemo. Maybe it's just a coincidence?" It didn't feel like a coincidence.

I studied the labels on the various drugs they had given me to combat the nausea. Bingo—one of the nausea drugs had a "side-effect of possible headache." Made it sound insignificant, but it wasn't—it felt like a caveman had chosen me for his mate and had hit me over the head with his club before dragging me off to his cave. I stopped taking that drug and within a few days my head, at least, was back to normal.

Once I nixed the pills, the headaches subsided, but the nausea still dominated the first week of the chemo cycle. On that week I could barely eat at all, just managed a few spoons of bland food at meal times. Even in the following week after the nausea had subsided I didn't really want to eat. Everything tasted strange and metallic. I'd always gained a lot of pleasure from the foods I enjoyed, and it made me extremely sad that foods I'd loved like sharp cheddar or dark chocolate now were way too severe for my palate. Would it ever come back? Would I ever enjoy food again?

I also learned from experience exactly why those cancer patients were so cheery on the day of their treatment. The treatment day for a cancer patient is usually their best day. For my first cycle of chemo (the most brutal), I was scheduled to come once every two weeks. The pattern was pretty much the same each cycle. I was more or less fine when I arrived at the Cancer Center. Then, a few hours later, the nausea would kick in. Each day until my next treatment I recovered a little more, until I felt almost fine by the time I was ready to go back. I remember joking with a nurse some months later, as she fumbled with my port to put in my IV. She asked how I was doing that day. "Fine," I answered, "but you're here to put a stop to that!"

About three weeks after my first treatment I started to lose my hair. I knew it was going to happen, but didn't expect it to start so quickly. I had gone to the hairdresser a few days before I'd started treatment. In a burst of bravery I had my long hair cut and gave my ponytail to Locks of Love, a charity that takes donated hair and makes it into wigs for children with leukemia. The hairdresser was the first person I told about my cancer outside of my immediate family. The girl nodded sympathetically and talked about all the cool hairstyles I could try after my treatment was over and my hair started growing back. I nodded politely but didn't really believe it. I could not imagine at this stage there ever being an end to the treatment which was laid out for months ahead of me, the treatment that might not even work.

My hair loss was what finally made the whole thing real for my son, Joey. Cancer was abstract; a bald mommy, not so much. I wore my wig (kindly donated from the Cancer Center) when I was out of the house, but at home, in the heat of the summer, despite my son's discomfort, I needed my head to be bare. The wig was just too itchy. I compromised when his friends came over to play by putting on a headscarf.

As I said before, it's amazing what you can get used to. Very quickly it all became routine—the treatments, the hair loss, the nausea. There were even moments of hilarity, like when my wig blew off while I was waiting at a bus stop one day. The look on the bus driver's face was priceless.

Very slowly my fear subsided into something more manageable. I'd talked to other cancer patients by then and survivors too. Breast cancer could be beaten. I also realized I was luckier than some; I had a family to support me. I met a woman in the Cancer Center about the same age as me, with an almost identical diagnosis. The difference was that she was on her own. There was no one to accompany her to the treatments and surgeries. No one to help at home. She had to try somehow between treatments and nausea to hold down her job, so that she could keep her insurance and continue coming to the Cancer Center.

The next round of chemo was easier, or maybe I just got used to it. Then the moment of reckoning—another round of tests to determine if it had worked. I held my breath and waited.

The toxic fluid that had been pumped into my veins for months now had been working its medical magic. Amazingly the lumps that had shown up like boulders on my first ultrasound were now all but gone, but still my oncologist was only cautiously optimistic.

I didn't understand. Surely it had worked. I felt the familiar flavor of fear rise up in my throat. I forced myself to swallow, to stay focused.

No, I didn't want to have a mastectomy. Yes, I would take my chances with a lumpectomy and radiation, though I wondered what in the world they were planning to remove as there was nothing on the ultrasound.

The prep for my lumpectomy surgery was extremely painful. Time seemed to slow during those minutes of pain. I truly don't know how long it all took, just that I was supremely glad when it was over and I was wheeled back downstairs to have my surgery. I sank gratefully into the oblivion of anesthesia and awoke to the welcome news that the operation had gone well.

After the surgery came radiation, and then finally nearly a year after I had first felt the lumps, I was done. The Cancer Center has a bell that survivors ring when they complete their treatment. I rang that bell gleefully. I had beaten it—I had beaten my fear. I had beaten the Big C.

* * *

For Liz - Now you get to jam with Bowie

Stardust, Always

Matronus

Cornelius Q. Kelvyn

"I have no idea what you're talking about," said the Otter.

The Swan fluttered its wings in reply.

The Otter intensified its tone. "No. Not a clue. Absolutely zero idea."

"But surely you can extrapolate?"

The Otter looked up at the Swan. He tapped his foot. "Look. The degree of sense you're making is minus two hundred seventy three. I'm talking zero *kelvins* clue."

The Otter was standing on a rock near the shore of a lake. The water was up to his neck. The water wasn't so crystal clear that the Swan would have been able to *see* the Otter's foot tapping on the rock beneath the surface. But the Swan could *feel* the subsurface vibration, and knew well enough what had caused it.

The Swan was on the surface of the glistening water. She skewed her head to her left. "Then it is still zero point one five of a clue."

"What?"

"Never mind. Just a temporal anomaly."

The Otter grinned. He let the grin fade so he could say, "You mean thermal."

"Actually, I meant temporal, but not as far as time or temperature, but the lobe of the brain." The Swan dove beneath the surface of the lake. The Otter followed suit. The two of them passed a pair of Crabs who were sparring. When the Crabs noticed the others, they swam toward the Swan. The Swan dove deeper to avoid them. The mammal chased the bird underwater and drove her to the top of the lake. They came up further from shore than they had been. The Crabs knew better than to come up to the face of the water. The Swan was floating on the glistening surface. The Otter rolled onto its back and floated with its head back and paws up. There was a black rope tied around its waist like a belt. It was the same color as the Otter's fur.

The Otter lay silent. He needn't speak. The Swan knew that he would chase her again if she tried to avoid it.

The Swan said, "I suppose I must tell you. A *matronus*."

The Otter's foot twitched as he said, "I already told you. I do not know what that is."

"Let's say you have never seen a tortoise before, and I ask you, 'Do you know what a turtle is?'"

"Of course," said Otter.

The Swan said, "A tortoise is the same thing."

The Otter glared at the Swan. "But I already know what both of those are, and a tortoise is not a turtle. It's not the same thing at all!"

"You must admit there are similarities," the Swan suggested.

A blur of brown flew past the Swan and landed on the Otter's belly. It was a Bat. It glared at its living raft's surprised face and spread its wings.

The Otter said, "Astrid, don't surprise me like that. I told you to call out before landing on me."

Astrid the Bat said, "You were in the middle of a conversation. I didn't want to interrupt." The Bat folded its wings beside its body.

The Otter said, "But you *did* interrupt—by *landing* on me."

The Swan said, "At least she changed from dragon form. I think you should thank her for not sinking you."

The Otter shouted at the Swan, "Watch it sister!" The Otter reached up and grabbed Astrid the Bat, and prepared to fling the Bat at the Swan.

"Or you'll do *what* exactly? Hit me with that fffffish?" said the Swan.

As the Swan had said the last word, the Bat transmogrified into a Fish, flopping in the Otter's paws. The

Otter tossed the fish, but it missed the Swan and splashed into the lake. The Fish swam away.

The Otter flipped over. As his back came above the surface, a small bag popped up into the air. It was bound to Otter's waist with the rope. The bag was the same color as the rope. Both bag and Otter splashed beneath the surface.

The Swan spread her wings. With a mighty stroke, she thrust upward. Two strokes later, and she was aloft. As she flew off, water dripped from her feet. Concentric ripples on the lake's surface formed from the droplets, making a path toward the shallows.

Otter burst out of the water. He nipped at Swan's feet, but bit at air instead. Otter turned and swam toward the shore. His Otter fur receded from most of his body except his head—the hair there grew longer nearly as fast as he swam. His shape shifted rapidly too. By the time the former Otter had reached the waterline, he had completely transformed into the human Girl, who now stood in the shallows. All she wore was a rope around her waist. The rope was much longer than it had been when she had been an Otter. As the Otter-turned-Girl walked ashore, she reached behind her and pulled the bag–also larger than the Otter's– to the front. She hadn't changed entirely to a human. Her ears resembled those of a hedgehog, though larger, proportional to her otherwise human head. At her back was a pair of wings, mounted on her shoulder blades. She shook them. Opening her waistsack, she pulled out some mercifully dry clothes and dressed herself.

The Swan had landed a few meters from shore. She stood a fair distance ahead of where the Girl had stopped to get dressed. The Swan wore an indigo amulet as a necklace which matched the color of her eyes. The Girl also had indigo eyes, even when she had been in Otter form. The Swan transformed into a large Tortoise.

"Oh, *must* you?" the Girl complained.

The Tortoise only seemed to hear the Girl when the transmogrification was complete.

"Very well," the Swan-turned-Tortoise relented. She underwent another change. This time she took on the form of a large white Rabbit. When she, now a he, stood up on his hind legs, the Rabbit's head barely reached the winged hedgehog-eared Girl's thighs, with the ears stretching up to her waist. The Rabbit pulled its amulet down from its neck and stretched the rope into a belt. Then he tugged at the amulet, like he was kneading bread, until it became a bag, from which he pulled a kilt and sweater, and put them on.

The Girl walked up to the Rabbit.

"Off this way, into the wood," the Rabbit insisted. He walked away from the lake. The trees became thick up ahead.

The Girl followed. "Late for tea, are we?"

"Not even funny."

"It's a bit funny." The Girl looked down at the Rabbit and said, "So you're saying that a *matronus* is like something else that I should know, just as a tortoise is like a turtle but also very different."

"Exactly."

"Well the only similar word that I can think of is *patronus*, like in those wizard stories," said the Girl.

The Rabbit, whose name was Aminah no matter what form she was in, looked up at Odette, her younger sister who was presently in mostly humanoid form. Aminah said, "That's it, exactly."

Odette looked down at the Rabbit Aminah. "You're saying we can have spirit guardians?"

"Maybe. A *matronus* is a little different. But we don't know if you can have one until you try."

Odette and Aminah had entered deep enough into the woods so that they had lost sight of the lake. The mesh of branches overhead blocked out much of the light.

Aminah continued. "If it is possible, *this* is a good place to try."

Odette asked, "Let me guess, I just say *'Expecto matronus'*?"

Aminah shook her head in that particular way to say both yes and no.

Odette clarified. "After waggling our wand in circles? But Aminah, we don't even *have* wands." She tapped her foot again. Then she said, "Where did you even *learn* this?"

"You remind me of the babe," Aminah sang before bursting out laughing.

"What babe?" asked Odette.

"The babe with the power," Aminah sang.

"Aminah!" cried out Odette. "Stop pulling my wing!" She was speaking figuratively, but her wings twitched as her anger rippled out. "This is serious. I'm trying to help my friends, and you're leading me on a wild fox hunt."

The two of them stopped walking. Aminah said, "I *am* serious. But you wouldn't believe the truth, because of how it resembles fiction."

"Oh, don't tell me more myths. My friends are dying. I need to help them however I can. Is this *matronus* thing real, and where did you learn it?"

Aminah told her sister, "I learned it from an owl and a doe. Otherwise known as a goblin king and a professor of potions. Or a messenger of the goddess, depending on her or his mood."

"Oh! I know the two you're talking about. They were in those forms? They were shifters like us?" Odette asked.

"Yes and yes. They were both shape shifters."

Odette glared at her Rabbit sister. "Then become an owl or doe or something and show me. How do we do such a thing without wands?"

Aminah bowed her Rabbit head to Odette, then took off the kilt and sweater. She stashed them away in the tiny duffel bag of holding, and then transfigured her body into the form of an Owl. Aminah the Owl spread its wings and launched upward. The dry leaves on the forest floor flitted about.

Odette raised her right arm and the Owl perched on the girl's forearm.

"You're a rather splendid owl," said Odette, admiring her sister's new form.

A blue Heron flew into the area and landed near some trees a fair distance away from the Owl and the Girl. The lean bird with slender legs looked out of place in the dark woods. The Owl took notice, then turned its attention back to the

Girl.

The Heron cocked its head back in the direction from which it had come. It tensed its legs as if it might take flight. There was rustling in the undergrowth. A sequence of shrubs and bushes shuddered. Whatever was causing it was moving toward the others. Some shadows scurried between the trees. Then a band of four Hedgehogs appeared from the undergrowth. They huddled around the legs of the great Heron, as if the tall bird would protect them. The Heron curved its long neck down and reached its head down to the Hedgehogs. The bird's sharp beak gently caressed each of the Hedgehogs. The Hedgehogs rolled over onto their backs. This game continued for a few moments as the Girl and Owl looked on. The Heron lifted its head and looked over at the Owl, who was still perched on the Girl's arm. All four Hedgehogs cuddled around the Heron's legs.

Aminah the Owl raised her right wing. She looked at Odette and said, "It seems that the Crabs have decided to join us again."

"Like the cancer that my friends are trying to battle," Odette sighed.

Aminah said, "Please be polite to our sisters. It is just one of their forms."

She turned her Owl head about and faced the Heron and Hedgehogs. "Listen up, Crab-critters. You could learn a thing or two."

It was plain to Aminah that the former Crabs had transformed into the Heron and the Hedgehogs. Their family of shapeshifters sometimes referred to one another based on their recent or frequent forms. Aminah knew that the Heron was their sister Arabella. The four Hedgehogs were a four-instance form of their sister Tavi. The Owl turned its head back toward the Girl.

Aminah addressed Odette. Her tone was deep and resonant. "About the *matronus*. It is a guardian, a healing spirit. Like the divine mother, she can take on many forms, each unique to the request and requester. We can request her presence ..."

Tavi interrupted. A chorus of four Hedgehogs called out in unison, "By saying *expecto matronus!*"

Odette snapped at them. "No! That's *not* it. You should have joined us *earlier*, you crazy Crabs."

Aminah spoke calmly. "Invoco spiritum matrem meum. At least that's the singular. That's what you should start with."

Odette whispered the phrase softly.

Aminah continued. "I shall use the plural, which you will understand in a few moments." As she had explained, Aminah performed the invocation. The Owl waved her wing in a circular motion. She repeated this continuously as she hooted, "Invoco spiritum matres mea. Invoco spiritum matres mea. Invoco spiritum matres nostrae." A blue aura emanated from the tip of her wing as she continued waving it around. It was as though she were swirling blue cotton candy in the air. Threads of phosphorescent blue spun together and accumulated until the bundle of light was larger than the Owl herself. Aminah ceased her wing spinning and became silent.

The blue cotton candy aura began to take on more of a definitive shape. Within seconds, the aura appeared to be a transparent blue Owl, bigger than Aminah. It hovered in the air. It spread its wings and cast a blue shadow of light upon Odette and Aminah. The blue Owl folded its wings behind its back and hovered there, facing Aminah.

Aminah said, "We wish to heal Odette's friends."

The holographic Owl transformed into a tall slender Man, taller than Odette's winged Girl form. He had long flowing hair, and his whole form still appeared blue but more opaque than it had been as an Owl.

"Odette," the Man said, addressing the girl. His voice was smoother than water off an otter's back, a familiar feeling that gave Odette chills at the same time as it warmed her with familiarity. Odette was nearly lost in the thin Man's voice when she heard him say, "So you are Aminah's sister?"

"Yes," Odette said, trembling.

"I like your ears." The Man looked over her shoulders. "And swan wings. Nice touch." He smiled to her. "You need not be afraid. I am Aminah's motherly angel of sorts."

"Of sorts," Odette mumbled.

The tall Man laughed. "You remind me of the babe," he said. Then he composed himself and told her, "Let's see if you can summon your own. Pay close attention."

Aminah the Owl leapt off of Odette's arm. She flew gently to the ground beside her sister's feet. Aminah transformed to her hatchling form, a bronze Dragon. In this form she beckoned to Tavi the Hedgehogs and Arabella the Heron to come closer. As they complied, Aminah transmogrified into a winged Unicorn that retained the bronze hide of her Dragon form and a bronze mane and tail to match. Tavi and Arabella remained in the forms they had maintained since entering the woods.

The blue aura of the tall Man shimmered as he spoke to Odette. "My dear swan-Girl, please extend either wing or arm in front of you."

Odette simultaneously reached her left hand toward the glowing Goblin King and extended her left wing four times the width of her body.

The Goblin King *matronus* smiled. "Good. Now swirl them through the air and recite after me." He chanted the same sequence with which Aminah had summoned him.

Odette rotated her arm and left wing in unison, forming ellipses with each. She chanted along with her sister's guide, "Invoco spiritum matres mea. Invoco spiritum matres mea. Invoco spiritum matres nostrae." This she repeated nine times, twenty-seven phrases in all. As she did, an indigo-lavender blend of colors swirled in the dim light of the wood.

Aminah the Pegacorn, Arabella the Heron, and the quadraphonic voices of Tavi's Hedgehogs all cheered with excitement as the purplish hues accumulated into an egg-shaped orb of glowing light. The concert master conducting Odette grinned giddily.

He said in a singing voice, "Enough. Be silent and fill it with your all your healing wishes for your friends."

Odette's indigo orb sparked and shimmered throughout the minute which seemed like an eternity. She stopped waving her wing and arm about.

"Let it be," said the Man. He stepped back three paces away from Odette.

Odette's orb transformed into the shape of a Doe, a deer, a female deer. The Doe hovered in the air before her. Then the Doe descended until its feet touched the ground. Her whole form was indigo. The Doe turned toward Odette and smiled as she winked glowing eyelids briefly over the orbs of her deep indigo eyes.

"Hello. Are you my *matronus*?" Odette asked the Doe.

A Doe-eyed glow smiled at her. The Deer raised up her front legs, and raised her neck and head above them so that she towered over Odette. Odette stepped back and tripped over a rock. She fell backward and landed on her wings and back. The Deer continued to transition. The Doe's front legs each divided in two, then differentiated into an arm and a wing. Her neck grew shorter and her snout shortened. The head seemed to absorb all the extra volume from her neck. When she had fully transitioned into the form of an Angelic Man, at one hundred eighty-five centimeters in height, Odette's matronus would have been slightly taller than Aminah's, were it not for the high heels worn by the Goblin King's image.

Odette got back on her feet and dusted off her clothes. She stared at the two figures before her.

"Good to meet you, my dear," said the Goblin King to the great winged Angel.

The Angel turned to the thin Man. "Always, my stardust friend," spake the Angel.

Aminah, Odette, Tavi, and Arabella watched the two glowing forms embrace one another in a hug of luminescence. When they parted, and became separate forms once again, the Angel addressed Odette.

"Thank you for summoning me here. There is much I can teach you."

Odette asked him, "Can you help me heal my friends? There are two of them, they each have cancer."

"My dear little swan, I often wish it were so easy. But surely, there is much you can do," said the Angel. The thin

Man beside him took his hand and they stood hand-in-hand facing Odette. "But the first step is to spend time with them. Share your smile, your touch, your stories, and your joy with them. Spend time with your friends. You can help them be happy. They will feel your love."

Odette asked, "Can you come with us?"

"Not looking like *this*, not in this form," said the Angelic one.

The thin Man spoke, "Aminah. Odette. You can carry us with you in your hearts. Remember us in your minds."

"Always," said the Angel.

The thin Man said, "And our light will shine through you." He looked at Aminah. "But for now we must part. You know how to summon us. You can do this silently at any time and we won't appear in *these* forms, but we *will* be with you. Practice. Carry us on. Carry us with you into your lives, and into those of your friends."

"I shall," said Aminah in her Pegacorn voice.

"We shall," said Odette in her Girl-swan voice.

The thin Man and the Angel parted hands. They turned away from the shifter girls. They rejoined hands and slowly walked away, hand-in-hand, as they faded into the soft light of the forest.

A Bat flew past the two figures and landed on Odette's shoulder.

"Cool it, Astrid," Odette scowled.

Astrid hopped off of her sister's shoulder and transformed into a red Dragon, now as tall as the Angel had been.

"Did I miss anything?" Astrid the Dragon asked.

Tavi the Hedgehogs replied in chorus, "Just Aminah and Odette summoning their *matronuses*."

Astrid asked, "*Matronuses*? Those spirit beings I flew by? But those looked like men. You must be talking about *patronuses*."

Aminah corrected her. "No, no. *Matronuses*. Don't be so narrow-eyed, you Bat. Like all of us, and any shape-shifters you know, the gender isn't the looks of the outside. It is what is in their hearts and minds that matter. The awesome people you met are genderless, and yet they have both motherly and fatherly gifts to share."

Odette explained, "They came to help me help my friends. You know, the ones who are fighting for their lives."

"But they just went away. I flew right past them," Astrid complained.

"Eternally ephemeral," said the four Hedgehogs.

"Always amorphous," said the Heron.

"Simmering stardust," said the Girl with the swan wings and hedgehog ears.

"We are all made of stardust," said the red Dragon.

"Their words, their songs, their spells, their style all live on in us," said the Pegacorn.

The Pegacorn turned into a Raven. She declared boldly, into the whole wood imploring.

Quoth the Raven, "Evermore."

What Am I to Do Without You?

Lora Hughes

Lost in life
No magic left,
No time to say goodbye.
No more to love; time has run out
No more smiles,
No more tears,
Nothing left but the dark of night
What am I to do without you?

How am I supposed to live alone?
Without your laugh?
Without your smile?
Even your frown?
No more hope,
No more care,
You left too soon
Life's so unfair,
Now nothing left; oh, how I despair!

Our time together now a mere flicker,
A photo, a video, no sound of you!
The darkest day of my life when I lost you!
What am I to do without you?

I look to the stars and hope and pray,
That maybe one day we shall meet again
Your smile,
Your dance,
Your infectious laugh,
Touched all our hearts!
And I shall dream of you,
As I learn to live my life without you!

Stardust, Always

Through The Mists

Michelle Valens

Her favorite thing in the world was gardening. She loved the way nature smelled and the way it calmed her down after a long stressful day. It was her way to unwind and relax, it was her happiness. Some people have music, others have painting; for Mary, it was plants. She had flowers, bushes, fruit plants and many more, and her backyard garden was something from the pages of Better Homes and Gardens. She took a lot of pride in the way her garden looked, as she should.

It was a beautiful and sunny afternoon, and she sat out in the garden looking over her flowers; another one of her favorite things was taking snapshots of her flowers. She loved her garden and cherished having it all to herself, but that didn't mean she wouldn't show off from time to time. She leaned down to get a particularly tricky shot of a flower drooping closer to the ground when she was interrupted.

"Come here, I've left you something," a voice she didn't recognize said softly. At first she thought it could have been one of the neighbors speaking but she looked around and nobody was outside with her. She went back to her flowers when the voice spoke again. "Come here." This time the voice seemed to have come from inside ... .She whipped around to look towards her kitchen door and then turned back to pick up her shovel; just about done here anyway.

She headed back into her stuffy house, opening one of the kitchen windows on her way to the living room when suddenly, the house started to shake.

She stopped and wondered what on earth was happening. The shaking grew more intense as she tried to drop under a table. She couldn't move her legs, standing in the middle of the kitchen as the house rocked like a ship on a stormy sea, as she looked around the small room she saw vines starting to slither up the walls, in mere moments the kitchen became overwhelmed with plants, flowers blooming out of the sink and roots breaking through the floorboards. She struggled to move as the plants enveloped her, vines hugging against her body and through her hair—She started to feel the vines tightening around her neck and just when her ability to breathe became difficult, several bright wisps circled her and she was taken in by the blinding light.

She hit the ground with a thud and scratched at her neck, gasping for breath only to find the vines were gone. She slowly stood and took in her surroundings, it was a beautiful; if not slightly overgrown forest.

"Hello?" She shouted out towards the trees, with no response. Dirt and moss covered her torn summer dress, the wisps from before were back and circling at her feet. She looked down at the tiny balls of light.

"Can you ... understand me?" She asked, The wisps flew up and down excitedly in response. "What am I doing here?" she asked them, they started to form a straight line and drifted off through a gap in the trees, beckoning for her to follow.

Several minutes into her trek through the trees found her having difficulty keeping up with the wisps, "You guys need to slow down!" she shouted as the wisps left her field of vision. She stumbled on a thicket of bushes and overgrown roots trying to catch up with them. She realized that her gardening shoes were hindering her pursuit of these strange guides. She kicked them off and carried them in her hands as she made her way through the trees. The ground beneath her was cold and a little damp and she worried about stepping on rocks. She kept walking on, cautiously. Wherever she was, time was no longer an element. The sun hadn't moved from its position in the sky since she was tending to her flowers in the garden and the walk seemed uncomfortably long. Finally she saw the wisps and called out to them.

"Hey! Wait up!" She climbed over a downed tree branch as thick as her waist and caught up with the wisps. "Where are we going!?" she asked. The wisps danced around her head. They felt warm and inviting, but they didn't answer her question.

"That's not an answer!" The wisps continued on their path through the trees and she reluctantly followed. After some time the dense forest seemed to give way to light and she found herself walking up a steep hill. The wisps swirled around her and started growing brighter, nearly blinding her before she shut her eyes tightly. When she opened them again; she was surprised to find herself staring at the base of a mountain that reached into the sky, she was standing in front of large stone staircase that wound its way up out of her vision.

"Am I supposed to go up there?" she asked the wisps. They answered by twirling around her head and floating up the staircase. She shrugged and followed them up the stone stairs.

It took what seemed like several days for her to approach the summit, broken up by time she spent passing out and nearly falling down the stairs. The wisps of light had stopped her from falling and waited with her until she felt refreshed enough to continue going. When she reached the top of the staircase, the sky was covered in the most stars she'd ever seen in her life, looking up in amazement when the wisps grabbed her attention by flying low around a small wooden table sat right on top of the mountain. There was a candle burning and beside it sat an unlit stick of incense "What am I supposed to do with this?" she asked the wisps. They flew around the candle; she walked to the table and knelt on the cold stone, the wind whipping through her hair and nearly blowing the incense off the table, she picked it up and held it over the flame until it lit the tip. She stood up and held the incense up to the night sky as bright white light came out of its tip instead of smoke. It transformed into a thread and connected all of the visible stars in the sky.

"I left you something," she heard the voice boom over the wind that was picking up speed behind her, whipping her hair into tangles.

"What?" she shouted "What am I doing?! Who are you?"

The wind grew so strong that it knocked her over, the

incense was blown out of her hand and the light that was connecting the stars dimmed and she turned to find the wisps slowly fading.

"What's happening?" she asked them as she slowly got to her feet, they twirled around sadly "What am I supposed to do without you?!" The fading little wisps glowed faintly and trailed off down the mountain. She looked over the edge. "How am I going to get down?" her question was answered as the foundation of the mountain changed. Right before her eyes a stone path down the mountain appeared and for what seemed like the hundredth time, she walked.

Her second journey down the mountain seemed to take less time than before. She tried to keep the wisps in sight but they seemed to be fading fast. Eventually she caught up with them at the base of the mountain, finding they were barely more than a mist at this point.

"How do I fix ... you?" She stood panting from the trip down the mountain. One of the wisps approached her and floated at eye-level. She learned in closely, as if she was listening to a whisper

"What?" She said "No! That's insane. I'm not going to do that." The wisp sadly trailed away from her and faded a little more.

"Wait!" She shouted after it. "No, come back. I'll do it!" The wisp floated back to her and she stood still as a statue, as it flew directly into her and she felt the warmth of the wisp in her throat, in her fingertips and toes. The other wisps brightened enough to light up an entire neighborhood but slowly dimmed to something that wouldn't blind her. As she followed them, she felt the wisp inside of her, guiding her. She kept going with the other wisps as the night became increasingly darker

After what seemed like ages, she and her wisp friends finally came to a halt.

"Why are we stopping?" She questioned, The wisps turned and glowed brighter as a response; up ahead stood an enormous wall covered in vines as thick as the ones she remembered from her kitchen.

"You can't go through it? Well, how am I supposed to get over that wall?" The wisps flew around the ladder-like vines.

"You don't expect me to climb over that thing, do you? It's huge!" She could barely see the top of the wall. Her wisp friends faded and twirled around.

"Alright, I'll go," she said walking towards the wall. Noticing her friends were still floating a ways behind her she turned. "What about you?" They brightened and faded, staying still. "You're staying behind? How will I find what I'm seeking without you?" They brightened and circled around her, indicating that she would be able to do it on her own, Turning away from the wall she approached her friends. She looked at each of the wisps and felt a sadness. "I guess I should say thank you." She blinked at the floating wisps "Thank you, for everything you've done." They brightened happily as she slowly walked towards the wall and grasped onto the first rung of the vine-ladder. She started to climb the wall and when she was a quarter of the way up she looked down to see that the wisps were gone.

The expanse of vine-covered stone seemed to go on forever. She felt like she should be near the top by now but it went on and on. Just when it seemed she couldn't do it, she crested the top of the wall to find more vines on the other side. She used them to climb down to the bottom and found herself staring at a large garden, with a shadow standing directly in front of her

"Come, I have left something for you." The voice seemed to come from the shadow. She hesitated, then took the shadow's outstretched hand.

"Where are we going?" she asked. The shadow didn't answer but continued on through the garden holding her hand.

She passed by beautiful flowers, large bushes reaching for the sky and covered with the most beautiful blooms she had ever seen. Her eyes dazzled; overwhelmed with the intensity of color as she passed the different sections of the garden. Somehow each new view was more breathtakingly beautiful than the last, until finally the shadow led her out into a large field. In the distance a stone loomed over the grass, and as the shadow led her closer, she found it was not as big as she imagined; just a small stone with white petals strewn around it.

It was a tomb. She looked around for the shadow but it was gone.

"I have something for you," the voice repeated. She touched her finger to cold granite and suddenly woke on her couch in the living room. The television blared in the background. It was daytime but the room was dark thanks to the overcast weather. A cool breeze quietly blew in through the open window and she sat up, running her fingers through her hair.

She stood up, turned off the television, and made her way into the hall to grab her car keys. She left the house and sat in her car for a few moments before starting the engine. It didn't take long to arrive at her destination. She got out of the car and pushed the door shut, making her way up the steep grassy hill crowned by a stone, not unlike the one in her dream. Wilted flowers were leaned against the stone and an unlit candle was placed on the ground in front of it. This was her father's final resting place.

As she came closer to the grave she saw something next to the unlit candle that seemed as though it had been placed there very recently, a small envelope addressed to her. She knelt and flipped it over. Words on the other side read, "Something for you." Inside, she found a piece of paper; a letter from her father.

"Dearest Daughter,

I know that things in your life did not turn out like you thought they would when you were just a little girl. I know there were moments you wish you could undo, or that had never happened at all. Things were not always easy for you—I'd be lying if I said I did not also have regrets—moments I wished never happened, chances I wish I took. I won't tell you to do things you don't wish to do merely for the experience of it all; what is experience worth if it doesn't make you happy? A life full of miserable experiences isn't much of a life. Do what you want, do what makes you happy. If it turns out sitting in your bedroom all day is a goal, that is commendable and you should do it. If your ultimate goal is just getting out of bed in the morning, be happy that you have. You don't need to be like other people any more than other people need to be like you, as long as you are happy. And it is my dearest hope that you are.

This will be hard. There will be things you wish you could have said to me, shared with me; movies, television, exciting moments in your life. I'm sorry I won't be there for them but your enjoyment of them is enough. You are your own person, a very wonderful and talented person. But you are an extension of your parents, and you take after me so very much. Don't feel sad that I won't be able to see new places and experience new things. You can do that, and it will be enough."

She felt the corners of her eyes sting as she read, but wiped her face before tears could fall on the letter. There was more.

"You are very much like me, you take after me, but please don't be who I was. Don't stay in one place for years when you want to be free,. I live on through the things you do, what you create, and the beautiful things you see.

Love from somewhere,
Your Father"

She had no idea when it was written or when it was placed at her father's grave but the letter gave her comfort. Ever since her father passed several years ago something was missing. She'd always wished that he had left her something, that there was more to remember him by. As she sat in the grass as in the wind and rain, she understood. The gift the wisps had guided her toward in that dream was knowing her father cherished the moments they had together.

She stood up and felt something drop out of the envelope. It was a single stick of incense, not unlike the one she'd lit in her dream. She walked back to her car, grabbed a lighter from her dashboard, then returned to the graveside. She lit the incense and held it up, releasing the smoke into the afternoon sky.

* * *

For my father, with the hope he knows I found my star

Silver

Laura Hart

Something didn't feel right. He sat up and looked around; everything appeared foggy. There was a grayish tint to the walls, the floor. He walked over and looked out the window, seeing only a vast silvery landscape.

"I'm still dreaming," he thought.

He blinked his eyes a few times, trying to clear this unusual fuzziness. He decided to climb back into bed and try to wake up again to see if that fixed it.

"What an odd dream," he murmured as he pulled the covers back over himself.

Moments later, there was a knock at his door. His eyes opened and his brow furrowed.

"Who's there?" he demanded. Who should be in his home but he himself?

The answer was only more knocking.

With a groan he rose again from bed and went to the door. The silvery haze was still everywhere around him; he gasped some when the door opened and he saw a cloaked figure standing in a stone hallway.

"This isn't my house," he half spoke under his breath. "Where am I," he questioned audibly.

Silence. The person headed down the hall and knocked on the next door. It was then he realized he was not alone in the hallway. He turned the other direction to see other doors; some of them open with silvery people poking their heads out of them. They all looked the same: same face, same eyes, same hair. A tinge of familiarity washed over him catching him by surprise. He wondered if he looked the same as the others. He looked down at his hands and they were silvery too.

He reacted as if he were gasping for air, only to realize he wasn't breathing in a traditional sense. He rushed back into his room, only to see it was not truly his room; just walls, a bed, and a window. He expected his heart to race, but he felt nothing.

"I'm dead?" he asked, though he knew the answer.

He replayed what he remembered from the day before in his mind. He didn't know what could have caused his death, so he must have passed peacefully in his sleep. He wasn't sick though, so why was he here? What happened?

He walked back to the hallway filled with the others like him. Silently, they all followed the cloaked figure that had woken them.

He tried to make small talk with the person beside him.

"Hello, I'm Gary."

No response. He tried to speak again, but his voice did not travel. In fact—for as many people gathered here—the silence was deafening. There was no noise of fabric and clothing swooshing as they walked, no steps echoing on the stone floors. The only sound was an occasional knock on the heavy doors.

At the end of the hallway was a huge gate ornately carved out of something metallic, but it didn't have the same silvery hue that covered everything up to this point. As each person stepped and made their way through the gates, shimmering foggy glow around everyone dissipated. They morphed into figures like he imagined ghosts to be; almost opaque, but with a touch of transparency. Each was clothed in a drab grey robe, and there was nothing to differentiate one from another. The mass shuffled about, bumping into each other, yet never really pushing or finding the space uncomfortable.

As the last person filed into the great room where everyone had gathered, an ethereal voice without hint of gender boomed from overhead. "Welcome home." The source of the voice glided to the front of the great hall. As the crowd was greeted, a warm glow fell over the room. Individual voices became audible, filling the room with cries of sorrow and confusion.

"What about my husband, who will take care of him?"

"Oh, no, please let me see my grandchildren one last time!"

"I should have done this a long time ago."

Gary shivered as he heard the voices and final thoughts of the others who had passed on with him. Each had their place in the puzzle of the world, each one a piece removed and a hole left in the lives of those they touched. Gary himself had lived alone and made few friends, so he doubted his piece would leave much of a gap. Instead, he focused on what the others were saying, until the great spirit at the front of the hall silenced them.

"Hush now, we must continue without further delay." came the ethereal voice.

"So, you're real? Who was right?"

The spirit at the front changed shape, first to a human with dark hair, then to an elephant, an eagle, a woman with many arms, and on to many forms before resuming the shapeless mass of golden glow it began as.

"Everyone was right, and everyone was wrong. I am all gods and I am none."

Voices blended into each other as the crowd took in the information presented to them.

"You are home. You all begin here, you all end here. Your return to this place gives you the chance to begin again or rest a while. The choice is entirely yours, but you must choose before the end of the thirteenth hour, or the choice will be made for you."

"Thirteen hours to choose if I want to live again? What kind of rule is this? How do they measure hours here?" He thought to himself. It bothered him that he didn't know what the rules were. If this was home, shouldn't he remember? As the questions filled his head, the familiar feeling he had earlier in the hall came over him.

"Gary?"

He turned, the being he saw there was just the same as every other spirit in the room, but he felt different.

"Sam!" He didn't exactly smile, but the positive feelings

were there, and evident to those close enough to pick up on them.

"Wait a second; we didn't just live that life together, did we?" Fragments of memories began to come to him, and he could look back on the entire life he just lived, as well as countless others. He was a little startled when he realized not all life was on Earth.

"Ah, no my friend. I spent the last century in a different galaxy altogether, one that I had never visited before. It was quite the experience and I highly recommend it. I am even considering going back for another round; it was quite entertaining. Fancy we got back here on the same round, eh?"

"Do you care to tell me about it? I'm still trying to recall the rules."

Sam smirked a little. "Gary, the rules are there are no rules. We come, we go. If we choose to rest, it is only for a while to investigate our options. Forget all that Earth talk. There are no lessons to be learned, no secrets to unearth. We head out, enjoy the ride, and come right back here. Think of it like a water slide, you had those on Earth, yes?"

Gary nodded.

"So you go up the stairs, ride down the slide, and go back up to start the ride over. The only thing is that the slide can go any direction you want it to go." Sam was full of excitement, like he was ready to start the next adventure.

"Where will you be headed then?" Gary asked.

Sam blinked at Gary and shook his head. "It hardly matters, does it?" With a wink, he took his leave and went to the great spirit to be sent on another mission, a new life anywhere.

"Well that seems a waste, doesn't it?" A new voice caused Gary to turn. Another ghost was there to speak with him.

"I suppose it does. All this at our fingertips and what do we do with it?" Gary replied.

"I agree. I feel like my last life on earth was too short, there are things I wanted try. I think I might go back."

"What kind of things did you miss out on?" Gary was

curious.

"Well, I didn't get to raise a family. I never knew what it felt like to hold my child, or see them grow in my guidance and care, and discover their dreams."

"I did," Gary said with a hint of sadness. "But, I didn't do it well. By the time my life finished, my children hadn't spoken to me in years." He tilted his head a little towards the other spirit. "May I ask why you didn't get to raise your family?"

There was a pause before she answered him. "I died too young. My daughter was just being born, but I was sick during her delivery. I saw her, I heard her cry, but then everything went dark."

Gary went to reply, but hesitated He felt he should comfort her, but didn't know how in this form. He focused on another conversation he could hear, listening to spirits who had become elderly and died in their sleep recount their experiences. Some were young and had died from ailments like cancer and other horrible diseases. Others were in accidents or were murdered.

"My name is Mary," came the voice Gary had uncomfortably not responded to. She was still beside him. Her voice startled him because he was focused on the other stories around him.

"Gary," was his reply, still a little distant in his thoughts. "You know, there is a theme among those who came from Earth," he said, not quite to her directly.

"Love," she replied in the same wistful tone.

The awkward tension between them fell away as they discussed how those who lived a life on Earth had a special kind of fulfillment in their lives; a fulfillment that seemed unknown to the other realms of being. They talked about what could be done differently, and examined the other stories they heard for ways to enhance a life experience. Before long, a warning chime sounded. The end of the thirteenth hour was upon them.

He felt a connection to the spirit, Mary, and reached his arm out to her. "Do you want to try again? As soul mates?"

A giggle escaped her. "Soul mates don't exist."

"We can make them exist, for this round."

She placed her hand on his extended arm and, as she did, they glowed together and walked to the great spirit for placement back on Earth; bound to find each other and love one another as only those on Earth can do.

Beyond the Stars

Mayra Pérez González

I was floating in the most peculiar way, sailing solitarily through cosmos unknown, ribbons of my long dark hair swirling softly, whirring whimsically, rolling gently around me.

I was soaring peacefully in the midst of stars.

They were just beyond my grasp. Outstretching my arms, I caressed them from a distance.

"There's nothing I could do," I whispered to myself without knowing why.

Immersed in surreality, a feather-light happiness grew within me, made me lighter as I floated higher and higher.

The sound of a distant tune, odd and soft, embraced me.

A nebula surrounded me. Two men floated just above. One, a curious and remarkable rockstar, played the guitar and sang with fluidity, painting landscapes with his voice; the other, a perplexing yet faithful wizard, looked around with quiet resolution, luminous magic running through his veins with electric brilliance, a slight glimmer just visible through his skin.

They both looked at me and smiled. There were stars in their eyes. Although surrounded by a wondrous cosmos, I knew the beautiful gleam in their eyes was not a mere reflection of our mystic landscape Their eyes emanated brilliance, entire galaxies contained within them.

They were like their striking, starlit eyes: they felt endless and evanescent, astonishing and shatterable.

An inexplicable sadness flowed into me; I had the sensation that I had been robbed of something beautiful, something intangible and intrinsic. I did not know its cause, but the sorrow invading me felt real and raw. I felt it more profoundly than a simple sadness. It reminded me of love, weariness, and acceptance. Peculiar. Ineludible.

I looked down as I let a tear escape and caress my cheek.

"We could be heroes," the rockstar confided to me, breaking the silence. "I feel," he continued, "we weren't given enough time. We can steal time. We can be heroes forever and ever. We're space oddities, you and I, floating amongst ethereal cosmos. And we could also be heroes. We could always be heroes."

The wizard looked at me with patient understanding, his compelling voice calm as he said to me, "We must remember who we are, why we are, where we come from, and what might be possible. An infinity of things are possible, but nothing else will be clear if we do not recognize our own strengths and frailties, if we let others be the judge of our character, and if we ourselves do not know who we are and what we stand for."

Silence.

We floated, the rockstar, the wizard and I, quiescent and contemplative.

It was time.

"There's a Starman waiting in the sky," the rockstar whispered as he picked me up gingerly and thrust me softly upwards. I began soaring slowly.

"I'm scared," my voice trembled.

"You've already proven yourself to be courageous," the wizard insisted reassuredly.

The rockstar, the wizard, and their voices became distant.

Their voices nearly inaudible, my own weak and breaking, I asked, "Will you be looking over me?"

The wizard whispered one word I couldn't quite hear. We were too far apart.

I ascended, floating in a way that felt like falling. The stars fell beneath me, Drifting away, a tear fell from my cheek and landed amongst the stars.

I was beyond the stars. I stopped moving, and in quiet reverie, I hovered. All movement stopped, the whisper of a song died away, my eyes closed, and although I could no

longer see the stars, I knew they were still there.
Everything else vanished.
Motionless.
Quiet.
Peaceful.

Stardust, Always

Distance, Speed, Time

D. R. Perry

The brightest stars move us with their absence.
Light from objects a billion years gone captures a million
eyes.
Miles and time stand ready, collecting their toll
Like bells whose voices depend
On shared heartstrings stretching across intergalactic
voids.
Each of us is an entire galaxy,
Collected souls in isolation walking the earth.
We love the phantom light because anything everyone
sees,
Feels,
Salves loneliness.
Love directed minds the gap, a lifeline of uniform motion.
Rate divided by time equals distance.
Two vanished kings cross it to help us rescue each other.
Always

* * *

For my old Star and my new one. You never steer me wrong.

Stardust, Always

Acknowledgements

Special thanks to Lora Hughes who really got the ball rolling, and to Laura Hart and Andrew Barber who kept it on track.

Initial Planning and Organizing
Lia Rees, Laura Hart, Andrew Barber, Clara Ryanne Heart and Lora Hughes

Beta Readers
Mayra Pérez González, D.R. Perry, Lora Hughes, Sandra Easter, Denise Peterson, Sarah Elford, Shanna Kate, Suzanne Wdowik and Gen Wren

Editors
Lacey Sutton, Ashlee Hetherington, Andrew Barber

Formatting / Typesetting
Lacey Sutton

Cover & Art Design
James Baldwin

Promotion and Release Party Contributors
Kelly Kuelber, Debbie Manber Kupfer, Lia ReesRyanne Heart, Kate Post, Virginia Carraway Stark, D.R. Perry, Janet Gershen-Siegel

Copy Proofreaders
Katelyn SweigartRyanne Heart, Debbie Manber Kupfer, Janet Gershen-Siegel, Trine Jensegg, Becca Bachlott, Ashlee Hetherington, Stacy Whitmire, Lawenda Tucker, Mayra Pérez González, Paula Hayward and Andrew Barber

And finally, thanks to Chelo. You know what you did.